Road Kill
Texas Horror by Texas Writers

Edited by
E. R. BILLS
&
Bret McCORMICK

Copy Editor
Misty CONTRERAS

Associate Editor
David ROBLEDO

EAKIN PRESS 🗡P Fort Worth, Texas
www.EakinPress.com

Copyright © 2017
By E. R. Bills & Bret McCormick
Published By Eakin Press
An Imprint of Wild Horse Media Group
P.O. Box 331779
Fort Worth, Texas 76163
1-817-344-7036
www.EakinPress.com
ALL RIGHTS RESERVED
1 2 3 4 5 6 7 8 9
ISBN-10: 1-68179-079-3
ISBN-13: 978-1-68179-079-4

Contents

Foreword

Dear Reader:

There are some really talented horror writers around these parts, and I'm pretty sure we weren't able to find—much less get in touch with—all of them. If we missed someone, I'm sorry. If we introduce you to someone you weren't already familiar with, excellent!

The mandate was simple: Texas horror by Texas authors. We scouted the state for voices, from the Panhandle to the piney woods, West Texas to the Gulf and the Rio Grande Valley to the hill country. We were able to land Texas legend and Champion Mojo Storyteller Joe R. Lansdale (Thanks, Joe!), old hand Michael H. Price, up and comers David Bowles and Russell C. Conner and cyberpunk newby Anna L. Davis. Plus several others. The tales we included are diverse and edgy and most will pack a punch or a paw, or give you pause. And that's what it's all about.

Enjoy.

E. R.

Acknowledgments

Special thanks to our families and friends for nurturing and putting up with the more acute symptoms and actual manifestations of our wayward and unconventional minds.

Shrine

By David Bowles

Marisa emerged from the little brick vault, blinking at the sun. Her back and knees ached from kneeling for nine hours at the makeshift *prie-dieu*. Her nose itched from the profusion of flowers. Her throat was worn raw from her hoarse prayers to Don Pedrito Jaramillo, the curandero who had died at this very spot a century ago after decades of healing the sick.

None of this discomfort overshadowed the migraine, a malevolent throbbing just beneath the skull on the right side of her head. It seemed to feed on the light and heat of the pitiless South Texas sun, blurring Marisa's eyes, sending the world spinning out of control until she doubled over and vomited up what little breakfast remained in her stomach.

"Are you okay, *m'ija*?"

Small, strong hands clasped her elbows and helped her to her feet. It was an older woman, perhaps fifty, a purple *rebozo* across her shoulders. Wearing a simple white blouse and embroidered skirt, she might have walked the streets of any border community during the last century and not been out of place. Letting Marisa lean on her, the woman guided her through a maze of tombstones to the shade of a nearby tree.

"*Gracias, señora.*"

"It's nothing, dear. Migraines?"

Marisa nodded, rubbing her blurring eyes. "Yes. Bad."

"*Ándale.* I've seen cases like this before. Let me guess. Doctors prescribed drugs, but they just made the attacks a little less frequent. So then you went to the *hierberías* and local *curanderas*, the *sobadoras* and shamans."

The pressure in her head made it hurt to speak or move, so Marisa bent her forefinger in slight affirmation.

"Where are you from?"

"Mercedes," she managed to whisper. "In the Valley."

The older woman lifted her left foot, scratched between the straps of her *huaraches*. "Damn ants. Hmm. None of that worked, obviously. So you drove up here to Falfurrias, hoping that whatever essence Don Pedrito left behind might cure you, or that he might intercede for you there beyond. *Bueno.* Problem is, the kind of migraine you have? It needs much stronger magic, much older rituals."

Marisa hushed the woman gently. "Right now, just need...to sit in my car a bit. Help me?"

Together they stepped through the cemetery's creaking gate and crossed the uneven gravel of the turnout. Marisa eased behind the wheel of her car, wincing at the hot touch of the seat against her back. Starting the engine and turning up the AC, she gestured at the woman to get in as well.

"It's starting to fade," she explained. "Sit with me a while."

Beyond the hum of motor and fan, there was relative silence for the better part of a half hour. The migraine unclenched itself, leaving Marisa feeling slightly hungover and depressed, with a soreness across her skull but no real pain.

"Thank you, ma'am," she finally said, giving the older woman's hand a brief squeeze. "Most people don't understand. They offer aspirin and advice and so forth, talking and talking, making it worse. It's like they can't believe such a thing actually exists. My dad used to tell me I was making it up to get out of chores."

"Oh, I've been around all sorts of ailments, *m'ija*. Very familiar with migraines, though you've got a special case, I think. Tell you what. Why don't you let me buy you dinner? There's a little place close by on 281, Rick's, not much to look at from the outside, but they've got great food. You really need to eat after spending the day in that little shrine in such pain."

Marisa was starving, so she agreed, heading for Business 281 and letting the woman guide her for about a half mile to a greasy spoon beside a run-down gym. It was dim inside, and cool, which lessened the disorienting after-effects of the attack. *Postdrome*, the doctors called this stage. Marisa always thought of it as the slumber of some unspeakable parasite lodged in her brain.

"My name is Sara Manso," the older woman said after they had ordered cold Mexican Cokes and *tacos callejeros*.

"Nice to meet you, Doña Sara. I'm Marisa Zabaleta."

"And what do you do there in Mercedes, Marisa?"

"I'm a paralegal." Worried that this sounded too haughty, she added, "At my Uncle Rosendo's firm."

"Boyfriend?"

Marisa pictured Bruno for a moment, features impassive as he told her he wanted to simplify his life. "Not anymore. I'm apparently too complicated. I have a dog, though."

"You're probably better off that way," Doña Sara mused.

"Yeah. Love's a little like the onset of a migraine. You get a weird euphoric feeling, start craving unusual foods, have mood swings. Your muscles tense up. Then the aura kicks in and you begin to see stuff. Your field of vision narrows and you go all numb. Not totally unpleasant, just odd and a little inconvenient. But major pain is just around the corner."

"Yes, that sounds like my relationship with my first husband, rest his brutal soul."

A woman emerged from the kitchen, setting plastic plates and frosty bottles in front of them. As Marisa ate, she thought back over Doña Sara's words in the cemetery.

"You said I needed 'stronger magic' and 'older rituals.' What did you mean?"

The older woman leaned back and adjusted her rebozo. "*Bue-*

no, m'ija, I was born in Boquillas del Carmen, Coahuila, but my ancestors weren't Spanish. No, my people are the Chizo, and we have lived in the Big Bend area for centuries, taking on Mexican customs and language to fade away from the eyes of Westerners. In secret, though, many of us have continued along the Path of the Ancients."

Marisa tapped the surface of the metal table. "You're a shaman, aren't you?"

"*Pos, sí.* Can't deny it."

"And you were hanging out by the shrine to see if anyone needed 'healing,' huh?"

Doña Sara lifted a hand as if to ward off suspicions. "I know what you're thinking, but that's not the whole story. I have an older cousin who lives in Premont. She's been pretty sick for a while, and I came to help her husband with her treatments. But, yes, I do visit these sorts of shrines around the state. Sometimes I meet people who can't be helped by anyone else."

"Uh-huh." Marisa didn't want to doubt this woman, who so reminded her of her own mother and grandmother, but quacks and frauds had already taken so much of her money that she just had to be cautious. "*Adelante.* What's your pitch?"

The shaman's eyes sparkled, not with anger, but amusement. "There's a shrine in Big Bend National Park. A holy place for the *Chizo* near the mountains that bear our name. I've taken tough cases out there. I perform a complex ritual, and by its end I have rid them of their pain."

Marisa glanced at her knockoff purse in the chair next to her. "And how much would this cost?"

"Well, I've got to head back anyway, so if you save me the bus fare by driving me, I'll just charge you sixty dollars."

"Hang on." Marisa dug around for her cell phone and then used an app to calculate the distance. Seven or eight hours. Two tanks of gas there, another two back. Add those eighty bucks to her fee . . .

"I'm inclined to say yes, Doña Sara. At this point, I'm willing to try pretty much anything. But do you know of a really cheap hotel nearby? There's no way I'm driving all evening and into the night."

A smile crinkled the older woman's eyes. "Hell, if you don't mind sleeping near a *vieja roncadora* like me, I've got a room with two beds at the Oasis in Premont. We could hit the road at first light. *¿Cómo ves?*"

It didn't take long to fall asleep. After calling her sister and asking her to watch Buddy for another couple of days while she sought treatment farther west, Marisa closed her eyes and slipped away from the waking world. Despite Doña Sara's warning about her snoring, she spent the night sunken into a deep, almost comatose slumber in which dark forms squirmed but no sound or pain impinged.

The next morning they packed and ate a substantial breakfast of *huevos divorciados*, refried beans and diced potatoes, loading up on flour tortillas to tide them over until a planned late lunch in Del Rio. Stopping briefly at Walmart to pick up some supplies, they headed east. The drive took them along aging two-lane highways, across the browning brushland, through sparsely populated towns.

Sara Manso was a spellbinding storyteller and attentive listener, like many of Marisa's own aunts, so it was easy to open up to her as the chaparral unfolded before them. They spent the first few hours swapping family stories, legends and recipes. Then the shaman spoke in general terms about her people, who once called themselves the *Tacuitatome* before others named them *Chizos*, a word that echoed with hints of forests, ghosts, arcane sounds.

Finally Doña Sara broached the subject of Marisa's condition.

"When did the migraines start? Puberty?"

"No. Doctors have told me that hormonal changes seem to trigger them in other women, which is why they're more severe when you're menstruating, but my first migraine came when I was seven. And they've been coming ever since, without any real rhyme or reason or predictability at all. *¿Quién sabe?* I think I'm a freak or something."

Doña Sara made a dismissive noise, but Marisa ploughed on.

"Seriously. For most of eighth grade, they disappeared. I thought going to CCD at church had cured me or something. But then came the day of my confirmation. When Bishop Peña touched my forehead with consecrated oil, a horrible burst of agony dropped me squirming to the ground. Apparently I started screaming all sorts of obscenities, insulting the bishop, cursing the Church, threatening everyone who tried to touch me. I don't remember any of it. The pain was so overwhelming that I lost consciousness. When I woke up, my dad was pissed and my mom inconsolable.

"Well, that scene made it tough to go to mass for a while, as you can imagine. My parents thought I was possessed or something, but our priest consulted with my doctors and they ruled that out, thank God. But the migraines were back. I didn't get another one that bad 'til, well, 'til I had sex with Freddy Higuera in tenth grade, which I think traumatized him for life, *pobrecito*. But they were back. Occasionally at first, then more and more often. I had to switch to a charter school to graduate. Couldn't manage normal classes. Needed self-paced modules so that I could work around the inevitable attacks."

"And now?"

Marisa gripped the wheel more tightly. The road seemed to disappear on the horizon, to fade into the brambles and mesquite, as if the car would soon reach the limits of civilization and careen off into the unknown.

"Hardly a day goes by without one, Doña Sara. My uncle lets me work as I can, but it's just . . . impossible. I won't be able to make it much longer if I can't find relief."

The desolation that had been hollowing out her heart for years crept into her voice like a bleak echo.

"But if no one can help me—I guess there is always one way out, no?"

The shaman reached over and placed her palm over Marisa's nearest clenched hand. "I swear to you again, *m'ija*: I will end this torment. The rites of my ancestors will set you free."

They had a quick lunch in Del Rio in the early afternoon, and then Marisa followed the calm yet insistent instructions of her GPS app until they arrived in Marathon around 4 p.m. In the distance, mountains loomed blue and craggy, stooped titans struggling beneath the weight of the cloudless sky. Marisa was unnerved by their age-old silent stare, but she drove for another hour, heading south on 385 until she hit the park entrance at Panther Junction Visitor Center.

"Okay, *m'ija*. Turn on Ross Maxwell Scenic Drive. The trail we're looking for starts about eight miles down."

Before long, they pulled into a parking lot that overlooked a drop in the terrain. Below, Marisa could make out the ruins of a ranch house amid the tall grass and cactus. The native stone walls were still standing, though the glass had long ago been shattered and the wooden porch weathered down to the dull gray of driftwood.

"Blue Creek Canyon," Doña Sara explained. "All this used to be the Homer Wilson Ranch 'til the government acquired the land. *Bueno, mira.* About three hours of sunlight. That's enough. But you're gonna want to put some tennies on if you've got them. We have some hard walking ahead of us."

As Marisa changed her footwear and shouldered her backpack, the shaman slid a couple of bottles of water into a large, brightly colored woven bag she slung across her chest.

"Come on. This is the smoothest part, girl."

The trailhead was right at the edge of the pavement, and the two women descended along the road's short, moderate grade with little effort until they reached the flat bottom of the canyon. The declining sun slanted indifferently across other abandoned structures: a storeroom, the ruins of a bunkhouse, a weed-infested corral, rusted chicken coops. The land, free from the tenuous grip of men and horses, had begun to reclaim the wood and stone once gouged from its arid flesh. Flickers of unseen life disturbed the ochre brush, but beyond those small movements, the canyon was unsettling in its stillness.

Doña Sara pulled at Marisa's arm, and they continued along the trail, the pebbly gravel twisting awkwardly underfoot. Before them, denuded hills thrust stubbly chins at the sky. Strange ridges like stony brows and fairy chimneys that grasped the air in arthritic paroxysms added to the sense that Cyclopean sentinels lay all about, buried beneath the sandy soil.

They headed north along a meager arroyo that sputtered over jagged rocks beside the dusty path. Marisa scanned the canyon wall closest to them. From time to time she noticed strange rust-red petroglyphs, primitive lines and spirals that hinted at shapes without ever finally merging into a discernible image. As she stared at one complex pattern, she felt a familiar fatigue settle over her, not normal exhaustion, but something more existentially draining.

"Another one's coming," she called to Doña Sara, who was setting a swift pace, even in her simple leather sandals. The shaman stopped, pulled a water bottle from her bag.

"Here, drink. How long 'til it hits?"

Marisa wiped her lips, screwed the cap back on. "An hour? I never know, really. Are we okay on time? I'd hate to hike back through this in the dark."

"Don't worry. It's only another two miles or so. But if we have to, if the ritual takes too long, we can camp up at Laguna Meadows. It'll be rougher than you're used to, *pero ya*. You can handle it."

The trail began a gradual climb. Odd cairns marked its increasingly indistinct margins. Soon they were walking between spindly hoodoos of copper-toned layered rock, strange twisted pillars that reared like intertwining serpents three stories overhead. As the late afternoon light scintillated against their narrow length, the spires seemed to change color as if slowly uncoiling.

Averting her eyes in sudden fear, Marisa tried to blink away the bleary patch in her vision, hoping it was just a result of sun glare. But no. It was her body, betraying her as it always did, bleeding her eyesight so that when the pain came it would find her floundering in a dim, grey limbo.

Her despair rose like a steady tide. *All these years. How many friends have I lost because this thing pushes them away? How much of life have I missed out on?*

Her family and a few close girlfriends had stuck by her, but she could see in their dispirited glances that their love was tired by the attacks.

Everything crumbles before it. Even my faith is unraveling. The santeras *and priests can sense it. They say that's why no one has been able to heal me. But what do they expect? How could God do this to me? Why? And if not Him, who? And if there's no one doing it, if it's just random shitty luck, then what's the point?*

They reached the arroyo's source, a small bubbling spring that sustained a thicket of oaks. Marisa rested for a moment in that shade, splashing the cool water on her face and neck.

Her field of vision was narrowing. As Doña Sara urged her on, the world shrank, encircled by darkness. "*Hemianopsia*," the doctors called it.

She stepped back onto the sunlit path. The air flickered around her, ambient light fritzing and jagging in black and white lines.

"Oh, God, Doña Sara," she cried out. "This is going to be one of the really bad ones."

"Keeping walking, girl. Not far now."

They continued climbing, heading toward the juniper-pinyon pine woodlands that encircled a blocky tor up ahead. Keeping her failing eyes on the shaman's back, Marisa forced her feet to move. A ringing started up in her right ear, low and persistent at first, then louder and louder until it became a dull roar. The landscape tilted. Marisa stumbled.

"Here." The shaman thrust a walking stick into Marisa's hand. "Lean on it. I can't carry you, *así que aguanta*. A little ways yet."

There was no way. She couldn't do it. Every step was like dragging her entire body forward, using the walking stick as a lever. The sky whirled dim and empty above her.

A hand on her shoulder. "Rest a second, child."

The canyon rim was a battlement. Dark forms kept watch. Beasts. Men. Demons. Roiling silhouettes against the deepening blue. Beyond them, all around, the behemoths raised their crooked backs to the cosmos, streaked with layers of limestone and antediluvian scars that hinted at stony fangs and claws.

"Do you see it? Look." The woman seized Marisa's jaw firmly, turning her head. There, a gaping hole in the wall, a black maw yawning above a brambly escarpment. "The shrine."

Pain erupted in Marisa's skull, a continuous, relentless stream of agony that unhinged her mind. Falling to her knees, she began to scream. Strong fingers forced something bitter into her mouth, squeezed water between her lips, roughly massaged her throat until she swallowed against her will.

The migraine did not subside. It raged against the walls of her skull. But Marisa no longer shuddered or moaned. Her body went numb, muscles refusing her broken commands. She tumbled into the weeds, unmoving.

Doña Sara grabbed her arms and began to drag her up the steep incline. Beneath the purple *rebozo* that shaded her face, the woman's eyes suddenly seemed devoid of sympathy, of mercy. And the sky was darkling.

Time lurched.

Chalky cave walls smudged black from fires. Rust-red enigmatic petroglyphs.

The shaman opened her bag, drew forth a small bow and a long shaft of bone ending in a hollow copper cylinder with jagged teeth.

Marisa tried to cry out, but her despair just gurgled weakly in a clenched throat.

"*Calla, madre,*" Doña Sara muttered, her impassive features softening for a moment. "'Blessed are you among women.' Isn't that the phrase? It must emerge, *querida*. You're the gateway and the sustenance."

The woman turned Marisa's face away, set the bow drill against her temple, chanted obscure words in a forgotten tongue. The sun was setting behind the south rim. The sky bled red and purple into the growing black.

Ecstatic shouts. "*Sinauhé! Sinauhé!*"

A sharp bite. The whine of metal on bone. And relief that brought tears to her eyes. The grind of the bow drill was unpleasant, but the excruciating gnaw inside her head started to subside.

The thing inside her uncoiled and slithered through the hole in her skull.

As the light failed, it reared above her, free but unrepentant, twisting and glistening black, before dropping back down to devour the husk of its unwitting mother.

Not from Detroit

By Joe R. Lansdale

Outside it was cold and wet and windy. The storm rattled the shack, slid like razor blades through the window, door and wall cracks, but it wasn't enough to make any difference to the couple. Sitting before the crumbling fireplace in their creaking rocking chairs, shawls across their knees, fingers entwined, they were warm.

A bucket behind them near the kitchen sink collected water dripping from a hole in the roof.

The drops had long since passed the noisy stage of sounding like steel bolts falling on tin, and were now gentle plops.

The old couple were husband and wife; had been for over fifty years. They were comfortable with one another and seldom spoke. Mostly they rocked and looked at the fire as it flickered shadows across the room.

Finally Margie spoke. "Alex," she said, "I hope I die before you."

Alex stopped rocking. "Did you say what I thought you did?"

"I said, I hope I die before you." She wouldn't look at him, just the fire. "It's selfish, I know, but I hope I do. I don't want to live on with you gone. It would be like cutting out my heart and making me walk around. Like one of them zombies."

"There are the children," he said. "If I died, they'd take you in."

"I'd just be in the way. I love them, but I don't want to do that. They got their own lives. I'd just as soon die before you. That would make things simple."

"Not simple for me," Alex said. "I don't want you to die before me. So how about that? We're both selfish, aren't we?"

She smiled. "Well, it ain't a thing to talk about before bedtime, but it's been on my mind, and I had to get it out."

"Been thinking on it too, honey. Only natural we would. We ain't spring chickens anymore."

"You're healthy as a horse, Alex Brooks. Mechanic work you did all your life kept you strong. Me, I got the bursitis and the miseries and I'm tired all the time. Got the old age bad."

Alex started rocking again. They stared into the fire. "We're going to go together, hon," he said. "I feel it. That's the way it ought to be for folks like us."

"I wonder if I'll see him coming. Death, I mean."

"What?"

"My grandma used to tell me she seen him the night her daddy died."

"You've never told me this."

"Ain't a subject I like. But Grandma said this man in a black buggy slowed down out front of their house, cracked his whip three times, and her daddy was gone in instants. And she said she'd heard her grandfather tell how he had seen Death when he was a boy. Told her it was early morning and he was up, about to start his chores, and when he went outside he seen this man dressed in black walk by the house and stop out front. He was carrying a stick over his shoulder with a checkered bundle tied to it, and he looked at the house and snapped his fingers three times. A moment later they found my grandfather's brother, who had been sick with the smallpox, dead in bed."

"Stories, hon. Stories. Don't get yourself worked up over a bunch of old tall tales. Here, I'll heat us some milk."

Alex stood, laid the shawl in the chair, went over to put milk in a pan and heat it. As he did, he turned to watch Margie's back. She was still staring into the fire, only she wasn't rocking. She was just watching the blaze and, Alex knew, thinking about dying.

After the milk they went to bed, and soon Margie was asleep, snoring like a busted chainsaw. Alex found he could not rest. It was partly due to the storm, it had picked up in intensity. But it was mostly because of what Margie had said about dying. It made him feel lonesome.

Like her, he wasn't so much afraid of dying, as he was of being left alone. She had been his heartbeat for fifty years, and without her, he would only be going through motions of life, not living.

God, he prayed silently. When we go, let us go together. He turned to look at Margie. Her face looked unlined and strangely young. He was glad she could turn off most anything with sleep. He, on the other hand, could not.

Maybe I'm just hungry.

He slid out of bed, pulled on his pants, shirt and house shoes; those silly things with the rabbit face and ears his granddaughter had bought him. He padded silently to the kitchen. It was not only the kitchen, it served as a den, living room and dining room. The house was only three rooms and a closet, and one of the rooms was a small bathroom. It was times like this that Alex thought he could have done better by Margie. Gotten her a bigger house, for one thing. It was the same house where they had raised their kids, the babies sleeping in a crib here in the kitchen.

He sighed. No matter how hard he had worked, he seemed to stay in the same place. A poor place.

He went to the refrigerator and took out a half-gallon of milk, drank directly from the carton.

He put the carton back and watched the water drip into the bucket. It made him mad to see it. He had let the little house turn into a shack since he retired, and there was no real excuse for it. Surely, he wasn't that tired. It was a wonder Margie didn't complain more.

Well, there was nothing to do about it tonight. But he vowed that when dry weather came, he wouldn't forget about it this time.

He'd get up there and fix that damn leak.

Quietly, he rummaged a pan from under the cabinet. He'd have to empty the bucket now if he didn't want it to run over before morning. He ran a little water into the pan before substituting it for the bucket so the drops wouldn't sound so loud.

He opened the front door, went out on the porch, carrying the bucket. He looked out at his mud-pie yard and his old, red wrecker, his white logo on the side of the door faded with time: ALEX BROOKS WRECKING AND MECHANIC SERVICE.

Tonight, looking at the old warhorse, he felt sadder than ever. He missed using it the way it was meant to be used. For work. Now it was nothing more than transportation. Before he retired, his tools and hands made a living. Now nothing. Picking up a Social Security check was all that was left.

Leaning over the edge of the porch, he poured the water into the bare and empty flower bed. When he lifted his head and looked at his yard again, and beyond to Highway 59, he saw a light. Headlights, actually, looking fuzzy in the rain, like filmed-over amber eyes. They were way out there on the highway, coming from the south, winding their way toward him, moving fast.

Alex thought that whoever was driving that crate was crazy. Cruising like that on bone-dry highways with plenty of sunshine would have been dangerous, but in this weather, they were asking for a crackup.

As the car neared, he could see it was long, black and strangely shaped. He'd never seen anything like it, and he knew cars fairly well. This didn't look like something off the assembly line from Detroit. It had to be foreign.

Miraculously, the car slowed without so much as a quiver or screech of brakes and tires. In fact, Alex could not even hear its motor, just the faint whispering sound of rubber on wet cement.

The car came even of the house just as lightning flashed, and in that instant, Alex got a good look at the driver, or at least the shape of the driver outlined in the flash, and he saw that it was a man with a cigar in his mouth and a bowler hat on his head. And the head was turning toward the house.

The lightning flash died, and now there was only the dark shape of the car and the red tip of the cigar jutting at the house. Alex felt stalactites of ice dripping down from the roof of his skull, extended through his body and out of the soles of his feet.

The driver hit down on his horn; three sharp blasts that pricked at Alex's mind.

Honk. *(visions of blooming roses, withering, going black)*

Honk. *(funerals remembered, loved ones in boxes, going down)*

Honk. *(worms crawling through rotten flesh)*

Then came a silence louder than the horn blasts. The car picked up speed again. Alex watched as its taillights winked away in the blackness. The chill became less chill. The stalactites in his mind melted away.

But as he stood there, Margie's words of earlier that evening came at him in a rush: "Seen Death once . . . buggy slowed down out front . . . cracked his whip three times . . . man looked at the house, snapped his fingers three times . . . found dead a moment later . . ."

Alex's throat felt as if a pine knot had lodged there. The bucket slipped from his fingers, clattered on the porch and rolled into the flowerbed. He turned into the house and walked briskly toward the bedroom,

(Can't be, just a wives' tale)

his hands vibrating with fear,

(Just a crazy coincidence)

Margie wasn't snoring.

Alex grabbed her shoulder, shook her.

Nothing.

He rolled her on her back and screamed her name.

Nothing.

"Oh, baby. No."

He felt for her pulse.

None.

He put an ear to her chest, listening for a heartbeat (the other half of his life bongos), and there was none.

Quiet. Perfectly quiet.

"You can't . . ." Alex said. "You can't . . . we're supposed to go together . . . got to be that way."

And then it came to him. He had seen Death drive by, had seen him heading on down the highway.

He came to his feet, snatched his coat from the back of the chair, raced toward the front door. "You won't have her," he said aloud. "You won't."

Grabbing the wrecker keys from the nail beside the door, he leaped to the porch and dashed out into the cold and the rain.

A moment later he was heading down the highway, driving fast and crazy in pursuit of the strange car.

The wrecker was old and not built for speed, but since he kept it well-tuned and it had new tires, it ran well over the wet highway. Alex kept pushing the pedal gradually until it met the floor. Faster and faster and faster.

After an hour, he saw Death.

Not the man himself but the license plate. Personalized and clear in his headlights. It read: DEATH / EXEMPT.

The wrecker and the strange black car were the only ones on the road. Alex closed in on him, honked his horn. Death tootled back (not the same horn sound he had given in front of Alex's house), stuck his arm out the window and waved the wrecker around.

Alex went, and when he was alongside the car, he turned his head to look at Death. He could still not see him clearly, but he could make out the shape of his bowler, and when Death turned to look at him, he could see the glowing tip of the cigar, like a bloody bullet wound.

Alex whipped hard right into the car, and Death swerved to the right, then back onto the road. Alex rammed again. The black car's tires hit roadside gravel and Alex swung closer, preventing it from returning to the highway. He rammed yet another time, and the car went into the grass alongside the road, skidded and went sailing down an embankment and into a tree.

Alex braked carefully, backed off the road and got out of the wrecker. He reached a small pipe wrench and a big crescent wrench out from under the seat, slipped the pipe wrench into his coat pocket for insurance, then went charging down the embankment waving the crescent.

Death opened his door and stepped out. The rain had subsided and the moon was peeking through the clouds like a shy child through gossamer curtains. Its light hit Death's round pink face and made it look like a waxed pomegranate. His cigar hung from his mouth by a tobacco strand.

Glancing up the embankment, he saw an old but strong-looking black man brandishing a wrench and wearing bunny slippers, charging down at him.

Spitting out the ruined cigar, Death stepped forward, grabbed Alex's wrist and forearm, twisted. The old man went up and over, the wrench went flying from his hand. Alex came down hard on his back, the breath bursting out of him in spurts.

Death leaned over Alex. Up close, Alex could see that the pink face was slightly pocked and that some of the pinkness was due to makeup. That was rich. Death was vain about his appearance. He was wearing a black T-shirt, pants and sneakers and of course his derby, which had neither been stirred by the wreck nor by the ju-jitsu maneuver.

"What's with you, man?" Death asked.

Alex wheezed, tried to catch his breath. "You can't . . . have . . . her."

"Who? What are you talking about?"

"Don't play . . . dumb with me." Alex raised up on one elbow, his wind returning. "You're Death and you took my Margie's soul."

Death straightened. "So you know who I am. All right. But what of it? I'm only doing my job."

"It ain't her time."

"My list says it is, and my list is never wrong."

Alex felt something hard pressing against his hip, realized what it was. The pipe wrench. Even the throw Death had put on him had not hurled it from his coat pocket. It had lodged there and the pocket had shifted beneath his hip, making his old bones hurt all the worse.

Alex made as to roll over, freed the pocket beneath him, shot his hand inside and produced the pipe wrench. He hurled it at Death, struck him just below the brim of the bowler and sent him stumbling back. This time the bowler fell off. Death's forehead was bleeding.

Before Death could collect himself, Alex was up and rushing. He used his head as a battering ram and struck Death in the stomach, knocking him to the ground. He put both knees on Death's arms, pinning them, clenched his throat with his strong, old hands.

"I ain't never hurt nobody before," Alex said. "Don't want to now. I didn't want to hit you with that wrench, but you give Margie back."

Death's eyes showed no expression at first, but slowly a light seemed to go on behind them. He easily pulled his arms out from under Alex's knees, reached up, took hold of the old man's wrists and pulled the hands away from his throat.

"You old rascal," Death said. "You outsmarted me."

Death flopped Alex over on his side, then stood up. Grinning, he turned, stooped to recover his bowler, but he never laid a hand on it.

Alex moved like a crab, scissoring his legs, and caught Death from above and behind his knees, twisted, brought him down on his face.

Death raised up on his palms and crawled from behind Alex's legs like a snake, effortlessly. This time he grabbed the hat and put it on his head and stood up. He watched Alex carefully.

"I don't frighten you much, do I?" Death asked.

Alex noted that the wound on Death's forehead had vanished. There wasn't even a drop of blood. "No," Alex said. "You don't frighten me much. I just want my Margie back."

"All right," Death said.

Alex sat bolt upright.

"What?"

"I said, all right. For a time. Not many have outsmarted me, pinned me to the ground. I give you credit, and you've got courage. I like that. I'll give her back. For a time. Come here."

Death walked over to the car that was not from Detroit. Alex got to his feet and followed. Death took the keys out of the ignition, moved to the trunk, worked the key in the lock. It popped up with a hiss.

Inside were stacks and stacks of matchboxes. Death moved his hand over them, like a careful man selecting a special vegetable at the supermarket. His fingers came to rest on a matchbox that looked to Alex no different than the others.

Death handed Alex the matchbox. "Her soul's in here, old man. You stand over her bed, open the box. Okay?"

"That's it?"

"That's it. Now get out of here before I change my mind. And remember, I'm giving her back to you. But just for a while."

Alex started away, holding the matchbox carefully. As he walked past Death's car, he saw the dents he had knocked in the side with his wrecker were popping out. He turned to look at Death, who was closing the trunk.

"Don't suppose you'll need a tow out of here?"

Death smiled thinly. "Not hardly."

Alex stood over their bed; the bed where they had loved, slept, talked and dreamed. He stood there with the matchbox in his hand, his eyes on Margie's cold face. He ever so gently eased the box open. A small flash of blue light, like Peter Pan's friend Tinker-bell, rushed out of it and hit Margie's lips. She made a sharp inhaling sound and her chest rose. Her eyes came open. She turned and looked at Alex and smiled.

"My lands, Alex. What are you doing there, and half-dressed? What have you been up to . . . is that a matchbox?"

Alex tried to speak, but he found that he could not. All he could do was grin.

"Have you gone nuts?" she asked.

"Maybe a little." He sat down on the bed and took her hand. "I love you, Margie."

"And I love you . . . you been drinking?"

"No."

Then came the overwhelming sound of Death's horn. One harsh blast that shook the house, and the headbeams shone brightly through the window and the cracks lit up the shack like a cheap nightclub act.

"Who in the world?" Margie asked.

"Him. But he said . . . stay here."

Alex got his shotgun out of the closet. He went out on the porch. Death's car was pointed toward the house, and the headbeams seemed to hold Alex, like a fly in butter.

Death was standing on the bottom step, waiting.

Alex pointed the shotgun at him. "You git. You gave her back. You gave your word."

"And I kept it. But I said for a while."

"That wasn't any time at all."

"It was all I could give. My present."

"Short time like that's worse than no time at all."

"Be good about it, Alex. Let her go. I got records and they have to be kept. I'm going to take her anyway, you understand that?"

"Not tonight, you ain't." Alex pulled back the hammers on the shotgun. "Not tomorrow night neither. Not anytime soon."

"That gun won't do you any good, Alex. You know that. You

can't stop Death. I can stand here and snap my fingers three times, or click my tongue, or go back to the car and honk my horn, and she's as good as mine. But I'm trying to reason with you, Alex. You're a brave man. I did you a favor because you bested me. I didn't want to just take her back without telling you. That's why I came here to talk. But she's got to go. Now."

Alex lowered the shotgun. "Can't . . . can't you take me in her place? You can do that, can't you?"

"I . . . I don't know. It's highly irregular."

"Yeah, you can do that. Take me. Leave Margie."

"Well, I suppose."

The screen door creaked open and Margie stood there in her housecoat. "You're forgetting, Alex, I don't want to be left alone."

"Go in the house, Margie," Alex said.

"I know who this is: I heard you talking, Mr. Death. I don't want you taking my Alex. I'm the one you came for. I ought to have the right to go."

There was a pause, no one speaking. Then Alex said, "Take both of us. You can do that, can't you? I know I'm on that list of yours, and pretty high up. Man my age couldn't have too many years left. You can take me a little before my time, can't you? Well, can't you?"

Margie and Alex sat in their rocking chairs, their shawls over their knees. There was no fire in the fireplace. Behind them the bucket collected water and outside the wind whistled. They held hands. Death stood in front of them. He was holding a King Edward cigar box.

"You're sure of this?" Death asked. "You don't both have to go."

Alex looked at Margie, then back at Death. "We're sure," he said. "Do it." Death nodded. He opened the cigar box and held it out on one palm. He used his free hand to snap his fingers.

Once. (*the wind picked up, howled*)

Twice. *(the rain beat like drumsticks on the roof)*

Three times. *(lightning ripped and thunder roared)*

"And in you go," Death said.

The bodies of Alex and Margie slumped and their heads fell together between the rocking chairs. Their fingers were still entwined.

Death put the box under his arm and went out to the car. The rain beat on his derby hat and the wind sawed at his bare arms and T-shirt. He didn't seem to mind.

Opening the trunk, he started to put the box inside, then hesitated.

He closed the trunk.

"Damn," he said, "if I'm not getting to be a sentimental old fool."

He opened the box. Two blue lights rose out of it, elongated, touched ground. They took on the shape of Alex and Margie. They glowed against the night.

"Want to ride up front?" Death asked.

"That would be nice," Margie said.

"Yes, nice," Alex said.

Death opened the door and Alex and Margie slid inside. Death climbed in behind the wheel. He checked the clipboard dangling from the dash. There was a woman in a Tyler hospital, dying of brain damage. That would be his next stop.

He put the clipboard down and started the car that was not from Detroit.

"Sounds well-tuned," Alex said.

"I try to keep it that way," Death said.

They drove out of there then, and as they went, Death broke into song. "Row, row, row your boat, gently down the stream," and Margie and Alex chimed in with, "Merrily, merrily, merrily, merrily, life is but a dream."

Off they went down the highway, the taillights fading, the song dying, the black metal of the car melting into the fabric of night, and then there was only the whispery sound of good tires on wet cement and finally not even that. Just the blowing sound of the wind and the rain.

Ten Digit PIN

By Anna L. Davis

A sudden scream from down the hall made the artist's hand shake. "Sorry," he said. "Want the mirror?"

Sawyer winced. Not the thing he wanted to hear from the guy holding a needle to his left shoulder. He shook his head.

"Nah, it's all right," he said. "Ain't like you're a newbie with the ink, man." Putting his head back down on the table, Sawyer let his dreadlocks fall forward as he stared at the dirty floor. "What's going on over there, anyway? Y'all got a torture room I don't know about?"

A chuckle.

"We brought in one of those biohackers. Owner thought it'd be good for business. But I gotta tell ya, from the stuff that comes out of there, I'm not so sure."

Sawyer closed his eyes to avoid looking at a suspicious reddish-brown stain on the floor. Maybe it was ink, not dried blood. "Biohacking? Like NeuroChip?"

The artist paused to replenish his needle. "No, we don't have the right licensing for that. This girl does street augmentations—stuff like magnets, radio frequency, infrared, antennae, cybernetic lenses, extrasensory tech—you know, your basic transhuman gadgetry."

"Sounds harmless enough," Sawyer said.

"Yeah, you'd think so, but she brings in a dark crowd. Calls herself Doctor Frankenstein. Uptown kids love her, and they got money, so we're not turning anyone away." The artist dabbed

Sawyer's shoulder with a sterile cloth. "About done here. This your, what . . . twentieth tattoo or so?"

Thinking, Sawyer took a minute. "Close. Eighteenth I think."

Another scream, followed by sobbing. Definitely female.

"What's that one getting?" Sawyer asked, motioning in the direction of the noise.

"Don't know. But the testing room is out front. Maybe if you hang around a while you'll get to see for yourself."

Sawyer stood up and assessed his new tat—a Native American thunderbird—a symbol of supernatural strength and power. He'd been drawn to it for months. "That's tight. Thanks, man."

"Anytime."

The artist cleaned his instruments and put them away.

Sawyer followed the artist to the front desk and swiped his wrist over the IDChip reader, reminding himself that tomorrow he'd need to balance his bitcoin account.

The click of high heels on concrete startled them both. "Speak of the devil," the artist said. "Sawyer, I'd like you to meet our newest addition—Doctor Frankenstein."

Sawyer swiveled his head but winced as his dreadlocks irritated the inflamed skin on his shoulder. An attractive, heavily augmented Goth woman held out her right hand. With jet black hair shaved short on one side, several facial piercings and tattoos down her neck and arms, she could've been Sawyer's female counterpart.

"Sort of a doctor, anyway," she said. "I don't create the biotech, but clean installation requires skill." The woman offered a cursory nod, shaking Sawyer's hand. "Happy with your ink?" She motioned to the bandage. "What is it?"

"Yeah, it's lit. A thunderbird."

"Ah, like the creature at the top of a totem pole? I have one of those too," she said, turning around and lowering her black jeans to reveal a small thunderbird at the small of her back. "What made you decide on that one?" she added.

The artist cleared his throat. "Sorry to interrupt," he said, "but I gotta get going. He might hang around a while for the freak show, if that's okay with you."

Doctor Frankenstein smiled and the light bounced off her lip piercing. "The more the merrier. I could use the backup." She turned and gave Sawyer a provocative grin. "Someone else on my side, if you know what I mean."

Was she flirting? Sure seemed like it, but she had at least fifteen years on him. Probably in her mid-thirties—not totally out of the question. But he suspected that older women who pierced their lips and shaved half their heads came with a decent amount of baggage. Not that his was a clean slate.

Sawyer sat down on a black leather couch near the register. "When'd you get the thunderbird tat?" he asked, internally chastising himself for his tentative judgment. Old programming died hard.

"A long time ago. I wasn't always Doc Frankenstein, you know." She surprised Sawyer by sitting beside him. "Back then I went by 'Jade.'"

"Jade. Much better. Do you mind if I call you that? Rolls off the tongue easier." Okay, he was definitely flirting back. Couldn't help himself.

"Sure," she said. "But don't spread it around, all right?"

"The secret's safe with me. So what happened?"

"Recreational biohacking doesn't bother me, but the idea of mandatory chipping . . . well, I got the thunderbird tattoo to show my resolve. The power to resist."

"But you caved." Sawyer meant it as a statement, knowing that she couldn't be a licensed, practicing biohacker if she hadn't complied.

Jade leaned forward and stared at the floor. Sawyer fought the urge to glance at her backside, in hopes that the upper edge of the thunderbird tattoo was visible over her jeans.

"Yeah," Jade said. "Same old story. Had to earn a living."

The door at the end of the hall slammed open, followed by footsteps, then the closing of another door.

"She just went into the women's restroom," Jade continued. "Probably to refresh her makeup. She'll be ready for testing in a minute."

"Should I brace myself?" Sawyer asked. "Are we talking 'Terminator' type stuff here?"

"Something like," Jade answered. "She looks normal and a bit high-end. But don't be fooled. She's barely human anymore. This one's had a lot of work done. Regular poster child for the Real Cyborgs of Dallas or something."

"What'd she do today? Sounded painful."

"Full tech manicure. All ten replaced from the roots."

The idea of it made Sawyer grimace. "Why the hell would anyone do that? Regular manicures can't be that much trouble."

"Drone control."

"With all ten fingers?"

"Nine actually. For her nine drones. The tenth one is for network control." Another smile. "Like I said, this one's had a lot of work done."

"I don't get it."

"Hang out a few more minutes. She can't leave until the tech clears testing room approval."

An uneasy feeling gnawed at Sawyer's stomach but his curiosity won out. "Fine. Y'all got anything to drink around here? That tat made me thirsty."

"Sure," she said, opening a hidden door in the wall behind her. "Pick your poison. Fortified water, amplified soda. And here at the back . . ." She reached past the bottles. "I think we even have some electrostat beer."

Eyeing the rows of drinks, Sawyer pointed to the fortified water. "What's in that? Just vitamins and crap?"

A frown. "Yeah, sorry. We're not licensed for chip amps yet. I mean, I could probably get some if you wanted, but . . ."

"Nah, that's fine," Sawyer said. She'd misunderstood. "I'll take it. No need for amps."

A door slammed. "Oh look," said Jade, turning toward the noise. "Miss Texas finally decided to grace us with her presence."

Sawyer's jaw dropped open when he saw the woman who'd emerged from behind the closed door. Tall, tan and shapely—with long brunette hair framing a symmetrical model-perfect face—she could've been a Dallas Cowboys cheerleader or a dancer for the Mavericks. Nothing looked augmented about this Lone Star girl-next-door, not even her cleavage.

Sawyer found it difficult to believe this was the woman who'd been screaming while he was under the artist's needle. The leggy brunette didn't have smudged eye makeup or splotchy skin. She wore tight white shorts and a black halter top, and everything about her was camera-ready, except for the bandages around her fingers, like puffy white gloves.

Jade smiled at Sawyer's reaction. "I'm gonna check her augments and then she'll be ready to test the tech. You gonna be around a few more minutes? We might need a volunteer test subject."

"Dang, lady. I don't know. You haven't exactly been reassuring." But Sawyer found the idea of this Miss Texas chick going postal with her cybernetic fingernails more than a little intriguing.

"Well, not everyone has the balls for volunteering in the testing room. It's a freak show."

Had to give her that. "Anything goes wrong and you'll step in, right?"

Jade nodded.

"Okay. Sure," Sawyer said. "I'll be her test subject." *And anything else they wanted him to be.*

Contemplating this opportunity, he tried hard to suppress his enthusiasm. Alone in a tattoo parlor with two attractive women, both of whom had a fetish for hidden body tech?

Hell, yes. He'd volunteer all night long.

Jade excused herself to attend to the woman's bandaged fingers. A few minutes later, she directed both of them to a door on the left, a black door with a chalkboard tacked beside it. In artsy, blood red chalk, someone had scrawled "Freak Show."

Jade laughed but the other woman didn't say a word. Sawyer squinted in the bright light of the testing area; it was much brighter than the lighting in the rest of the parlor. When his eyes adjusted, he saw two distinct sections in the room. On one side, several armchairs and a bistro table. On the other, a glass enclosed control center that reminded him of a recording studio.

"If you'll have a seat," Jade said, glancing at both of them. "I'll get everything set up in the control center."

The brunette clutched her turquoise handbag closer to her side when she realized that Sawyer would be there with her.

"Don't worry," he said. "I don't bite or anything."

She smiled at him, revealing perfect teeth. "I'm not worried. My name's Vivian. And you are?" Her voice was just the right balance of friendly and detached.

"Sawyer. Doctor Frankenstein said you'd need a test subject." He flipped a dreadlock out of his face.

Another wide smile. "Aww, thanks sweetie. Bless your heart. You don't need to spend the rest of your evening with my silly whims. I'm sure you have a girl waiting for you at home . . ." Vivian's brown eyes twinkled as she leaned back in the armchair and crossed her shapely legs.

Sawyer's mouth went dry. He cleared his throat. "Uh, no. I don't mind helping you out."

"You're the best," Vivian said, clutching her purse tighter. "I've never had my nails augmented before. I'm so incredibly excited to show Teacup what I can do."

"Teacup?"

"My dog." She pointed to her purse. "She's so tiny, I call her Teacup. But shh . . . she's sleeping now."

Sawyer was about to respond when the lights flickered. "Ready?" Jade asked, her voice coming over the intercom.

"Yeah," Vivian responded. "Can't wait." Her eyes met Sawyer's and she smiled.

"Good," Jade said, from behind the glass. "Alright. Let's start with your ten digit PIN. The augments use an invisible screen, so it works best if you pretend that you're using a keyboard."

"Easy enough," Vivian answered, raising her fingers into the air as if putting on gloves. Besides some redness and swelling at the base of each nail bed, her hands looked normal.

Jade's voice crackled in the room. "Start with the far left pinkie finger and work your way to the right." A pause as she waited for Vivian to comply. Sawyer stared.

"That's right," Jade continued. "Very good. Now the other hand, starting with your right thumb . . . excellent. Now the right pinkie finger, that's the one you're using for network controls?"

"That's correct," Vivian answered, her right ring finger suspended in front of her. "Should I keep going?"

"Yeah, I'll make a note here in your file." Another pause. "Okay, you're all set up. Ready to test them?"

Vivian grinned, then giggled. "Oh my, yes. I've been beside myself all day."

"Umm hmmm." Jade didn't sound enthusiastic. Sawyer wondered how many times she'd walked uptown socialites through this routine. "I'm all set. Go for it."

Vivian smiled then turned to Sawyer. "Can you pretend like you're asking me out? But . . . be rude about it. And maybe act like you're going to rough me up a bit?"

No way would he try to take advantage of this girl, not even for an augmentation test run. "I don't think so," he said.

"Please?" She smiled again and Sawyer reconsidered.

"Fine. Okay, so I'm supposed to hit on you. Got it." He pulled a few dreadlocks forward over his eyes and lowered his voice, trying to be menacing.

"Hey pretty lady," he said, affecting a Southern drawl. "Whaddaya' say you and me get to know each other a little better? I think I could make you real happy." He laid it on thick, grabbing her slim wrist for effect.

Vivian didn't say a word. With one swipe of her left index finger, her hoop earring came flying out of her earlobe, turned from vertical to horizontal, and transformed into a small drone.

It headed straight for Sawyer's face and stopped in front of and between Sawyer's eyes.

"Oh my God," he shouted, jumping out of the chair and stumbling backwards. "Dang, woman. Never mind, I didn't mean it. Go find someone else to cuddle."

Vivian swiped her finger to the side and the small drone floated away from Sawyer.

"Geez," Sawyer continued. "You got problems with old boyfriends or something?" He tried to play it off, but the drone scared him.

"It works," Vivian said, giggling. "It really works."

She swiped her finger as if to return the drone back to earring form, but nothing happened. It simply hovered in mid-air. She swiped her finger again and yelled at the control center. "It's not coming back. Why isn't it—"

The drone whizzed past him and lodged in Vivian's head at her ear. Her hand flew up to the wound and she jumped up and down, yelling for help.

At first Sawyer thought she was joking, but seconds later he saw blood oozing from between her fingers.

"Help her," Jade said, abandoning the control panel on the other side of the glass. "Help her!"

Sawyer went to Vivian to retrieve the drone, but when he got closer he realized it was already lodged in the side of her head. Vivian screamed, her eyes twitching wildly, her weaponized, perfectly manicured nails now digging at the wound. As Jade entered the test room, Sawyer tried to grab Vivian's hands and she jerked them away.

"Back off," she screamed. "Don't touch me."

Vivian raised her left ring finger, sending the other hoop earring flying out of her ear as it transformed into an identical drone.

"Stop, for God's sake—stop," Jade yelled.

The second drone flew past Sawyer and went straight for Jade.

"You!" Vivian screamed, holding her gushing ear with one hand. "You did this to me. Now it's your turn."

Jade instinctively held up her arms to block the drone. It sliced through her left forearm, deflecting off of the interior edge of her radius bone. It entered her body in the center of her chest and Jade gasped and collapsed.

Sawyer scrambled on his hands and knees over to her, checking the severity of her wounds. He could still hear the drone in the center of her chest—it was spinning, penetrating. Heart racing, he quickly lifted her up, just as the drone exited her back and bounced off the linoleum floor.

He carried her into the control room and slammed the door. He laid her down on the floor near the control panel. He heard Vivian groan softly through the speaker.

"Jade?" He wanted her to be okay, but knew she wasn't.

"Hey, Thunderbird Man," she said weakly. "I never got your name. Sorry."

"Sawyer. My name's Sawyer. But I don't think you should talk."

"I like that," Jade said. "Sawyer." Her eyes rolled back in pain, but she fought through it. "Listen, Sawyer. Everyone thinks that the thunderbird is special because . . ."

She struggled to complete her thought.

"The sound its wings make," Sawyer finished for her. "Like thunder."

"Yes. Like thunder." Jade exhaled shakily, as if she wanted to add something else but couldn't.

Blood appeared at the corners of her mouth.

"But thunder comes after lightning," she finally continued. "It's the lightning that's dangerous, not the thunder. Understand what I'm saying?" Jade glanced back and forth between the control panel and the door. She lifted her hand to motion him closer, then groaned with the exertion. "Lightning takes out the cyborgs," she murmured. "Bots and borgs—all of them. Everything except IDChip."

Jade began to shake violently with shock, and Sawyer cradled her head.

"A gentleman," she quipped, the blood now dripping from her lips. "Lightning. That's how we'll win the war. A sudden power surge, flashes of lightning . . . Mighty Thunderbird."

"What war?" Sawyer asked, trying to hold her steady.

"The war against the human race. Soon. It's coming." A deep, jagged breath. "They're going to kill me. I did it—oh, God. I helped them . . ."

"Helped who? What's happening?"

"The bots."

Metal flashed at the glass window in front of the control panel. Two drones appeared and hovered at eye level.

Jade winced and shivered. "They're going to get me. Remember what I said." The muscles in her core contracted and she spat up a splash of deep red. "It's called a thunderbird, but the lightning in its eyes wins the war. Lightning first, thunder second."

"Jade, you're not—"

A whirring sound.

"Promise me," she whispered.

He nodded. "Okay, I promise. Lightning wins the war."

One of the drones withdrew about five feet from the window and then reversed. It sped up and smashed through the control center glass, but it was damaged by the impact. It fell and hit the blood-slick floor, still whirring less than a foot away. The second drone rose and entered through the break.

Sawyer paused and stared, struck by this semblance of teamwork and intelligence, but jumped when the second drone darted for Jade. He slapped at it, and a sharp pain enveloped his hand. He drew back, his palm gushing blood.

"Make it stop," Jade gurgled. "Shut it *dow*—"

The repositioned drone slashed into one of her jugular veins, cutting her instructions short. She contorted and slumped flat. Dead.

The drone, bloody and relentless, raised back up.

He knew he had to get out of there.

As the drone floated, Sawyer grabbed some paper from a shelf and hastily wrapped it around his wounded hand, then ripped a few long pieces of tape from the nearby dispenser and cinched the paper closed.

Clutching his paper-bandaged hand, he realized he needed a distraction.

"Hey Vivian," he yelled, hoping she could still hear him. "You never showed me your little dog. What was her name? I can't remember."

The drone continued to hover, tracking his every move.

He continued. "I'm sorry I didn't get to see your sweet little puppy—I'm sure she does some great tricks."

Retreating, the drone stopped at the hole in the window glass. Sawyer exhaled in relief.

"Teacup." A soft voice came through the speaker. "Her name's Teacup."

Sawyer risked a look through the window. He leaned up and stood on his toes and saw Vivian crumpled at the base of the armchair, blood dripping from the side of her face as she cradled her purse. With her right hand, she pinched her thumb and index finger together, as if holding something, and held out her pinkie finger. The tenth one, the one she used for network controls.

"See? Like a dainty teacup." She swiped her pinkie finger in the air.

A tiny robot emerged from her purse.

Her dog. It was a robot.

"Come here, little Teacup. I told you I'd train you one of these days . . . "

A growl. Low at first, then stronger.

"Now Teacup," Vivian said. "Mommy's hurt real bad, don't be mean to me. Can you fetch me a drink? No, bad Teacup, don't bite me, don't—"

Another growl. Sawyer stepped to the control room door, but the drone at the broken glass rose and drifted above his head again, still dripping Jade's blood.

Then, one vicious bark and a long, shrill scream.

Shivers ran down Sawyer's spine and he scanned the room for a power switch or something—anything—to use against the drone and Teacup, but nothing caught his eye. Jade's body blocked most of the buttons on the underside of the control panel.

Wait.

Her lifeless, bloody arm rested near a yellow button with a symbol on it.

A lightning bolt.

Without thinking, he reached past her and punched the yellow button, praying it'd stop the machines, hoping it wasn't too late.

The small drone fell to the floor, bouncing off the control panel like a quarter.

Thank God, Sawyer thought.

From the test room, a murmur. "Teacup, oh Teacup."

Sawyer stood up and peered out. Vivian was covered in blood, her face slashed, her ear missing. She spotted him out of the corner of her eye.

"You killed her," she said. "My poor Teacup. I hope you have a good lawyer—that poochbot cost me a fortune."

Sawyer sunk below the counter and took a ragged breath. Beside him, Jade was motionless, her blood still dripping down the cabinet doors and leather chair where the drone had left a trail. The two broken drones lay at her feet, mere inches from Sawyer.

A voice from the speaker.

"Can you get me a bandage?" Vivian said. "I'm bleeding all over my clothes, I'll never get them clean."

Sawyer's chest heaved, and he almost threw up.

Without a word, he stood up again and steadied himself. He walked straight to the front door, swiped his left wrist in the ID-Chip exit reader and fled.

Sad Potatoes

By E. R. Bills

Ben watched unhappily.

In his simple mind, this was the saddest funeral he had ever seen.

The old woman wheezed and moaned. The middle-aged man sniffed and sobbed. The preacher's soothing voice seemed to somehow complicate their grief, and Ben wanted him to stop; but all he could do was cry.

So much pain, he thought. So much hurt.

Ben had been to seven funerals in the last three months, and each one dismayed him more.

At first he was only slightly sad because he was mostly mortified. The ritual was frightening and freakish to him. At his second funeral one of the mourners had propelled herself onto the deceased's coffin as it was being lowered and screamed "Take me, Lord! O please, Lord . . . take me instead of him."

The spectacle had terrified Ben. He had wrapped his arms around his head and cried out.

Others in attendance had simply panicked, not knowing whether to dislodge the leaping woman or console the screaming half-wit. The last few funerals were uneventful. Ben had been mostly just sad.

When Ben was sad, one of the older, blue-haired ladies would sometimes pat his shoulder to comfort him, or look up at him and say things like *"There, there,* it's okay. He's gone on to a better place . . . we should only envy him."

Ben would nod and swallow, wiping his tears with his shirt-sleeve.

Ben knew they were right. His Aunt Ruby had told him so.

Before every meal and at bedtime, they thanked the Lord for his blessings and prayed for forgiveness and salvation. Aunt Ruby constantly impressed upon Ben the importance of the Lord in their lives, and Ben often felt blessed and forgiven and salvaged. He prayed for preachers and worshipers and neighbors and Aunt Ruby and all the kids he could remember on the milk cartons. Sometimes he even prayed for his dead dog, Larry, and his parents, even though he knew that they, too, had gone on to a better place. Aunt Ruby's heart was filled with warmth-eternal when she watched her huge nephew kneel next to his bed and pray like a child.

"Blessed are the meek," she whispered, when she crept by later to check on him.

Ben's funerals came afternoons after working in Aunt Ruby's garden. His devotion made it a Parker County landmark.

Encompassing most of Aunt Ruby's back yard, the garden yielded some of the area's largest melons and cucumbers, and the county's sweetest potatoes. Ben was the first to till every spring, and only the Sabbath kept him from weeding and raking and watering. He carefully concocted every compost and patiently attended to every stalk and sprout.

Ben's potato crop was his pride and joy; Aunt Ruby's soil was made for his spud slivers and every tuber section—placed six to eight inches deep and spaced fourteen to eighteen inches apart—sprouted in no less than two weeks, and every eye produced at least a half-dozen Bliss Triumphs. And when Ben's Bliss Triumphs went head-to-head with Irish Cobblers and Idaho Russets, he still brought home blue ribbons for the region's greenest thumb.

When it became too hot to work in Aunt Ruby's garden, Ben would usually clean up and have lunch. Sometimes he went to town to browse through the local hardware shop.

Ben loved the Ace Hardware shop and he kept a clipping of the latest John Deere 42-inch Hydraulic Tiller in his wallet. It had a reversible till design that allowed for forward and backward tilling, and he enjoyed sitting on the store model and imagining himself plowing through monster pigweeds, rabid dog fennels and threatening buckthorns.

Lately, however, Ben had been spending his afternoons at the town cemetery. He discovered it one day after following a slow, winding procession of cars and trucks into the pasture the cemetery occupied. The crowd had piqued Ben's interest, so he'd followed them. Being part of the procession had made Ben feel somehow important.

He often cleaned up, put on his church clothes and headed to the cemetery. When Aunt Ruby asked where he was going, he would smile and say "the church place." Aunt Ruby assumed he meant the church and she would remind him to avoid strangers and stay off the road.

"Remember what happened to Larry," she would add.

But Ben could never remember what happened to Larry.

The first time he tried to recall what happened to Larry, he had nightmares for a week. He envisioned the bloody, white, passenger-side quarter-panel of a 1977 AMC Pacer. It was sort of like the "white-light-at-the-end-of-the-tunnel" dream that Aunt Ruby and her friends occasionally discussed at the Quilt Club gatherings that she held in their den every second Tuesday of the month. Except when Ben got to the end of the tunnel—which invariably smelled like mulch and the sulphur stuff he sprinkled on the squash to protect it—the bright light was really the blood-smudged, white quarter-panel of the Pacer. It scared him and made him sad. He didn't understand.

The walk to the cemetery was short, but it gave Ben time to think about things like the garden, the quarter-panel and the hurt he witnessed. Even in his simple mind there was a sense of wrongness about the hurt and a desire to fix it, and on the afternoon of the saddest funeral he had ever seen, something clicked.

"Harvey was a good man," the preacher said, in his soothing tone, the drone of his voice floating off as surely as Harvey's soul. This particular preacher was Ben's favorite. He was always dressed in black with his hair combed back, perpetually solemn and serious; and he always concluded the service with personal remarks, anecdotes—stories that repeatedly made Ben wish he was the man or woman being lowered in the coffin, the lucky one, on his or her way to a better place.

"Harvey was a good man," the preacher repeated, as if remembering. "He's left us for now, but he's gone on to a better place." And in Ben's mind—at first murky and indiscernible, but now perfectly clear—it finally made sense.

As Ben stood there behind the wheezing old lady and the sniffing man, looking over their shoulders at the preacher and the open grave, he had a revelation, like the ones Aunt Ruby read him from the Bible.

Ben thought of the hereafter. He imagined the Elysian Fields, green and flourishing. He saw all the happy souls arranged in row after row, acre after acre (like his Bliss Triumphs), and it all came together. All the unhappy, weeping mourners were sad because they had been left behind. All the poor old people and pitiful young people were hurting because their friends and loved ones had gone on without them.

Ben finally understood, although it was an understanding he would never be able to put into words. He knew what the Bible said about man being made from the dust of the ground; and he knew from the garden that a seed had to be planted in the ground before it could grow. As he stared at Harvey's coffin and surveyed the grave that it would soon be placed in, he realized what he had to do. He wiped his eyes and slowly stepped forward.

He was smiling tearfully, compassionately, when he seized the old woman and middle-aged man in mid-whimper and brought their heads together with a loud "thwack."

They fell away like discarded marionettes, their innocent glares seeming to confirm Ben's theory. He smiled wider and held his arms out to the preacher.

The preacher's soothing drone broke when he recognized the approaching hulk to be the screaming half-wit from the frightful memorial where the hysterical widow had launched herself onto her husband's coffin. As if that wasn't nightmare enough, he thought, and then trembled.

Ben only beamed.

For a short instant he thought the preacher seemed unsure about his own deliverance to the sweet by-and-by, but the preacher quickly regained his composure and started to speak. As Ben embraced him and squeezed, the preacher attempted to say "My son," but he never got past a hiss of the "S" and his cracking spine and death rattle were accompanied by a shrill, long "A" groan and a guttural slur.

Ben released the preacher from his embrace, but took the lucky man's face in his large hands and kissed it. There was only love in his deliverance, and he was well-pleased that the preacher seemed to recognize him for what he was as his back snapped: *a savior.*

To keep the sun from parching his new strain of spuds, Ben peeled away their sackcloth and moved them into the nearest shade. After a quick trip home to change back into his work clothes, he returned to the cemetery with his tools.

Ben spent the rest of the afternoon preparing tuber sections and readying the new garden to receive them. When the early evening breeze came, he carefully planted them six to eight inches deep, fourteen to eighteen inches apart. He finished just after dark.

On the way home Ben marveled at all the suffering he would now be able to cure. And he felt—maybe for the first time ever—a grown-up sense of righteousness.

Working two gardens would be difficult. But he was inspired.

The False Face
of Donovan O'Grady

By Stephen Patrick

Donovan O'Grady was my first attempt at becoming human and the experiment seemed to be working. It was a nice enough name, particularly compared to my demon name, *Kihatomen*, the Flayer of Souls. Less a name than a curse, it had been cried out to the soaring moon by lesser beings in times of weakness.

My life as Donovan O'Grady began outside a loud, smoke-filled saloon in a remote part of the Texas Panhandle. Spurs jingled across the dance floor while skirts flared and whirled to the delight of twenty half-drunk cowboys, all eager to tame the frontier before civilization tamed them. Cheap, hard liquor was the lifeblood of the place, fueling the basest human instincts. It was a distraction and a necessity, one of the few escapes from a life of sun-bleached days as ranch-hand labor.

One of them, a transplanted Irishman, wandered outside, searching for a private place to relieve his beer-bloated belly. One of his companions called to him, "Donovan O'Grady, you hurry back. I aim to win some more of your money!"

The proclamation was followed by raucous laughter.

The Irishman found his way behind the saloon and into the shadows, my shadows. As the darkness swallowed him, I was reminded of the painful rules for mortal transformation by the Great Spirit of the Underworld.

Un-bartered flesh will rot from the inside. Flesh will only be suitable when it is given freely.

I was still finding my way and sought not flesh, but vestments for my journey. The Irishman's size and attire were perfect. His needs were even more basic, and as he relieved himself on the cracked Texas soil, I remembered that a bandana and wide-brimmed hat can only hide so much. He heard nothing until I was upon him, sliding my claws across his throat and spilling his blood onto the dirt. I was careful to keep my marks beneath his collar, so I could harvest the face and hands from the quivering body. They would not last long, decaying as soon as I slipped them on, but I hoped the town might bear enough fruit to satisfy all my needs.

How naive that sounds now.

My secret spot behind the stable was discovered too quickly, thanks to a Yankee tack dealer with a weak stomach. As he re-gurgitated his last drink onto the crimson ground, he learned of the Irishman. I silenced his screams, but not before a murmur ran through the saloon and then through the town, until the doors of every building burst forth with intoxicated gamblers, immoral dancers and a few criminals. Worse, they were joined by a pair of badge-wearing lawmen, both confident that the pistols dangling from their hips could handle any disturbance.

My false-face dripped with fresh blood and when the first dancing girl saw me and screamed, I knew that no bargain could be made with this group. Bullets tore through my newly acquired flesh before passing through my demon-form. I rushed into the gathering crowd, letting fear overcome them as they continued to fire. Quickly panicked and backing away and turning as they shot, they created a crossfire and soon most of them lay at my feet. I chased down the stragglers (mostly women and children) who positioned themselves beyond the fray. I dispatched them to my master forthwith, and then lamented the now rotting flesh that began to drip from my face and hands.

I left the silent town behind me, never noticing the eight-year-old son of a prostitute who had been hiding in the attic of the saloon. When I arrived amid cattlemen in Fort Worth, news had already spread about a bloodbath to the west. The accounts concluded with reassuring reports that the Texas Rangers had been called in to investigate a lone stranger who'd wandered into the town. Apparently, the boy had told the story to a post messenger who arrived with a sack full of letters, only to return with his arms full of death notices.

The Texas Rangers were a determined group.

Despite my efforts, they dogged my heels at each turn. My search for willing flesh turned into a frantic dash across the state, sustained by impromptu flayings of necessity, the acquired flesh quickly obsolete. The Great Spirit's rules were inviolate, and I left a trail not unlike that of the muleskinners chasing the bison herds. My fleshless countenance was too terrible to be safely beholden, and borrowed flesh, though fleeting, offered my sole opportunities for flight. Escape meant time to hunt.

The Rangers pursued me from a brothel outside of Fort Worth to a miller's cottage near Waco and finally a cattle company near San Antonio.

I found a willing donor in the company cook. He was a short, squat fellow whose liver had been eaten away by disease. He was quite willing to negotiate when I offered him relief from his pain.

He survived the initial part of the process. He even thanked me as I peeled the flesh from his right arm and slid it over the misshapen appendage that dangled from my right shoulder.

I also took parts of his torso, fulfilling my promise by removing the wretched disease that wracked his liver. But that torso was soon taken from me, ripped away as three pistol shots rang out in the fading light.

Our pact unbound, I tore the throat from my startled companion, releasing him from his fate. A damnable Ranger named Captain Barr stepped from the shadows, his smoldering pistol waving in front of him. It was only the settling darkness and the limitations of human vision that had kept him from perceiving my true nature.

A second volley tore through the chill night, ripping the cook's vibrant flesh from my grasp. I feared discovery as much as defeat.

The Rangers' pursuit had turned countless "volunteers" against me, so I slipped away, hoping to lose them on a long chase in the dark. But they rode well under the moon; even with my allies (the vermin and the night fliers) to guide me, these men stayed close behind. Before light, I spotted a large wooded area and realized the Rangers' pursuit might provide a unique opportunity.

"There he is. Kill him!"

Four gunshots pierced the stale midnight air. They echoed through the woods, sending a dozen sleeping birds into flight.

The shooters kept their aim, scanning for any reaction in the murky landscape.

I peered out from behind the tree that had absorbed the four shots. Unlike the hunters, my vision was unhindered by the misty darkness. I could plainly see their faded denim tucked hastily into worn leather boots and their short beards, stained by chewing tobacco. Their spurs chimed softly as they stepped. These men were more comfortable on horseback than tromping through the woods and, under normal circumstances, I would have turned the forest into a slaughterhouse, feasting on the marrow and entrails of my pursuers. But I did not lust for blood; I sought longevity.

Pulling my right hand back from the tree, I flexed my fingers, relishing the warmth and tightness of my most recent gift. The cook's hand was calloused and tanned and much older than I would have preferred, but it was my first. I treasure it, even now.

"There he is! Fire!"

The first two bullets cut deep into the tree behind me, showering me with splinters. The final two caught me square in the chest, leaving two gaping holes smoldering beneath my shirt.

"I think we got him," the youngest one said.

A smile crawled across my lips. The hunt had truly begun.

Deeper in the forest, the chase became slow-going for the Rangers. Even skilled frontiersmen slowed when crossing briars and thickets.

Despite the temptation to flee, I slowed my pace, keeping the Rangers in sight, enticing them to continue the hunt. I regularly draped a few shreds of my clothing over the thorns and scattered just enough of Donovan's blood to entice the hunters to continue.

When the Rangers drew closer, I heard frustration and reluctance in their voices. The youngest one, a dainty cherub I would learn to call Thomas, wore his discomfort on his face and it soon spilled over into his words.

"Captain Barr? Maybe we should turn back. Ain't no way he'll find his way outta that briar. Let the buzzards have him."

The tall man in front turned back on Thomas with a fire blazing in his eyes. The man riding beside Thomas, Andrew Lassiter, was only a few years older and might have agreed with the young man's concerns, but his lips grew tight under the gaze of the leader.

"We didn't ride this far to let a murderer go because of a few scratches," Captain Barr said. "If you're scared, you can go back and wait with the horses. Just leave your star with me. I'd hate for anyone to confuse you with a real Ranger."

I made a silent wish from the darkness. Thomas may have been afraid, but I certainly had a use for him.

"Captain, sir, it's not the brambles. It's just that this guy's already taken two slugs. I saw it. And he's still going strong, maybe even stronger than us."

Captain Barr turned to the lanky rider behind him, the final member of the party, a loyal man I'd learned was named Benjamin Widger. He was dedicated to his profession, but tormented by the brutal murder of his wife and daughter.

"Mr. Widger, will you kindly relieve young Thomas of his burden?"

Widger, the group's second-in-command, stepped toward

Thomas and, in a single motion, tore the gleaming silver badge from his shirt. Thomas stared down at the torn strip of flannel dangling from his left shirt pocket.

I could see a thin smile of satisfaction on the Captain's face.

"Thank you, Mr. Widger," Captain Barr said. "Now, Thomas, get out of my sight before I decide to shoot you where you stand."

Thomas's head slumped to his chest as shame flooded over him. He turned slowly, hoping, waiting for belated words of forgiveness from Captain Barr.

I knew Thomas's wait would be a long one, but the walk home through the woods would provide an opportunity for us to get better acquainted.

Utterly disheartened, Thomas walked with his rifle hanging loosely at his side, only a single round left in the magazine. Some might assume that I toyed with him or tormented him, but it was not so. I merely offered him the things he had been unable to achieve in his life.

Thomas spied a flash of movement to his left. He turned, but saw only the softly swaying trees and rustling bushes that had been his companions throughout the trip. He muttered something about his family's small store in Odessa.

Maybe his Pa could help him find work, help him find a life without the Rangers.

"Having trouble finding yourself?" I called out from a dark thicket in front of him, just to the left of the trail.

"Who's there?"

"Just a friend. I think you've been looking for me."

I stepped from the thicket, relishing the awe and fear on his face.

Thomas raised his rifle, leveling his sights on my chest. The barrel was shaking, but he gathered himself. I tried my best to calm him.

"You reckon your last bullet will stop me where all the others have not? And won't you look foolish when they arrive to find you with an empty gun in your hands, your head missing?"

"Listen, Mister."

"No, Thomas. You listen. You were punished for being the smart one back there. Be the smart one now."

"Now just stay where you are."

"Oh, I intend to. I wouldn't think of crossing a lawman. Maybe we can make a deal. Perhaps I have something to offer you."

"What are you saying?"

"I'm saying you're moments away from becoming an immortal Ranger, the greatest hero in Texas."

"How is that going to happen? Especially if you're not afraid of my gun."

"A deal, Thomas. A deal between friends. I'm willing to give you everything you've ever wanted: fame, fortune, even that shiny star. All in exchange for the one thing that I want."

"You're a murderer. You killed that man in that mess hall."

"It was not murder. He begged me to do it. To free him from a life that had grown uncomfortable. The disease that wrecked his body was a symptom of a darkness that was eating at his soul. He was a reprehensible man and long-suffering. Even he deserved the mercy I gave him." I ran the back of my right hand across my cheek. "And he is serving a much better purpose now."

"Is that how you want to reward me? By killing me?"

"There are many things worse than death, Thomas. And a number of uncomfortable options if we can't come to an agreement."

Thomas gripped his rifle even tighter, his finger shaking as it hovered over the trigger.

"A gentleman shouldn't enter into a bargain with a rifle. If a bullet is your answer, pull the trigger and get it over with. It's a deal-breaker, but if I die, you're a hero. If I don't, then we'll consider you in a much less favorable bargaining position. Either way, I think we can both get what we want."

I could see thoughts racing through Thomas' head. He considered his abrupt demotion and his bleak prospects back home.

"All it takes is a leap of faith, Thomas."

"How do I know you won't crawfish on your end of the deal?"

"It would hardly suit my purpose. I need your help."

Thomas thought for a moment and then his rifle dropped to his side. It now hung from the leather strap around his neck.

"Well, now," I said. "I'm glad you've decided to negotiate. Let's see if I can fulfill your greatest desires."

I discovered the intrepid Captain Barr floundering through the briars looking for an easier passage while his men waited back in the clearing. They were close enough to hear his screams and I did not want to take the chance of spooking them.

I don't know if it was an errant footstep or a branch snapping beneath my hand, but he turned toward me prematurely. His pistols gleamed in the moonlight.

"Hold it right there," he demanded, turning his head to alert the others.

It was his choice, of course. Not mine. But it was as ill-advised as his decision to ignore Thomas, and I was forced to dispatch him to the master before we could barter.

The Captain had instructed the remaining men to hold their positions while he scouted an easier route through the briars. True to their code, they obeyed his orders.

The remaining two Rangers had fashioned a quick camp in their leader's absence. They had gone for hours without food, their rations still lashed to their horses. A stale bit of tack from Andrew's pockets and a quick draw from Mr. Widger's flask made them feel better.

The sound of three sets of horses' hooves sent them diving into the shrubbery, each leveling their guns toward the disturbance.

Thomas had collected their horses and was astride the lead horse. I was lashed to the second horse, my hands and feet bound by coarse hemp rope. The third followed in tow. I saw Thomas swallow hard to gather his courage. He lifted his head high in mock pride and called out to his companions.

"Gentlemen, I've got something to show you."

The men lowered their muzzles at Thomas's voice and stared at us as we rode into the clearing.

"Thomas! You found him . . . and you caught him?"

"It wasn't easy. He took down the Captain before I got there." Thomas turned and gestured toward the horse blanket lashed behind his saddle. The blanket was bulky and lumpy enough that the other Rangers accepted him at his word.

"Oh my God!" cried Andrew, his youth and inexperience betraying him.

"We'll take the Captain's body in for a proper service tomorrow," Thomas said boldly. "In the meantime, does anyone know where I left my badge?"

Widger pulled the star from his pocket.

"It's right here, Thomas. Or boss, I reckon. Seeing as how you are the man that bagged that mongrel."

Widger twirled it in his hand for a moment before tossing it to Thomas.

It arched through the air and struck him in the chest, bouncing down his left arm before falling to the ground. He didn't even try to catch it.

"Are you okay, Thomas?" asked Andrew.

I forgot my place in this charade and let a thin smile sneak out. Although my hands were bound, I could still rub my new thumb across the fresh, tender flesh of my left palm. Thomas was quite taken with his role in our game.

"I'm all right, Andrew. I'm just a little tired."

"Let me get that for you."

Andrew retrieved the badge from the dirt and tried to hand it to Thomas.

"Thanks, Andrew," Thomas said, nodding towards me. "This

hombre didn't come easy. Nothing I can't handle but maybe you should just pin my badge on my saddle. I'd hate to lose it again."

"I won't let that happen. Hell, you're a hero now. You got the drop on this maniac. It's like the stuff in the dime novels."

Widger tipped his hat up and pursed his lips, studying the situation.

"You'll be a Captain for sure," I said, playing my part. I could see that Andrew's praise made Thomas uncomfortable, particularly with Widger, Captain Barr's right hand man standing nearby.

But Widger just lowered his hat and let his face turn from its usual scowl into a broad smile.

"Captain, huh?" Widger said. "I can see that. You'll do as well as anybody, I reckon."

"Yes, sir," Andrew added. "Let me be the first to report to your command. Andrew Lassiter, at your orders, sir."

As all eyes were on Thomas, I allowed myself a small pleasure, softly stroking my shirt, relishing the new flesh that now adorned my upper body, finely attached to my treasured hand. I reveled in the sensations, but longed for the complete transformation, the completion of my human shell.

Thomas shifted on the horse in front of me. His demeanor transformed.

"Mr. Lassiter, I'm sure that you will do your duty. As my first action, may I suggest that we get the hell out of these woods?"

"A good idea, sir," answered Widger. "You lead the way. I'll take care of the prisoner." Benjamin grabbed the reins to my horse.

"Yes, do take care of him, Mr. Widger." Thomas nudged his horse forward and Andrew followed, holding the reins of the horse transporting Captain Barr's covered corpse.

Widger turned back toward me, finally getting a closer look at Thomas' prisoner.

"You don't look so tough now, boy."

Benjamin inspected my clothing. He found a burnt hole at my left shoulder and another in my abdomen. Neither showed any blood and the flesh beneath looked healthy.

"How you manage to dodge them bullets that tore your shirt?"

"Just lucky, I guess."

"Are you lucky enough for this?" Benjamin grabbed his rifle from his horse, gripped the barrel with both hands and swung it like a club, slamming it into my face. I fell backwards from the horse I was on, my bound hands unable to break my fall. I crumpled to the ground, the rough earth scuffing and bruising my tender treasure.

"What's going on back there?" called Thomas from the clearing.

"Nothing, boss. Our friend here just had an accident. No worry, though, I'll have him ready in a minute. We'll catch up."

I heard Thomas and Andrew press on through the brush, and then the soft clink of Benjamin's spurs brushing the ground.

"Sorry about that, neighbor. My rifle must've slipped. I'm sure you understand, on account of all those folks you hurt."

"Oh, I understand, Benjamin Widger. You have felt that pain. I can see it in your eyes. You seek revenge—cold revenge—against the man who killed your wife and daughter."

Benjamin's left fist smashed into me, crushing my borrowed face and dislodging one of my ears. Then a pistol in his right hand tore open my forehead and sent me sprawling across the dusty ground.

"Don't you ever mention my family again, you slick bastard!"

"I bet you'd give anything if he was here in my place, so that you could have revenge."

"You have no idea what I'd give for that moment. But since he's not here, you'll have to do."

"Do not be hasty, Ranger. Revenge is a simple thing, often found by the simplest of means."

Another flurry of blows crashed into my head, ripping through the tender flesh and beginning to reveal my rather grisly, true visage.

"Who are you?"

"Let's just say I'm someone who can grant you the revenge you seek," I said, spitting blood.

I had never seen the murderer of Widger's family, but I was certain that he hadn't either. As my face was already torn open, something shifted inside him and he eyed me warily, wondering.

Was I the dark remorseless killer of his nightmares?

I goaded him.

"What would you give for a chance at revenge?" I said, smiling at him through the blood and collapsing flesh.

"Son of a bitch! You're the one! You want to know what I'd give? I'd give anything, even my life, to see you suffer!"

"Very well," I said. "We have a deal. *I killed them both.*"

To Widger's credit, he was both vicious and complete. When his arms grew tired of smashing the accursed face with his fists and his pistol, he stabbed his knife into the Irishman's side. I let his fury continue unabated until he turned his attention to my hand, my newfound, beloved hand. When he raised his blade high, I simply rose from the ground and unsteadily confronted him in my torn clothing and borrowed, putrefying flesh. He was somewhat taken aback.

"Enough, Benjamin Widger!" I commanded. "You have wrought your vengeance and I have fulfilled my part of the deal. Now, I shall collect payment."

Widger put up a valiant fight, but his body had grown weary.

Despite all his hacking, his knife was still sharp.

Very sharp.

Thomas and Mr. Lassiter had refrained from a full gallop, but kept a constant pace until I could catch up. I was well past the need for stealth, so I simply rode up to meet them.

"Thank you, Thomas. Our agreement worked perfectly."

I had not completed my transformation. Widger's person had afforded most of what I required, including new leg coverings and a second hand. All I lacked now was the smooth, soft skin of a younger man to complete my face.

Andrew turned in his saddle, his hands instinctively snatching the pistols from his holsters.

"Holy God! Hold it right there, mister! You're under arrest!"

"You have a smooth, youthful face," I said. "It would be a shame. Perhaps you should ask your commanding officer what to do next?"

I expected Thomas' voice to break, but he took on the stern, solid tone of a leader. "I'm sorry, Andrew. But you're obliged to follow my orders, aren't you?"

"Yes, sir."

"You're a Texas Ranger, aren't you?"

"Yes, sir."

"Then holster your weapon."

Andrew Lassiter completed my transformation.

I lost track of Thomas in the woods as the new false-face merged with my previously acquired patchwork of bartered flesh. It was not pretty, but it was mine.

An assortment of humans had each contributed to making Donovan O'Grady the man I was. And so I would remain, at least until I found something nicer.

Daniel's Dilemma

By Carmen Gray

As he attempted to peer beyond the trees obscuring his view of the Austin sky at night, he put out his last Parliament. A large, shiny cockroach scuttled quickly by a urine-soaked mattress that he'd left out on the porch months ago.

That mattress had seen a variety of butts in its day. He'd found it by the curb in front of the apartments behind his place. It had been in perfect condition, save a tiny tear and he'd hauled it to his bedroom.

Butts on parade. Heart-shaped, bell-shaped, dimpled, firm, black, brown, freckled, you name it. Now, it just lay in a heap next to his bucket of discarded cigarettes and it had become many a stray cat's favorite place to piss.

Daniel was a butt man. Boobs he could take or leave. As long as he could mount a woman from behind, he considered it a win and that's what got him hard, regardless of the woman's physique. It was solid technique to focus on the back end, especially if the woman wasn't so easy on the eyes. Women kept Daniel from thinking too much. Women and his dependable plastic pint of vodka and his guitars. Sex, drugs and rock and roll. The Holy Trifecta of Escape.

He stumbled back into his place, a coffee mug half-full of vodka in hand. He was buzzing nicely and just about ready to collapse into oblivion on the couch for the night. The A/C unit working extra hard to keep the front room at a tolerable temperature.

He pulled a plateful of crispy fish sticks out of the oven to help soak up the alcohol before passing out to a song he'd recorded two days before. Vivid streams of purple entered his mind when the minor chords hit. He loved those haunting sounds. He was a self-taught musical genius in a city that was drowning in musical talent, which made him quite anonymous really. But not to himself. He was somebody in his mind, or would be, someday. Someday was a cottage industry in Austin.

He dozed off thinking about one woman or another, and then drifted into a recurring dream.

The dream took place in the same house always, a nice house. A house in the hills. He would walk in, feeling as though this amazing place was his sanctuary. Then, he strolled through each of the familiar rooms. They were nicely furnished with all of his guitars and musical equipment. His favorite guitar, the Sunburst Jagmaster, was leaning against a bright red leather couch. He always touched it before rounding the corner into the kitchen, with its vintage woodgrain and spacious refrigerator. Then he would go to a back door. The same door, which, when he opened it, led to a side of the house he'd never realized was there before. On the unfamiliar side, the floor was uneven, the plumbing was in need of repair, the walls were cracked and unpainted and the rooms were empty, except for one with the old, broken-in mattress from his front porch. It was there he began to hear the melancholy strings of a cello and see faint ripples of light green. He could see another door leading to the exterior, but it was always locked. As he approached the door, the cello played a little louder, still light green. Almost olive. But the walls and the entire sky outside would begin dripping a deep shade of scarlet.

That's when he woke up.

Daniel's heart was beating wildly and his forehead was beaded with sweat. He still thought he could hear the cello.

He looked at his clock. Just half past twelve.

"Godammit!" he said aloud. "Why can't I get more than two hours of sleep a night?"

He was still too shook up from his dream to go back to sleep again easily, so he went out to his front porch for another smoke.

He was taking his last drag from his second final cigarette for the night and sipping the last dregs from his mug of vodka. A gray and white cat wandered up to get a pet from him and add his own scent to the cat piss mattress. Only this cat looked injured.

"Hey, buddy," Daniel said. "I relate to you, my friend. What's going on here?"

The porch light revealed a slick, red contusion on the cat's right shoulder.

"Damn," Daniel added. "What have you gotten yourself into?"

There was a collar with a tag around the cat's neck. He took a look at it.

"Sr. Rey," Daniel observed. His owner's name was Maya, and there was a phone number. "Hmmm," he continued. "Excuse me your highness, but do you think your owner, Maya, is a pussy I'd like to meet?"

Daniel put out a dish with some leftover fish sticks for Sr. Rey and went back inside to try to get more sleep. At 5 a.m. his alarm would summon him to get up and ready for his menial, yet dependable job at a neighborhood coffee shop . . . like the thousands of other struggling musicians in town.

"Live Music Capital of the World, my ass," he said. *Struggling artist capital of the world, more like.*

"Daniel!" Megan shouted as she handed him a slip of paper.

"Ugghhh . . . what is this?" He responded grudgingly. He was still a tad hungover from last night and wasn't keen on being sociable just yet.

"It's the name of that band I want you to check out. Reminds me of your style of music." She gave him a wink and leaned over, purposefully brushing her ample breasts against his arm.

Megan sure did put it out there for him. If his dry spell continued, he decided he might just have to flip her over one day. On the other hand, you don't shit where you eat. It might complicate his paying gig. He put the paper in his pocket and they got back on task getting the front of the shop ready for business.

The day dragged on, as it usually did. And it was a Monday.

Daniel and Megan were a synchronized team. They had worked together for two years.

As their shifts came to a close, she snuck up behind him and gave him a bear hug. He felt a sickening feeling rush in and he reacted before he could stop himself. "STOP!" he yelled at her. He saw bright red blotches.

"Dude, what's your problem?" she asked him.

"Haven't I told you at least a hundred times I can't handle when people sneak up on me? Don't get in my space. Please."

Megan looked hurt, her eyes cast downward. "I'm sorry," she said. "I just wanted to give you a little hug before heading out for a few days off."

"Next time," Daniel said, "ask me for a hug and if I'm in the mood, I'll oblige you. You know I have this thing. Please don't touch me unless you give me a heads-up."

"Fine," she said as she started to head out the door. He caught up with her in the parking lot.

"Look, I'm sorry. I'm just tired. How about a beer on my porch before you leave town?"

"Ummmm . . . okay. I have time for a quickie." Megan gave him her big-toothed grin. He rolled his eyes.

"Just a beer, lady."

Everything had sexual undertones with Megan. It's just how she was. But she was a good sport and she put up with a lot of his shit.

On the way to his place, Daniel decided that there couldn't be a dry spell long enough for him to flip her over. She just didn't do it for him. She was too flirty with every guy that came near her. She enjoyed that power, and it turned him off.

On his porch, they toasted to the end of a boring day on the job. They shared a few laughs about some of the regulars who had come in.

Megan was a natural comedic talent. Her imitations of some of the assholes that neither of them enjoyed dealing with were spot on. Despite her big teeth and heavy-handed salaciousness, he could have a good laugh with her. But laughing was the extent of it. Laughing and drinking.

"Who is this gorgeous boy?!" she exclaimed, when the same gray and white cat showed up looking for another plate of leftover fish sticks.

"Oh, that's Sr. Rey," Daniel said.

Megan saw the gash on his shoulder. "But damn, what the hell kind of fight did he get into?"

"I know, I noticed it last night."

"Daniel, you need to call the owner . . . he has a tag with a name and number on it."

"Yeah, I was kind of waiting to see if he would show up again and then I was going to call."

"Well, then, call," Megan insisted.

"Wait, wait, this song is almost over," Daniel said. "I'm seeing yellow swirls." He was listening to the last refrain of "Cosmic Dancer," by T Rex.

"Dude, did you take a hit of acid without me? What do you mean?"

"No, it's my superpower. I have chromesthesia. I told you that."

"Oh, yeah . . . the great guitar player can see melodies in color. I just heard a story about some obscure musician with that on *The Moth Radio Hour*. He works at a coffee shop." Megan arched her eyebrow at him, teasingly.

"As a matter of fact, I can," Daniel said. "I perceive a lot of things with color, not just music. It's a rare phenomenon, as I'm sure you're aware."

"Oh, I'm hip, *Rain Man*. But you got your signals crossed.

That's not T Rex swirling in your brain. That's the smell of that nasty mattress ol' Sr. Rey and every other cat in a twenty block radius has been pissing on for three months"

Daniel laughed. That was the nice thing about Megan. She was intelligent. And he felt he could talk to her about certain things that he wouldn't share with just anyone. He was a loner because he was smarter than most people he knew and more talented. Definitely more talented. But there were a few exceptions and Megan was one.

Sr. Rey yowled at them before the song completely ended.

"Grab your phone," Megan said. "Let's take care of this poor sailor."

Daniel called the number. It rang a couple of times and a young girl answered.

"Hola?"

"Hi," Daniel said. "I'm looking for Maya?"

"Yes."

"Yes, is this Maya?"

"Si."

Daniel motioned to Megan, who he knew could speak a little Spanish because her father was Mexican-American.

She took the phone. *"¿Tenemos un gato que tiene tu nombre?"*

"Yes," replied Maya.

Megan gave Daniel an inquisitive look and handed the phone back to him.

"Okay, well, so you understand? We have your cat and called you. He's been wounded."

"Yes," replied this Maya person again.

"Well, your cat is wounded. Your address is on here. It looks like you live in the apartments just behind my house. Can we bring him to you right now?"

An almost inaudible "Yes." Then, the phone went dead.

A flash of red raced through Daniel's mind.

"That was a little weird," Megan said. "Either she spoke Spanish and didn't want to use it with me, or she was just trying to brush us off."

"Yeah, whatever," Daniel replied. "Let's just get this over with. I want to get back to my drinking."

They coaxed Sr. Rey into an old cat carrier Daniel had in the storage shed. He didn't use it anymore, but once upon a time, he'd nursed a stray kitten back to health and had borrowed it from a girlfriend to take it to Emancipet. The girlfriend didn't last, and neither did the cat. But evidence from his past was piled up in the storage shed and all around his place.

Megan walked with him over to the run-down apartments behind his house.

"Seriously, this place is nasty," she whispered.

"Yeah, I thought my storage shed was bad, but this is worse".

It was bleak and there were piles of cast-off, broken furniture and refuse piled near the dumpsters. They approached the address listed on the tag and knocked on the door.

A beautiful young waif of a girl, twelve or thirteen years old maybe, cracked the door open. She had brilliant green eyes and they were naturally highlighted by her café au lait-colored skin and dark hair. Daniel was struck by her eyes, but averted his own. He wanted to get this over with.

"Are you Maya?" Megan asked.

"No." the girl responded abruptly. "But he's mine."

There was a hint of an accent. Her eyes kept peeking around Daniel and Megan, as if she were making sure no one was watching them.

"Well, you need to get him to a vet, if you can," Megan said, pointing at Sr. Rey's wound. *"Mira, su hombro—hay una herida."*

The girl nodded her head and locked eyes with Megan for a brief second.

A man's voice boomed from inside the apartment. *"¿GUERA, QUE HACES?"*

The girl flinched and grabbed the cat carrier.

"Whoa, I need that back!" Daniel chirped as the door was slammed closed.

"Dude, let her keep it," Megan chided. "You don't even have a cat and they have to get that cat to a vet."

Then they both heard a man arguing with the girl from behind the closed door. Daniel had a flash of his recurring dream.

"Let's go," he said, wanting to avoid the bad vibe. "Our Good Samaritan duty is done. I'm ready for more beers."

Megan leaned her ear closer and tried to make sense of the indistinct chatter. Daniel was suddenly annoyed with her meddling.

"This is not my problem," he said. "I don't want to know this person's story. I have my own life. And I'm ready to get back to it."

Daniel started to walk away, but the door opened and a man stepped out. He looked to be in his early forties, with a bit of a paunch and a distinct scar above his right eyebrow. His breath smelled of alcohol, but theirs did as well.

"Thanks for returning Sr. Rey, man," the man said. "He's my daughter's cat."

Daniel and Megan nodded and said "You're welcome." Then, they headed back to Daniel's front porch.

"What the hell?" Megan said. "I don't think that's his daughter. He's pasty white and she's Mexican."

"How do you know? *Your* mom is lily white and you're *half*-Mexican. Maybe she's just half, like you? Didn't you see her eyes?"

"No way. He had dark eyes, looked too ugly to have such a pretty daughter and didn't seem like a dad. You don't think something's up?"

"I don't think. It's none of my business. If you're going to fixate on the freak show back there, just leave."

It was not his problem. He just wanted to settle into oblivion for the evening, which was rapidly approaching. Besides, he had songs to re-record before it got too late.

"Whatever, Daniel," Megan replied. "Sometimes you're a real

asshole. But then, you know that. I'm outta' here."

He shrugged his shoulders as she took off.

"Papi, I'm sorry," Maya said sweetly as Tony's jaw twitched. She knew that look on his face meant he was in a dangerous mood.

"What the hell was I thinking, letting you have this cat? You cannot answer the door or the phone. Those are the rules, Maya. *¿Te acuerdes?"* He slammed his hand on an end table, making his half-full quart of gin jump.

Maya flinched again.

"It's okay," Tony said. "It's okay. That guy is a burnout. He's harmless."

"Sorry, Papi. But Sr. Rey is hurt."

Sr. Rey was sitting at Maya's feet. Tony picked him up and petted his head.

"He'll be okay, I think. I'll get some ointment for it later. Listen, Maya, there's a friend coming over tonight. He's going to get you primed for ACL. You need some practice so you'll be ready."

Maya's face crumpled.

"Oh, he'll be gentle, *chiquita.* And just think of all of the money you and I will make from the wasted foreigners coming here for the 'music.' We'll buy Sr. Rey a giant kitty tower. He'll live like the Rey he is meant to be!" Tony laughed, sat Sr. Rey down and offered the quart of gin to Maya. She held the bottle with both hands and took a long swig.

It warmed her and Tony handed her a pill. She took another long draw on the gin, swallowing the pill. It calmed her nerves, so she always took it eagerly. Lately, though, one was not enough. But it did keep her from completely losing her mind. Sr. Rey brushed up against her leg and purred at her.

"That's right," Tony said. "You know how to make men purr. It's a talent. Now, go take a shower and make yourself pretty for John. He likes a clean *concha."*

It had been a good month of watching TV and zoning out on the new Nintendo 3DS that Tony had bought her. He'd even taken her to Ulta to buy as much makeup as she wanted. He was good to her and provided her with things she'd never had before. And no men for two weeks was a nice break.

But lately Tony was drinking a lot more and the food he was bringing home was minimal. The other girl, Leti, had run off, leaving Maya to make the money until Tony met with *El Coyote* to find another Leti to join their family. Cash was low. That's why Tony refused to take Sr. Rey to the vet.

"We are running out of money," Tony had said. "Luckily, for us, Maya, the festival is almost here. You're going to need to be on your best game. Don't you want Sr. Rey to live like he should? It's up to you."

And it was. She knew that.

She dried off from the shower and put on the red lipstick and dark black eyeliner that made her green eyes even more alluring. She hoped that this guy John would not be able to get it all the way up and he'd just want to pleasure her instead. Many older guys were like that. They didn't care so much about being inside her as they did about just touching her and playing with her, because she was young and forbidden. She could escape into her mind and pretend it was some cute boy her age touching her instead some panting, overweight man who had trouble getting an erection and was hoping for a miracle in the form of a womanchild.

She was putting the finishing touches on her eyes when she noticed a movement outside of the small bathroom window. She thought it might be Sr. Rey, so she opened it to double check.

It was.

Tony had thrown the cat back outside as soon as he felt like the people who found him were gone. He never liked Sr. Rey, but he had coaxed Maya into his place with him. Sweet Sr. Rey, who loved her vibrato on the cello.

She wondered who the man and woman were. She had the guy's phone number on the call history of Tony's cell phone now. If Sr. Rey went missing again, she could just sneak the phone and call when Tony passed out, which he basically did every night by 10 p.m. if they weren't working. Unless he changed the passcode to unlock the phone. He did that from time to time so that she couldn't use it.

Maya peered out of the window, and sure enough, there was Sr. Rey, trotting off to the back of the house that belonged to the annoyed guy and his girlfriend. She decided that as soon as she was done with her job with this "friend" of Tony's, she would sneak the phone.

But John never showed up and Tony got mad and took it out on her. He snarled at her and called her names. He knew exactly how to break her down. He was her only connection to survival and the world and she depended on him. So he knew he could do whatever he wanted. Even discard her. Which is what she began to think had happened to Leti. Maybe Tony had gotten rid of her.

Maya missed Leti, especially at times like this. When Leti was there, they at least had each other to hold on to when Tony ranted. Now Maya was all alone.

She withstood the name calling and the humiliations. Tony kept slamming down more and more gin and eventually she saw the telltale sign of him soon passing out: his eyes shook involuntarily when he looked at her. He was just minutes away.

Once Tony was passed out on the bed, she found his phone and unlocked it. He had not changed the passcode.

She searched in the recent phone calls and found the last incoming number and hit call. She snuck into the workroom to talk. The workroom was the extra bedroom where she had to do her job with the men that Tony brought in, if they didn't take her to their place for the night—which Tony discouraged. He liked to keep a close eye on her.

It was empty in that room and creepy. The walls were cracked and the floor was uneven. The only thing in it was an old mattress and her most beloved possession, an old, out of tune cello that she somehow knew instinctually how to pluck. It felt like she did. Broken and sad.

Daniel was in his front room finishing up his latest edits on a song when he noticed his phone lighting up with a call. He'd turned the sound off so he could focus on finishing his music.

"Godammit, Megan," he barked into the phone. "What do you want?"

There was a silent, awkward pause.

Daniel realized that he hadn't checked the number and looked at it. A Houston area code.

Shit, he thought. What if this was the hot girl he'd talked to at the coffee shop a couple days in a row last week? He tried to repair his mistake.

"Um, hello? Is this the Megan who has been prank calling me? If so, I would appreciate it if you would stop this nonsense."

To his surprise, a very demure voice spoke. "Hello? Do you have my cat?"

His mind flashed olive green and he saw the bed in the empty room of his recurring dream. If he'd just stayed in bed last night instead of going out on the porch for a smoke, he'd never have met the cat or this kid.

"Is this Maya?" he said. "I don't have your cat."

"Oh," she whispered. "I saw him go from the window."

Daniel could detect an echo, as if Maya were sitting in an empty room. "Well, why don't you go outside and look for Sr. Rey? He was a little exasperated. She was interrupting his alone time.

"I can't," she replied.

This piqued his interest. Had Megan been right? "Because of him?"

"Yes," she said.

"Then how are you able to talk to me? Where is he now?" Olive green was doing the wave in his head now, like the inside of his skull was a packed soccer stadium. He felt an awful feeling pressing in on him, not unlike the one he'd had after Megan grabbed him.

"He sleeping in the other room," she answered very quietly.

"Leave now!" he found himself saying as he massaged his temples with his free hand. *"Get out of there, man!"*

"But, he will kill me."

Daniel's vision blotched red behind his eyelids and the phone went silent. Now he was meddling. It was highly uncharacteristic of him. He found himself wondering what to do.

Should he keep drinking his vodka and forget about this situation and the awful feelings it was invoking in him, or should he call her back?

He called Megan.

"I need your help," he said.

"What? Are you kidding? You were a jerk. Sometimes I think you are a nice guy. You're funny, sarcastic, smart, talented, but you are ultimately a jerk to me. Why should I help you?"

"Because you were right. That kid with the cat called me."

"Maya?"

"Yes."

"And?"

"I think she's in trouble."

"Why?"

"Because she said—because I know."

"You know what, Daniel?"

"I know things. Things in my head. *I know.*"

"I'm on my way over. I knew something wasn't right."

Why had she done it? She'd never done anything like this before. It jeopardized her situation.

"¿Güera, que haces?" Tony hissed.

He closed the door behind him and grabbed the phone out

of her hand. "I told you not to answer the phone. Who were you talking to?"

"*Nadie*," she said shakily.

"Yes, it was someone," he replied. "And you told this person that I was going to kill you."

He grabbed her face with sausage-fingered hands and pressed her cheeks so hard she thought her jaw would break. "If you weren't so pretty I'd snap you in half, *Güera*," he breathed in her ear.

His breath was steeped in alcohol and Maya's stomach lurched.

"It's okay, I won't. I need your pretty face. We need it. Come on, it's time for bed. You're sleeping with me."

He dragged her to his room, which was normally off limits. She usually stayed in the front room, with her Nintendo 3DS and makeup and TV.

She did not want to be in his room. He had never done this to her.

In her entire time with him, he'd never taken her for himself. He kept her, like a shiny trophy on a shelf, charging others to play with her or admire her, but never for himself. She was scared. Really scared. About as scared as the night she met him after running from *La Migra*.

She heard that guy's voice in her head. *Leave now.*

Tony pushed her onto his sweat-soaked sheets. "Stay here, Maya," he warned, before stumbling toward the bathroom.

Maya had a choice. Leave now, or let Tony slobber over her like the rest. And more soon, ten, twenty. They paid big money to Tony. Or maybe she would disappear like Leti. But not until ACL was done. They rode her through the big events. It got them through most of the year. He wouldn't get rid of her yet.

Maya made her decision. She bolted from Tony's putrid bed and ran to the front door. When she opened it, a tall muscular man filled the doorway.

She gasped.

"Hello, there," the man said. "I'm assuming you are Maya? I am John, Tony's friend."

Her heart fell.

She could hear Tony stumbling toward them from behind. "Oh, you made it!" he said. "Yes, here is our lovely Maya."

She felt Tony's large hand land on her shoulder and give it a squeeze, while his other hand shook John's and they exchanged money. It was too late.

Maya became sullen as Tony led them to the workroom. Anger boiled up inside her as John removed his clothes and she mechanically removed hers.

"What's wrong? Why the sour face? Tony promised a sweet, easy girlfriend for me."

Maya continued to pout. It made a muscle in John's cheek twitch and Maya knew she would be in trouble, but she didn't care.

John began to fondle her and grab her boyish hips. She remained still, like a statue. He flipped her over to take her from behind.

Her body was rigid and he was not, as she had hoped, having trouble with an erection. But he could not enter her, because she was clenched tight.

John began to slap her and command her to open up, but Maya wasn't playing along.

"Alright, honey," he said. "Take this . . . it will help you relax." He cupped a handful of bluish powder under her nose and told her to inhale.

She did.

If she couldn't leave this place physically, she could at least leave it mentally.

A rush of bright orange washed her vision as he moved his dusty fingers around her lipstick-smeared mouth. His fingers tasted metallic. She stared at the broken, out of tune cello in the corner. The drug he had given her was making her eyelids feel incredibly heavy.

Maya began drooling and fell limp like a ragdoll.

"What the hell?" John yelled. But she was far away.

By the time Megan arrived, Daniel was pacing on his porch.

"What's going on?" Megan asked.

"I am pretty sure it is too late."

"What do you mean? Did you see something?"

"Olive green. And then orange washing red. Deep red in an empty room."

"Ummm . . . I don't know what that has to do with this, but let's call the police".

"NO. I have a warrant out for my arrest for an unpaid ticket and there's a shitload of pot here. They'll take me in. How about you call on your phone and say you were walking down the street and heard a scream."

"Screw you, Daniel. They aren't going to come over here and talk to you."

"They might . . . especially if something happened. Which I think it did."

"Fine. I'll do it and then I'm going back home. It's late and I'm supposed to be leaving early for Houston."

Megan left after reporting the incident and Daniel smoked a couple of bowls of Indica to help calm his nerves. He heard the police sirens in the distance as he drifted off to sleep on his couch.

The phone woke him up. A cello was playing, then a dial tone. He drifted back off.

The phone rang again. He answered and held it to his ear. The cello was playing again.

"Hello?"

The cello was barely audible. It was the music from his dream.

"Maya?"

No response.

He looked at his phone and found a call from the Houston area code the girl had called from. He set the phone down and stepped out into his backyard. The police were at Maya's place with an ambulance. A stretcher appeared with the slim body of a young girl on it. Then, two men were led out of the house in handcuffs. One of them was Tony. He saw Daniel and glared at him.

Daniel decided he needed to smoke more pot and drink more vodka until he could forget all of this. He went back inside and, within an hour, he was passed out on his couch. He had the dream again. Only this time, there was no music.

When he woke up, he checked his phone. Five missed calls from the Maya number—and two voicemails.

Oh shit! Voicemails?

He was shaky and getting shakier.

He stepped outside on his porch, rubbing his eyes in dismay, hoping to lose the pressing feeling that was squeezing in on his whole existence. He spotted Sr. Rey sleeping on the pissy mattress next to a bloodstain.

His phone rang again and he answered it without holding it up to his ear.

He could hear the anguished cello strings.

Crepuscular

By Bret McCormick

Journal Entry—September 29, 2010

I was in pretty bad shape when I came back to stay in Fort Worth at my Mom's house. My arm, the left one, was broken and I guess I looked a lot worse than I really was with all the bruises on my face.

The family treated me the way you treat an elderly person with dementia, sort of overly conciliatory, never expressing doubts as to what I claimed had happened, but also not bothering to conceal the fact that they thought I'd gone round the bend. I could see it in their eyes.

But they were super nice to me, as if they were really worried about my welfare. Like I might fall and break a hip or descend into a state of detachment. Hell, I can't blame them. How would I feel if I was in their shoes?

To make my Mom feel better I agreed to some counseling at a clinic that lets you pay on a sliding scale, based on how much you make. Since I'm not making anything right now, the price is damn cheap. Not free, but cheap enough. This doctor I've seen a few times, Joel Henshaw, suggested that I write a journal about it. I might've done that anyway. I like to write. That's probably part of the problem with my family. I was always the creative one. The one who dreamed up fantastic stories. The stork dropped me in the wrong nest. If any of them ever had a creative impulse, maybe they'd be a bit closer to understanding. They're all good Christians and they believe all manner of mystical and miraculous stuff if it's in the Bible, but anything like that happens to a living person, especially someone they know, and every last one of them is a doubting Thomas.

Yeah, I see the anger in the words I'm writing. I suppose that's normal, too. Back to the point; this journal about my unbelievable experience is supposed to help me work through my feelings and come to grips with all of it. Maybe it's supposed to make me realize none of it ever happened. At least that's what my family's probably thinking. Who knows? Maybe someday I'll decide it's better to pretend it didn't happen. Maybe I'll pretend to snap out of it one morning and return to my senses. That'd make everyone a lot more comfortable with me. And I may do that.

But, I know what happened.

Journal Entry—September 30, 2010

The town is called Fodice. It's located in the southern part of Houston County. Some of the locals say the name is a corruption of the phrase "four dice." Another version of the story says that most of the town's founding members were from a plantation in Fordyce, Arkansas, and that they gave their new home in East Texas a name familiar to them. All agree that the town was a freedmen community. In other words, it was comprised of former slaves who had left the site of their enslavement in search of new opportunity and a new identity. I've lived in Texas most of my life. Even so, I'd never heard of Fodice until I was well into my forties.

I'd been leasing a great old three-story house that was built in 1889 on Galveston Island when Hurricane Ike came along and displaced me. My book business came to an end when forty thousand dollars' worth of uninsured inventory was destroyed in the flood. For a time after that, I made a modest living selling used merchandise of every description at pseudo-garage sales. I call them that because I'd set up in various friends' driveways and sell all sorts of stuff I'd acquired at Salvation Army auctions and at other garage sales. There was a motel in South Houston owned by an Indian family and they'd let me hold a sale in their parking lot once a month in exchange for ten percent of the take. It wasn't a booming business, but it helped me keep my head above water while I searched for a better, more permanent solution to my financial situation. I rented a storage unit to house the merch and I slept in my minivan in the parking lot of whatever Walmart was nearby. Sometimes I slept at the homes of friends when it didn't feel like I was imposing.

In March of 2009 I did a sale in my cousin Michael's driveway in the Houston neighborhood known as "the Heights." Mike's got a lot of friends in the arts community, painters and sculptors, and some of them came to my sale looking for junk they could turn into art. That's how I met Sean and Julie. Sean was a thirty-something, good-looking guy from a wealthy family who pretty much dabbled in whatever struck his fancy. His wife, Julie, was a knockout from a middle-class family in Waco. They were both artists and had met while attending the University of Texas at Austin.

I talked with them the better part of an hour as they foraged through the glassware, framed art by amateurs (from the Salvation Army), toys and kitchen utensils. I learned that they'd recently purchased an abandoned school building in Fodice. They intended to turn it into an art studio and gallery of sorts as a weekend destination for curious Houstonians. Really tired of sleeping at Walmart, I went out on a limb and mentioned that I had a lot of experience as a handyman and if they ever needed an on-site caretaker for the place, I'd be interested. I told them I'd done repairs for lots of folks over the years and could provide them with references.

For the next couple of months, every time I ran into Sean and/ or Julie, I'd bring it up. About the time I realized I was probably being a pain in the ass and determined never to mention it again, they called and asked me when I could move in. Turns out someone had broken some windows and vandalized the building and they'd decided it might be good to have me living there to keep an eye on the place.

I liquidated as much of my pseudo-garage sale merch as I could.

What I couldn't sell I returned to the Salvation Army. It made me wonder how many times some of those things had been recycled through that place.

The second Saturday of May I moved into the empty school building. I replaced all the broken glass the first few days I was there and began cleaning up the interior. There was a room with a sink and some counters and cabinets which I imagined had been the school's kitchen. I used this room as my bedroom because it was the easiest to put into livable order; plus, it kept my stuff concentrated in that area and out of the way as I worked on the larger rooms.

The first two nights I slept there I had bad dreams. Nothing real solid or linear, just dark shapes swimming through the atmosphere and me in a disembodied state, but feeling a bit like a small, wounded fish surrounded by sharks.

For the first couple of months I stayed busy cleaning, building shelves (and a few partitions), patching old plumbing and landscaping the grounds. When I say landscaping what I really mean is mowing, eliminating unwanted trees and putting in a small vegetable garden. Sean and Julie had lots of ideas for improving the property and they had the money to pay for it. They set up a bank account for building supplies and such and gave me a debit card to use.

In addition to money for materials, they gave me a modest stipend for food and other necessities. It was a win-win. They were getting the improvements they wanted at a bargain rate and my presence discouraged any further vandalism. I was glad to be out of the pseudo-garage sale business.

I enjoyed working with my hands and I had plenty of time to work on some writing projects I had in mind. Well into middle-age I was still fantasizing about earning my living as a writer; and there, at the schoolhouse in Fodice, I felt a bit like Henry David Thoreau. I sometimes went three or four days without speaking to another human being.

Does that sound funny?

Well, that's just the way I meant it. I did plenty of talking; to myself, the trees, the small animals and to my hammer when it hit my thumb. I just didn't talk to other people much.

There was a platform outside the back door to the place, just under the window over the sink in the kitchen where I was sleeping. It had been built of sturdy wood. The supports were mostly good, but I had to replace a lot of the decking. When I got it in reasonably good shape I bought a cheap charcoal grill and started cooking out there. The place had no A/C, not even electricity really, just what I got from the small generator Sean had supplied. The long-term plan was to install solar panels, but that was still a ways down the road. So, around sunset I'd sit out there and grill a piece of meat and listen to the crickets, cicadas and birds. It was pleasant after a strenuous day. I'd usually have a little cooler with some iced down bottles of water and beer.

I've often wondered if everything would have still happened if I hadn't decided to kill a couple of squirrels for dinner one night. There were plenty of squirrels around and I'd heard my grandfather talk about growing up eating mostly squirrel meat. I'd never tasted any and I just thought I'd try to grill a couple. I still had a pellet rifle I'd had no luck selling at the pseudo-garage sales. When I saw the condition of the old place and the raccoon droppings everywhere, I decided to hang onto the gun to discourage small animals that might make it into my new home. Anyway, the pellet gun was perfect for hunting squirrels. I made a marinade out of oil and red wine and soaked the squirrel carcasses in there a while, then rolled them in a southwestern rub before throwing them on the grill. They smelled great.

While the squirrels were cooking I noticed the place got real quiet. No cicada or cricket noises. No birds. The sun was sinking low and I thought I saw people moving around the trees on the east property line, but there was nothing there. No people anyway.

I remember musing for a while about cleaning the meat; removing the head and feet, gutting the torso, peeling the skin back. Most people would be put off by the task. In fact, I'm pretty sure most modern Americans would give up eating meat if they had to kill and butcher everything they ate. Or maybe they'd just eat a lot less of it. I was realizing that life and the way it is sustained is really not a very pretty state of affairs.

I dug a hole and deposited the cast off parts of squirrel into it. I don't know why, but something made me decide to keep the tails. I tied a string to each one and hung them from the eaves of the roof above the kitchen window. If I'd hung them somewhere else or if I'd never killed those little animals, maybe things would've been different.

After I washed up, I sat on the platform in the growing darkness and drank beer. When the squirrel meat smelled done, I took it from the grill, let it cool a bit, then tasted it. I liked it. I didn't feel so bad about my poor granddaddy growing up with nothing to eat but squirrel. It tasted fine. Granddaddy probably never had it marinated and rubbed, but that wasn't my fault.

Gradually, the natural sounds of the place returned and I remember feeling satisfied as I sipped my beer, my stomach full of squirrel meat.

After I was certain the fire was out and the ashes cool, I went inside and stretched out on my cot. I had one of the beers with me and I was just nursing it along. I pulled out one of the spiral notebooks that I use for writing first drafts and I may have written three or four paragraphs, but my heart wasn't in it, so I closed it back up and slid it under my mattress.

For a couple of days before sleep I'd been reading *The Three Stigmata of Palmer Eldritch* by Philip K. Dick. It was a battered paperback I'd picked up the summer before. Dick was one of my favorites. Twice, as I read the pages of the musty-smelling book, I could've sworn I heard sounds like a crowd of people talking, but distant, faint, the words unintelligible. The second time it happened I actually got up and went out onto the platform to take a look. Even as I made the effort, I knew I wouldn't find anything. I was far away from any parks or churches or any other place where people might congregate this time of night. But, there was a breeze stirring and a rain smell in the air. I saw a flash of lightning to the south. I just stood there a minute, taking it in, appreciating it. Rain would cool the summer night and make it easier to sleep.

Going back inside after a bit, I don't think I read anymore that night. I finished my beer and fell asleep.

Now, I distinctly remember the dream I had that night. I was wandering through an old building, really old, maybe even a castle. It was dark and dusty and I was searching for something. I noticed a tapestry stirring on one of the walls and as I neared it, I was taken by the colors and the quality of its execution. I thought to myself, *Wow, I didn't know they could do tapestries of this quality back then.* Although, I wasn't even sure when 'back then' was. I reached out and was about to touch the thing when it suddenly came to life. In an instant it became an animated movie. The key figure in the tapestry was a large horse. The horse began to gallop and as it went along, it was gobbling up everything in its path; first vegetation, then small animals, then larger animals, other horses and people even. Finally, it came upon a dragon and the dragon tried to fight it, but the horse ate that thing, too. Still, it galloped along; seemingly no less hungry than when it started. I muttered to myself, "What the hell is this?" As if in response, my mind was filled with an idea not in language, but clear as a bell and emphatic. It was this: Everything is eating everything else. This is the first rule of life.

When I woke up it was pouring rain outside. Lightning flashed and thunder shook the walls. I looked through the window above the sink and saw the squirrel tails whipped around by the wind. I stared at the tree line along the east end of the property. My eyes kept going to the big oak tree that stands about midway along that boundary and I seemed to have this anticipation of seeing something or someone. No one would be out in a storm like that. Still, I watched for a long time, certain that I would see something. Something that shouldn't be there.

Of course, there was nothing.

Then, just as I was turning to go back to my bed I thought I saw a pair of hands trying to grab the squirrel tails. They were little hands and dark, like a small black child was on the platform, jumping up in an effort to reach the tails and pull them down. The hallucination or vision was so convincing that I went back to the window and stood on my tip toes so I could look down onto the platform below the window. There was no child.

I lay on my cot a long time, listening to the storm. I even drank another beer thinking that would help me get back to sleep. I felt really creepy, like there was something wrong, but it was something I did not understand and could do nothing about. It wasn't a good feeling.

Most of the time I believe whatever the problem is, you can take steps to fix it. Maybe small steps, but positive steps nonetheless that lead to progress, a solution to the problem. Lying on that cot I felt like a man drifting on the open ocean in a life raft without a paddle. The worst part was that I didn't even know why.

The following morning I got a visit from Sean and Julie. I'd allowed myself to sleep in because of the weirdness of the night before and the heavy rainfall. Most of the work I had planned to do that day was on the exterior of the building and I needed to let things dry out. So, I was still drinking coffee and reading my Philip K. Dick paperback when I heard the approach of their car.

At first I wondered who it was, then I heard Sean cursing about the red mud as he climbed out of the vehicle. I met them at the platform.

Sean was growling and looking down at his expensive boots as he made his way through the standing water. Julie was bright as ever, smiling and carrying a brown paper bag that I knew contained food or some other gift for me. They came into the kitchen area, Sean shaking my hand and Julie giving me a friendly hug.

"Damn, you got some serious rain," Sean said.

I pointed to some rags piled near the end of the counter. "You can clean your boots with those," I suggested and right away he took my suggestion, leaning on the counter top with one hand and using the other to carefully wipe the mess from his lizard skin boots.

"The place is looking great," Julie beamed and placed the bag on the counter next to Sean. "I brought you some goodies."

"And it's not even my birthday," I said.

Julie liked to be playful. "It's not? Damn, I got my dates confused. I'll have to take this home and bring it back on your birthday."

"On second thought, it is my birthday," I said. "What'd you bring me?"

"No big deal." She waved a hand in the air and wandered away from the kitchen to check out my progress. "Just some snacks and stuff."

When she left the room, I joined Sean at the counter and peered down into the bag. It contained a six pack of beer, some corn chips, dry-roasted peanuts and some tins of sardines. All things I enjoy. "Thanks for the grub. How's everything going?"

Sean dropped the dirty rag on the floor. "Everything's okay. We're on our way to the airport, wanted to let you know. We'll be out of the country until mid to late September."

This was a surprise to me. "Really? Where you headed?"

"Italy. My uncle has a place on the Mediterranean that he's offered to us for the summer. It was too good a deal to pass up. Julie's got a couple of art dealers in Europe interested in her stuff, so we'll try to do a little business, too."

"Great, man." I was genuinely happy for them. Plus, the better things went for them, the likelier I was to continue to have the run of the school.

"Here," he said, pushing a wad of money toward me.

"What's this?"

"We appreciate everything you're doing here," he said, and though Sean wasn't big on handing out compliments, I could tell from the look in his eyes that he meant what he was saying. "Call this a bonus. We want you to have a good summer."

"Thanks." I slid the roll of bills into my jeans pocket.

"I've put enough money into the special account to keep you going until we return. Here's an email address you can use to let us know if anything comes up. I can always have Mom put some extra cash in the bank for you."

"I'm sure everything will be fine," I said.

"I love this place," Julie called from the area I'd come to refer to as the grand gallery. "Sean, come see."

I'd incorporated some found objects into one of the walls I'd erected. Julie was impressed, as I'd hoped she would be. They spent an hour or so with me before heading on to the airport, complimenting me on my work, suggesting things they'd recently thought about adding. They were happy and so was I. The more work I did, the more ideas they got and the more work I had ahead of me. None of us had talked about what would happen once the place was finished and opened up to artists and art collectors. There'd be time enough to think of that later. I hated to see them go, knowing I wouldn't get to visit with them again until the fall. But, I also imagined the fun they'd have in Europe and in a way felt like I was a part of that.

"Take care of yourself," Julie said, giving me a goodbye squeeze.

"You, too," I answered.

Sean took my hand. "Great job, man. We're glad the place is in good hands."

"Thanks, Sean. I appreciate that. Here," I said, handing him a few of the rags from the counter. "Use these to keep from getting mud in your car."

He smiled and nodded and followed Julie to the car. He honked the horn before pulling away, Julie waving rapidly through the windshield like a kid. I laughed and waved back, and then they were gone.

I felt a little depressed, so I popped the top on one of the beers they'd brought me and sat down on the platform. I don't mind being alone; quite the opposite, really. Most of the time I enjoy my solitude. It's always been that way. Maybe I just needed to make some friends in the local community. Someone with whom I could play an occasional game of cards. As a last resort, I could attend a church. There would be social interaction there, but not really the kind I wanted. There would be potluck dinners. Those were good. I tabled that internal discussion and looked out at the old oak tree on the edge of the property.

A couple of beers later, the sun was setting and I was still sitting on the platform, doing nothing but vegetating. I didn't feel like reading or much of anything else. I considered for a minute or two what I should do about dinner, but then determined I'd just eat some of the snacks Julie had given me.

I'd set up a compost bin not far from the platform near a cluster of shrubs and a family of field mice had adopted it as their own personal cafeteria, enjoying the scraps I tossed on there almost daily. As the sun sank lower, the rodent family ventured out onto the compost heap, sniffing about for tasty morsels. They watched me, but not with fear. I really think they'd come to accept me as a sort of benefactor. I'd never frightened or harmed them and I left a lot of stuff for them to eat. They probably felt toward me a bit like I felt about Julie with her bag of beer and snack foods.

When I mention field mice, most folks think I'm talking about the little gray things they typically see. The first time your average American lays eyes on a field mouse, he or she usually exclaims something like, "My god, look at the size of that rat!"

They're almost as big as bunnies, some of them. To me they're cute, though I know most folks don't think of any rodents as cute. Smiling as I mused about the field mice, I heard a scuffle nearby and turned to see a couple of small, black children near the edge of the platform to my right.

The sight of the boy and girl confused me at first. I couldn't imagine how they'd gotten so close to me without my hearing their approach. "Hello," I said.

"Hi," the girl replied softly. The boy beside her just waved his hand in a noncommittal arc. The girl looked as if she wanted to smile at me, but hadn't yet. The boy, a year or so older than her, just studied me with a blank expression.

"I'm Richard," I said. "What's your name?"

The girl twisted her body in an expression of self-consciousness and replied in a voice that was barely audible, "Anna Mae."

"Anna Mae?" I asked, making sure I'd heard correctly. She grabbed at the hem of her dress and nodded. "That's a nice name. I like it." Anna Mae smiled a real smile now. The boy still stared expressionlessly. "How about you? What's your name?"

The girl looked at him to see if he was going to speak and at first it seemed like he wouldn't.

"It's okay," I said. "I don't bite."

Anna Mae smiled big at this, almost laughing. The boy smiled in a tentative way, almost a smirk. "I'm Calvin."

"Calvin. That's a good name, too." Anna Mae looked up at him smiling. "Are you Anna Mae's brother?" The two of them nodded. "I thought so," I said.

There was a noise to my left and I looked over to see a couple of the field mice fussing with one another, probably fighting over a choice nibble.

"What's those?" Anna Mae asked, pointing at the compost bin.

"Oh, they're just field mice." I said. "They won't hurt you."

"They big," said Calvin.

"Yeah, they're fat from eating my scraps." I said. Then a word popped into my head and I thought I'd share it with the kids, the way my grandmother and my mother had done with me when I was young. "They're crepuscular. Know what that means?" I'd picked the word up from a college biology professor I'd met when I was working for an organic restaurant in Arlington.

"Cruh . . ." Calvin started, crinkling his nose with the effort. "Cruhhh . . . "

"Crepuscular," I repeated. It means animals that like to come out at sunset to feed and water themselves." The kids said nothing. I looked at them and actually noticed for the first time how they were dressed. Anna Mae was in a shapeless, light brown dress, probably something her mother had sewn. Calvin was wearing overalls that were too small for him, pant legs only reaching halfway down his calves and a single gallous draped over his left shoulder. These kids must be poor, I thought. And maybe hungry. "Would you like some corn chips?" I asked.

Anna Mae looked up at her brother, then they both stared at me as if they were uncertain how to respond. Maybe they'd never had corn chips? It seemed unlikely, but I assumed it was possible.

"They're good," I said, standing up. "Wait here and I'll get you some." I stepped toward the door.

"Are you a good white man?" Anna Mae asked.

Not a good man, but a good white man.

I turned back and looked at both of the children with as much benevolence as I could muster.

"I like to think so," I said. "One thing's for sure. I'd never hurt you or your brother."

They stared at me and I hadn't a clue what they were thinking.

"I'll be right back," I continued. "I'm going to get you some chips." I went into the kitchen and opened the bag of chips. Then, realizing the salty chips would make the kids thirsty, I got a couple bottles of water. Through the window over the sink I heard them laughing.

"Crepulsive!" Calvin exclaimed. "You're crepulsive."

"I'm not crepulsive. You're crepulsive." Anna Mae giggled.

I couldn't help but laugh myself. "It's not crepulsive," I called through the window. "It's crepuscular. Rhymes with 'muscular.'"

The rhyming thing was a trick my folks had used to help me remember words way back when. The kids fell silent and I wondered what they were up to as I gathered up their snack and headed back out to the platform.

Outside, I was surprised to see that they were no longer beside the platform. I looked about, then I saw them almost to the oak tree. It seemed impossible to me that they could have gone so far, so quickly. They were laughing loudly to themselves.

As I watched, Anna Mae turned and looked back at me and, just for an instant, I saw something dangling from her mouth. It looked like a black shoelace.

Then they were gone in the trees.

Well, I thought, maybe their folks had taught them not to take food from strangers. That was good advice, but the kids sure looked hungry. I wondered where they lived and why I'd never seen them before.

Returning to the kitchen, I put the bottled water away and grabbed a beer. I resumed my perch at the edge of the platform and ate the chips I'd intended to give to Anna Mae and Calvin.

Journal Entry—October 4, 2010

There's a store called Howard's Gas 'n' Go about five or six miles from the school. They sell some grocery items, the usual convenience store fare, but they also sell some damn good barbecue that Howard himself cooks in an old smoker on the back patio. The day after I'd first seen the kids I got a hankering for Howard's ribs and went down there that afternoon for lunch. Howard's brother-in-law Grady had a business salvaging building materials from old houses and there's a fenced yard beside the store where Howard sells some of the used lumber and old hardware like door knobs for Grady. I thought I'd have lunch and look through the stuff to see if there was anything I could use.

I grabbed a beer from the cooler and went up to the counter. After a couple moments Howard came from the back, wiping his hands on a rag that he kept hanging from his belt.

"Hey," he said, smiling and pointing his chin at me.

"I'm hungry for some ribs," I said.

"Aw, man, I'm sorry. Just sold the last of the ribs little while ago."

"Got any brisket?"

"Oh, yeah. Plenty of brisket."

"In that case I'll take a brisket sandwich, bag of chips and this beer."

He rang it up, told me the total and as I dug the money out of my jeans pocket, he said, "How's things going out to the school?"

"It's shaping up pretty good. You should stop by and take a look sometime."

"Maybe I'll do that. I'm glad somebody's doing something with that old place. Any of the locals nosing around in your business out there?"

"No, hardly anybody comes around. This week the only people I've seen were the owner and his wife." Then it occurred to me to add, "Oh, Anna Mae and Calvin were playing around the old loading dock." I figured he'd know who the two children were. Everybody in Fodice seemed to know everybody else in town. Hell, in the county for that matter.

Howard just stared at me over the tops of his glasses as I handed him the money. "Yeah, right," he said.

"Mind if I take a look at your building materials?"

He gave me my change and said, "Help yourself."

"I'll take a look and be back for my sandwich in a minute," I said, heading for the door. Howard went into the back to put my sandwich together.

Out in the fenced-in salvage yard there was everything a carpenter might need; studs and siding, bins of hinges and all sorts of hardware. I took the notepad out of my hip pocket and jotted down a few reminders for future reference. A lot of the stuff I could use later, but I wasn't ready to buy it then and there. The prices were a handyman's dream. It beat the hell out of driving twenty-five miles to one of the big superstores. After poking around, I went back inside to pick up my lunch.

The bag was sitting on the counter by the register, grease stains already darkening the brown paper. I didn't see Howard, so I grabbed my food and called out, "Thanks, Howard. I'll see you later."

"Hey," he said softly, rising up from where he'd been bent over pricing merchandise on an aisle to my left.

"Whoa!" I said, jerking the paper bag to my chest. "I didn't see you down there. You scared the crap out of me."

"Were you serious before?" His eyes were solemn, almost mournful, peering over his glasses.

"Hmmm?" I didn't have the slightest clue what he was talking about.

"Anna Mae and Calvin."

He stared at me. Stared hard. "Who told you about them?"

I was confused. "Who told me? Nobody told me anything. Like I said, they were playing around by the dock. I talked to them a bit, then I tried to give them some chips and water, but they took off."

The way Howard just stood there staring made me uneasy as hell. It went on for so long, I finally felt obligated to say something. "Is there something wrong? I don't understand."

Then, it was like he just snapped out of it and he was good old friendly Howard again. "Naw, naw, nothing wrong. You enjoy your brisket. See you soon." Stooping back down, he began clicking the price gun in his hand, sticking little white labels on the cans in front of him.

Outside, I climbed into the van, popped the top on the beer and unwrapped my sandwich. I just sat there in the gravel parking lot, satisfying my hunger and puzzling over Howard. The sandwich was good as usual and when I'd finished eating and sipping the last of my beer, I wadded my trash up in the bag and tossed it into the floorboard. I started the van and headed back to the school, but I couldn't stop thinking about the two children and how weird Howard had acted.

Late in the day I was out on the platform assembling a little wooden cabinet when I heard the scuffing sound of shoes on the gravel behind me. I turned and had just enough time to see a big black man in a dirty T-shirt before he stepped up on the platform and hit me. It wasn't exactly a punch in the face and it wasn't a slap. It was a smack from the back of his huge fist that connected real good with my right cheek bone. That smack carried enough power to send me to my knees. While I was down on all fours, trying to clear my vision, the man talked. He had a deep, rumbly sort of voice.

"You don't talk about Anna Mae and Calvin, white man. I hear you mention 'em again and I'll mess you up. Who the hell you think you are?"

He took an angry step toward me and I raised an open palm to ward him off. "Listen, man," I said. "I didn't do anything to hurt those kids. What's the problem?" I looked up at him and saw the same expression on his face that I'd seen on Howard's earlier that day. It was faraway and mournful, frustrated and panicked in a wordless, quiet way.

The man's pain was tangible. I could feel it. He looked to be about my age, big and brawny; a man accustomed to hard work. His cheeks were flecked with little dark spots, his eyes red and puffy. I'd never before seen anybody look both sad and terrifying at the same time, but he did.

The man shook his head violently, let out an anguished, angry sound something like a dog coughing, then just turned and walked away. He disappeared behind the corner of the building and I heard a car start and drive off. I wondered how I hadn't heard the car arrive in the first place. I'd been busy with the little cabinet I was building, distracted and preoccupied. It wasn't so strange. It wasn't strange by itself, that is, but everything that had been happening was starting to add up to a serious pattern of strange. What the hell?

I stood up and touched my sore cheek. He'd walloped me good. Pissed off and not in the mood to do any more work, I went into the kitchen and got a beer. I held the cold bottle against my face. In the bathroom, I checked my reflection in the mirror and saw a red, swollen lump that made my whole face look lopsided. Yeah, I knew that would be one massive bruise in the morning.

I spent the rest of the afternoon drinking beer and reading a bit in my Philip K. Dick novel. Leaning against the building, seated on the old loading dock, I was on my fourth beer when the sun began to set. It had the usual soothing effect on me.

I decided a philosophical approach was best. Somehow, sometime, I'd figure this mess out. The man was obviously disturbed, maybe with good reason. I'd seen torment in his eyes. I was in the process of breathing deeply and releasing my negative emotions when I heard the sound of laughter. Children's laughter.

The laughter came from the bushes near the compost bin. It was the two kids, I knew it. Now, a lot of shit ran through my head. Was the man who hit me their dad? Had they run away from home? Would he come back and try to finish what he started? All of this and more in a couple seconds.

"Calvin?" I called. "Anna Mae? Is that you? I don't think you're supposed to be here."

The only response was more laughter.

"Hey! What are you two doing over there?"

What I saw is something I'll never forget. Little Anna Mae stepped out from behind the bushes, eyeing me with a sort of taunting expression. In her hands was one of the big fat field mice, squirming and trying to get free. The wiggling rodent was terrified, but the little girl was having fun.

It sent a chilly tremor through my entire being.

Anna Mae grasped the animal firmly by the tail and held it up, looking from the mouse to me, measuring my reaction. I wish I could unlive, or unsee what happened next. It was completely impossible. I know that. Still, I know it happened.

Anna Mae opened her mouth wide, I mean really big and wide—like a boa constrictor getting ready to swallow a pig—and she dropped the fat mouse, almost as big as a bunny, into her face.

I almost fainted. Anna Mae closed her mouth and grinned at me, the rodent's tail whipping between her lips in its last futile expression of the desire to stay alive.

Then, Calvin stepped out from the cover of the bushes and stood behind his sister. There was a frantic mouse in each of his hands. The children just stared at me. They said nothing, but I knew their intent was to frighten me. They wanted to scare me. And suddenly I got the distinct impression that they were feeding on my fear as much as they were feeding on the rodents. When they turned to go, another seemingly impossible thing happened. They were there by the compost bin, then instantly, out by the old oak tree.

Then it was black as night but there were three bodies hanging from the tree; one big one and two small ones. I heard a crowd of people shouting. And I spotted a little white girl standing below the old loading dock, sort of leering at me. Gloating.

And then it was all gone. The sun was setting and I was sitting alone with a beer in my hand.

When I say I was goddamned scared there's no way you can know the depth of terror that washed over me at that moment. And if Calvin and Anna Mae and whoever the little white girl was, if they were feeding on my fear, then by God they were having a feast.

Next thing I know, I'm in the van driving. Don't know if I locked up the school before I left. I just can't remember.

I drove to the interstate and went to the first motel I could find. I used some of the cash Sean had given me to pay. There was no way I could sleep in the school that night. I barely even slept in the motel. I tossed and turned, sometimes wide awake, other times half asleep but tormented by flashes of nightmare imagery. My mind kept trying to make sense of it all. Maybe I'd fallen asleep on the platform and dreamed it. Maybe the blow to my face had given me a concussion. Maybe I'd ingested some hallucinogenic substance without knowing it. Maybe I had a brain tumor. All that kind of garbage ran through my head all night long.

But, deep down, in my heart of hearts, I knew the truth. Everything had happened just the way I described it. Something dark owned that schoolyard. Something the locals didn't know about or maybe knew but didn't like to think about it. That something had a hold of the place. It had a grip on that little spot and it was hanging on, trying to drag itself more into our world. If I was sure of nothing else, I knew that.

I woke up when a maid barged into the room to clean up. I told her to give me a minute.

So, at least I'd slept. I felt nominally better. The sun was high and the terror I'd known the night before seemed distant. I got in my van and drove back to the school.

It looked normal when I arrived. It was just an old building. Hell, it was my home. Had been for many weeks now.

I went into my room and got my Bible. Holding it in my hand, I walked the perimeter of the property, praying and saying whatever popped into my mind that might disperse the dark energy I believed was living there. When I passed under the oak tree it was like my right arm suffered a spasm. The Bible fell out of my hand. I picked it back up and held it close to my heart. "You may think you own this place," I said. "But you don't. There's a higher power that owns this place and everything else. There's nothing here for you. There's only light in this place."

Not perfect. But not bad.

I waited to see what might happen next, but nothing did. I went back inside.

It wasn't long before I heard a car pull up. *Great,* I thought, *just what I need. The big guy is back to kick my ass some more.* The only weapon I had was the pellet gun, so I picked it up and carried it with me out onto the old dock. I was relieved to see it was Howard. It was only then that I realized it was Sunday and his store was closed. I leaned the pellet gun against the wall and stepped down off the platform.

"Thought I'd take you up on your offer to see the old place," he said as he closed his car door. Howard walked toward me grinning, but the grin disappeared when he got a good look at my bruised face. After sighing, he said, "That's a hell of a shiner."

"Yeah," I said, offering my hand.

He shook my hand. "Listen, man, I feel like that's my fault. See, I told Luke you saw Anna Mae and Calvin."

"You did?"

He nodded solemnly.

"Come on in and sit down," I said. He was my first real guest since I'd been living there. "Want a beer?"

"No. Thank you, though. I don't drink beer on Sundays."

"How about a bottle of water?"

"Okay."

We went into the kitchen area and I fished a bottle of water out of the cooler for him. It was fairly cool, though all the ice had melted. He took it, screwed the top off and took a good, long drink. Then, he stared at me a long time. His face twitched and he seemed to feel genuinely guilty about my bruised face.

"I shouldn't have said nothing to Luke. He's touchy. You had no way of knowing. I saw you were telling the truth. Nobody around here'd have any reason to tell you the old stories."

"Stories?"

"Yeah. Lots of folks have seen Anna Mae and Calvin. That's why there's plenty of locals think this place should be tore down."

"Really?" This was news to me.

"Yeah. See, Luke's granddaddy was Silas Dowdell. He was Anna Mae's and Calvin's little brother. Silas and his mama was hiding under that sink there the night the Alvin KKK lynched his daddy and Anna Mae and Calvin." Howard gestured with the water bottle toward the sink.

"My God," I said.

"You can see why he's upset. He wants to believe his grandfather's brother and sister can rest in peace. It hurts him to think that little murdered boy and girl are trapped here outside heaven. You know?"

"I understand." But even as I said it, I wondered. That's not them. It's something that uses their images to generate fear.

"Nobody knows for sure what got the white boys over in Alvin all riled up. But a bunch of them come out here one night and made an evening of it. Brought their families. Hell, it was like a picnic. They were some sick bastards."

I said nothing. I couldn't think of anything to say that would be appropriate in this situation. I guess you could say I was stunned.

"Miss Hattie said tell you to come on over this afternoon if you want to."

"Miss Hattie?"

"Miss Hattie Tanner. She's an old lady lives nearby. Never married. Used to teach school. She's sort of a historian for the town. She wants to talk to you."

"Think I should go?" I asked. "I don't want to make things worse."

He nodded. "I think you should go. Come on. I'll go with you."

We both got into Howard's old Chevy. It smelled of motor oil, perspiration and barbecue smoke. He drove and we spoke sparingly for the ten minutes or so that it took to reach Miss Hattie's house. Under different circumstances I might have laughed when I saw the place.

It was down a red dirt, county road, but, unlike the other houses in that part of Houston County, it was freshly painted. There was a picket fence, also freshly painted, and a variety of yard decorations like birdbaths and a wisteria arbor. The place was full of flowers and fruit-bearing trees. Miss Hattie had spent a lot of time making the little frame house attractive.

We moved up the walk and onto the porch, the steps creaking a bit under our weight. There was a nice bench swing with a cushion. On the swing lay a copy of the *Saturday Evening Post*. This place seemed like a monument to simpler and gentler aspirations from a bygone era.

Howard rapped at the door frame. A sweet, high-pitched voice responded.

"Yes? Who is it?"

"It's me, Miss Hattie. Howard."

"I'm on my way," the old woman called from the interior. It was a few moments before the door finally swung open to reveal the slight form of Miss Hattie. She was dressed in her church clothes, complete with a hat that had a flower made from cloth attached to one side. She smiled big. Her eyes were bright and welcoming.

"I'm so glad you came," she said. "Come inside. I have a fan and it's cooler in here. I just made some lemonade."

Howard introduced me and held the screen door while I stepped into the house. It was a good deal cooler inside. Cooler than I'd expected. I remember thinking the place must've been really well-insulated. We walked into the living room (which I suspected Miss Hattie called a parlor) and Miss Hattie indicated that I should sit on the sofa.

The room was packed with furniture and I carefully maneuvered my way. The paths between chairs and the coffee table were an appropriate size for a little woman like Miss Hattie, but a challenge for most grown men. Howard accidentally let the screen door slam shut and Miss Hattie stared at him sternly over her spectacles.

"*Howard,*" she cautioned.

"Sorry, Miss Hattie," Howard answered quickly. "It slipped out of my hand," Howard reverted to his eight-year-old self for a moment. It was hard not to laugh, seeing him stare uncomfortably at the little woman.

"Make yourselves at home," Miss Hattie said. "I'll be right back."

Miss Hattie went into the kitchen. I sat on the sofa and Howard perched uneasily on a rocker like he was afraid he'd break it.

Miss Hattie returned with a tray containing a pitcher of lemonade and three plastic tumblers. I expected glassware, but I suppose her experience with Howard dictated plastic. It would never have occurred to me that Howard was clumsy or self-conscious, but in the presence of Miss Hattie, he was both.

She seated herself on the sofa beside me and after she had poured each of us a serving of lemonade, she scrutinized me for a time. Not harshly, but with a benevolent half-smile.

"You know, I was worried about you moving into the old school," she continued. "I knew the bad things that happened there had not yet exhausted themselves."

I found her choice of words interesting. "Miss Hattie," I said, "all I know about what happened there is what Howard told me today about a lynching."

She nodded with pursed lips and gave my knee a reassuring pat with her small, bony hand. "You walked into something you couldn't possibly understand."

In silence, I agreed.

"Howard says you're a good man. I can see for myself that's true. I hope you won't hold a grudge against Luke. He's still full of pain and hate over what happened even though it happened before he was born."

I don't remember everything Miss Hattie said that day, but a lot of it had metaphysical overtones. She spoke of "energies" and "resonances" and said it's up to those of us who will, to hold the light on this planet up to the darkness. There was a power to her presence that seemed very real to me.

As I sat there listening to her talk, I felt that I'd rediscovered the true nature of humankind, that Miss Hattie was what all of us had come here with the intention of being. At one point, she pulled a large photo album out from under the sofa, scooted closer to me and opened it up across both our laps. It was filled with amazing old black and white photos of early members of the Fodice community. She quickly passed over those until she came to a horrifying photo that, although I'd never seen it, was all too familiar to me.

In the photo Model A and Model T Fords were gathered around the old oak tree behind the school. There was a bonfire and torches scattered throughout the scene. Three bodies hung from the tree. One big, two small. There were people sitting on blankets and eating and drinking like it was a church picnic. A tiny little blond girl was nibbling at a chicken leg and staring directly into the camera. It was the little girl I'd seen.

"My God," I muttered. The photo sent a chill down my spine.

Miss Hattie sighed heavily. "I don't know why they felt like they had to kill the children. Normally, they would've just made them watch, to terrify them into toeing the line for the rest of their lives. I've prayed over that place many times and I know in my heart that evil will eventually dissipate . . . sort of like the lingering radiation after an atomic bomb. The evil there has a half-life. A real long one."

"Miss Hattie, you're a remarkable woman," I said.

She smiled. "And you're a remarkable man. I never would've thought anyone could live in that place. Not yet. And least of all a white man."

I pointed to the little girl in the picture. "Who's that little girl? I've seen her at the school."

Miss Hattie drew in a quick breath and turned her head sideways, shooting a look at Howard, who grimly nodded. With lips squeezed tightly together, she shook her head slowly. "Mmm— mmm mmm . . . well, it doesn't surprise me that you saw her. But you're the first one who has, that I know of anyway."

"Who is she?" I asked again.

"That's Phoebe Warner. Her daddy was the head of the Klan back then. Folks say she's as dark-hearted as they come. Pretty little thing back then, but evil often comes in attractive packages."

I couldn't help but notice Miss Hattie used the present tense when she referred to Phoebe Warner as dark-hearted. "You mean she's still alive?"

"Barely, but yes. She's in a nursing home over in Alvin. Hanging on very tenaciously. Maybe she's not too eager to go wherever she's headed when she leaves."

"How old is she?"

"I don't know for certain, but I've heard she's close to a hundred. Might be over a hundred by now."

The three of us were quiet for a time. I was the one who broke the silence. "Miss Hattie, you wanted to see me. Well, I came. What now? What am I supposed to do?"

She traced the line of her jaw with a thin index finger, then wagged the same finger at me. "That's a good question. Are you a religious man?"

"No," I admitted.

"Didn't think so. Do you have faith in a higher power?"

"You mean God?"

"Doesn't matter what you call it, him or her. Have you ever experienced the intervention of a higher consciousness in your life? Have you ever had faith in something or someone you could not see, but you knew was there all the same?"

"Yeah," I said. "I think so. I'm not sure it's what you or anyone else would call God, but I know there's something watching over me."

"Good." She clapped her skeletal hands together. "That's faith, the knowledge of things unseen. That's your protection."

Without saying anything about it, I recalled how I'd grabbed my Bible as if it was a charm when things got crazy at the school house. I didn't really believe the book could protect me, but that it somehow represented a connection to something that might.

"All I can do for you is pray," Miss Hattie said. "But, I know from experience how powerful a tool prayer can be."

"Amen," Howard muttered.

"I'll call my prayer group and have them all pray for a circle of divine protection around you. Howard and his family will be praying for you, too."

"That's right," he agreed.

"We're done here." Miss Hattie smiled at me and patted my knee again. As I rose from the sofa I thanked her for the lemonade. "You are so welcome. And you are welcome to come back and visit anytime." As we moved toward the door she added, "Howard, I know you are not going to let my screen door slam."

"No ma'am," he answered.

Neither Howard nor I knew what to say, so we rode in silence back to the school. When he showed no intention of getting out, I thanked him for checking on me and introducing me to Miss Hattie.

"Least I could do," he answered, offering me his big, hard hand. "You're a brave man."

"Brave?"

"Well, yeah, I think so. You're gonna spend the night in this place aren't you?"

I nodded.

"In my book that makes you brave. Don't think I could do it. And we will be praying for you. I'll talk with Luke again and make sure he doesn't bother you anymore."

"Thanks."

I climbed out of the car and he drove away, waving as he left the property and turned out onto the red dirt, county road.

Time passed slowly. I was restless. I placed the Bible over my heart and lay on the bed. Again and again I tried to read *The Three Stigmata of Palmer Eldritch*, but I was easily distracted. Every little sound drew my attention. Finally, I set the paperback aside and just lay there. After a while it began to rain. The sound of the rain on the roof was somewhat comforting. There were a few flashes of lightning and the thunder rumbled out many miles to the east. Sometime after the rain began I fell asleep.

Laughter woke me. High, shrill giggling. It was the mischievous titter of a little girl. I was pretty sure I knew who was laughing. I woke with a start, but was afraid to move. My hand went to the Bible and pressed it to my chest.

"Hello . . ." the little girl's voice called from out there in the rain.

Journal Entry—October 7, 2010

I may be reading too much into it now, with distance and perspective; but I sensed that my life was at a crossroads. My situation and mindset, coupled with the history of that place, had created an opportunity for something from somewhere else to try and get a foot into the door of our world. I thought about Miss Hattie.

Knowing that she and the others were praying for me, helped ease my consternation a bit. I realized the little girl I heard laughing was not a little girl at all; just something dark and malevolent, trying to frighten me. It was using the forms of Anna Mae and Calvin and Phoebe Warner because the contrast between its own evil and the innocence of children was bone-chilling, deliberately grotesque and confusing to the human mind.

What was it? Had it ever been a living thing? Was it always a parasitic something that latched onto unsuspecting people and made them do things like lynching Anna Mae and Calvin and their dad?

Thinking again of Miss Hattie and her prayer circle gave me a bit of courage. Still holding the Bible, I sat up on the bed.

As I write this I realize it sounds like I was mulling it over the way one might consider a bit of information from a magazine or textbook. It takes longer to write it than it took to experience it. Though these insights flashed through my mind as quickly as the lightning flashed in the rainy night outside, mostly I was just plain terrified. The dread that had hold of my mind would not be shaken off by rational inquiry.

I heard the sound of something, tossed by the wind, bumping against the glass of the window above the sink. Not wanting to, but knowing I had to, I turned my eyes in the direction of the repetitive thump. There, where I'd seen the squirrel tails dancing in the wind before, I saw two little black hands, one slightly larger than the other, tied by string and hanging in front of the glass.

Something pounded on the door that led to the dock. I heard the little girl's tittering laughter.

"Let's plaaayay . . ." she called. "I won't hurt you . . ." She laughed louder than before and I knew better than to believe her.

The bolt snapped in the door and it creaked open until it was far enough out for the wind to catch and slam it against the outside wall. Lightning illuminated the yard and I saw the little blond girl peering over the edge of the dock. She smiled playfully and laughed, covering her mouth as she did.

I stood and moved toward the open door. At that moment I wanted nothing more than to bolt it and shut the thing out. I stepped cautiously toward the opening. There was a stirring at my feet.

My head automatically jerked downward to see what had brushed against me. It was a large rodent. I guess it had come into the school to escape the storm. But, now it ran like an insane thing straight for the little girl. Phoebe opened her mouth impossibly wide and the rat jumped right in, tail and all. She chewed with satisfaction, her eyes never leaving mine, savoring my disgust and fear.

She swallowed and wiped her mouth with her little forearm. "Hungry?" she said. "Let's have a snack."

The lightning flashed again and I saw the three bodies hanging in the oak tree. Phoebe noticed me noticing them. "They're my friends. Do you want to be my friend?"

Water swept into the kitchen through the open door. Already there was a large puddle at my feet. Again, I felt movement. I looked down to see a large snake weaving between my legs, headed for the girl. It slithered onto the dock and, like the rat, willingly sprang into her mouth. "Mmmm," she moaned as the snake's head slowly disappeared between her lips.

I sort of lost it then. Like a frantic animal trapped in a cage, I rushed to grab the door and pull it closed. I could clearly imagine being the next snack to disappear into Phoebe's mouth.

Seizing the door handle, I pulled against the wind. When I looked down at Phoebe I saw, not a little girl, but a hideous old hag clad in a worn and filthy night gown. The snake was still slowly making its way into her mouth, and there was a smile in her eyes.

My feet slipped on the wet linoleum and I went down. A burst of pain shot through my back. The wind shifted and flung the heavy door in my direction. I tried to move, but I was too late. The door slammed on my arm. I heard the snap of the bone over the sound of the storm. Then the pain in my arm made the pain in my back seem like nothing.

The old woman was up on the platform now, crawling toward me in the pouring rain. The snake's tail still dangling from her lips, writhing and slapping against her face. For an instant it seemed like I heard the sound of many voices, speaking in unison, though I couldn't make out what they were saying.

Then a hellacious bright light and a bolt of lightning came down smack dab on the old woman. The sound of the atmosphere being ripped by thunder was deafening.

And that's all I remember.

I woke up in the county hospital.

For what seemed like the longest time I was alone in the room, but it was clean and dry and represented a reality with which I was familiar. I could hear voices in the hallway and on the intercom. Tell the truth, I wasn't sure I was still alive. Maybe I was in some sort of waiting room for heaven or a purgatory or something? I really didn't care. I felt safe.

Later I learned that Howard had come by in the morning and found me on the dock. He's the one who called the ambulance. That evening after he closed the store, he and Miss Hattie came to see me.

"Sorry I couldn't be here when you woke up," Howard said,

"but my profit margin at the store doesn't allow for unscheduled days off."

I told him not to worry about it and thanked him for checking on me. Miss Hattie quizzed me about everything that had happened. I told her everything she wanted to know. Then she told me something every bit as strange as what I'd told her. Seems her niece or great niece is a supervisor at the nursing home where Phoebe Warner had been living for years. The night before, during the storm, the staff heard a shriek coming from the old woman's room. Two or three of them rushed to her bed immediately. All they found was a scorched sheet and part of a hand lying on the floor beside the bed. There was no trace of the rest of her body.

Journal Entry—October 9, 2010

Okay, so now I'm at my mom's place. When I've healed enough I'll look for a job. Maybe I'll go back to school. I don't know.

I haven't told Sean and Julie everything that happened, just that I had a bad accident and I'm recuperating in Fort Worth. They're understanding and supportive. I wonder if I'll ever be able to tell them the truth.

I spend my days reading a lot and watching a little TV. Mom's always been the suspicious type. She hasn't come out and said it, but she's hinted at the idea that maybe I got crosswise with some drug dealers or thugs of some other stripe. Other than her suspicions, she's been real good to me.

I've had plenty of time to think about what happened and the larger implications of the whole presence of evil in Fodice. One thing that occurs to me is this; most people never get a good close look at evil. Maybe that's one reason that our world is as sane as it is. It's like once you notice evil and it has your full attention, then it's able to slip into this world through the smallest crack.

With all the thinking I've done about evil, I've come to the conclusion that there are four types. First, there's evil with a lower case "e." That's the way we think of mean bosses or people who cheat us in a business deal of some sort. Then, there's B-movie evil. That's largely a literary construct used to educate children. The guys in black hats in an old western movie, or Ming the Merciless, or maybe a murderer from an episode of Perry Mason. Hollywood evil. They illustrate evil in an entertaining and understandable way, but keep it out there at arm's length. It's always someone else and hardly ever us. The third kind is what I call the King-Lynch kind of evil. Stephen King and David Lynch. This evil is informed by an understanding of what it is to be evil. The evils these guys present in their work is disturbing to lots of people because it clearly points out that evil is not a foreign entity, but a part of us. We don't want to believe that it's hiding down deep somewhere, waiting to get out or that maybe it's the bulk of the iceberg and the tip, or what we normally think of as ourselves, is just the smallest, but most visible part of what we are. And lastly, there's true evil. That's what the Allied forces experienced when they liberated the Nazi concentration camps. It's the damning realization that our attempts at civilization are fragile at best. That at any moment, the sum total of our collective good can be swept away and replaced by our worst nightmares.

I think the forces that we identify as evil are allowed in when a human soul is in twilight. I'm not a religious man at all, but I think I understand good. It's the light. Its clarity and a sense of community. We're social creatures because we need the company of others to help us stave off the darkness. I don't know what would've happened to me if Howard and Miss Hattie hadn't intervened. So, if you're not focused on the light, you can drift like I did into a twilight region where evil can step up and shake your hand. I guess you could say evil is crepuscular. It lives in the darkness, but it feeds in the twilight.

Pretty Deaths

By Russell C. Connor

The trip took nearly an hour on their bikes, which they left hidden in a clump of bushes by the highway more than a mile from their destination. From there, the three of them tromped into the woods so they could circle around and approach from the far side, where they couldn't be seen from the road. The smell hit them when they were still fifty yards from the fence, a stench so harsh it seemed to sear their nasal passages. Mandy made them turn off their flashlights after that, and they stumbled through the last stretch with only the moon to guide them.

"See?" Mandy said. "I told you. There it is."

Mandy pointed at the chain link fence cutting through the woods with one bubblegum pink fingernail.

Tight coils of razor wire lined the top of the barrier. On the opposite side, more trees stretched out, but when Willa leaned around Mandy and peered along the fence, she spotted a sign attached to the chain link. It was barely legible in the moonlight.

PROPERTY OF TEXAS STATE UNIVERSITY
HAZARDOUS BIOLOGICAL WASTE CONTAINED WITHIN
KEEP OUT!

"Are you sure there's no one here?" Willa asked. The whole thing sounded like a bad idea to her earlier at Mandy's house, but she had played along. She thought Mandy and Kit were kidding, testing her, seeing if she was cool enough to hang with them.

"Totally," Mandy assured her.

Mandy smoothed the front of her immaculate Hollister sweater over her budding breasts. The former San Marcos Junior High homecoming queen looked out of place in the middle of the woods dressed like someone from an upscale clothing catalog. "Sara Collier's brother says the scientists or whatever only come out here every few days," she added. "There aren't any guards. All they have is a few cameras."

"Cameras? That's even worse!"

"Move." Kit shoved between them to get to the fence.

Of the three, Kit was the only one outfitted for a covert mission, wearing all black with a hoodie pulled low over her face. But, then again, she'd been dressing like that pretty much every day for the past six months.

Without a word, she pulled her hood back, put her backpack on the ground, removed a pair of wire-cutters, and set about clipping a vertical seam in the square links of the fence one at a time. The metal made a quiet clink as the sharp blades snipped through.

"Look, I don't think we should do this," Willa tried again. She found it hard to think straight in the stench. There was no escape from it; it hung over everything like an invisible fog.

"Would you chill out?" Mandy told her. "The cameras aren't to catch people, it's for, like, their experiments or whatever. They need to . . . you know . . . it's so they can—"

"It's to document the decomposition," Kit snapped, without stopping her work.

"Right. If they see us on them at all, it won't be for weeks. And even then, they'll have no idea who we are."

"But . . . it can't be that easy to just break into a place like this . . ." Willa looked at the gaping slash Kit had opened in the fence.

"Why not?" Mandy shrugged and tossed her brown curls. "They prob'ly figure the only people who would want to get in here are perverts and freaks."

Willa started to say something but thought better of it and remained silent. She still felt lucky just to be spending time with these two. She'd known them since kindergarten, but they had always been part of the upper echelon of the girls their age. And now, of course, they were sophomore A-listers who sported clothing labels like police badges. They occupied a completely different social and economic strata than Willa, whose current ensemble had a retail value of maybe thirty bucks at Target.

But Kit's father had died last year, and things had begun to change.

Kit finished her work on the fence and wrenched at the chain link, pulling aside a long flap. The opening looked as dark and deep as an ocean abyss.

Mandy put a hand on the small of Willa's back and gave her a shove. "Go on."

"Why me?"

"I thought you'd wanna go first."

"I don't wanna go at all!"

"I'll go first," Kit grumbled.

She pulled back her long, greasy hair (Willa could remember when those flowing auburn curls were the envy of every girl in the seventh grade), tucked it back into her hoodie and then got down on her hands and knees to crawl through the hole she'd made. Willa went next, sliding her palms through the dirt. She stood up on the other side and gazed into the dim woods while they waited for Mandy to join them.

"C'mon!" Mandy said, after bouncing to her feet. Her rosy cheeks practically glowed with excitement. "Let's go find them!"

They kept their flashlights off as they continued through the woods, all of them attempting to peer in every direction at once through the trees. Willa didn't know what to expect or what the object of their morbid quest would even look like when they found it, but she had the eerie sensation that she was on an Easter egg hunt. That smell got worse the farther they went, so thick that Willa felt like she was swallowing the air rather than breathing it.

The land sloped sharply downhill, the trees replaced by a tangled bed of brambles. Kit led the way with robotic determination, her pace so quick that the other two had trouble keeping up. Willa tromped after her, unable to see where she planted her feet, and then felt the toe of her sneaker snag on a root. She tipped forward and lost her balance. Her hands snatched at the air, but there was nothing to save her.

Willa performed a silent, oddly graceful swan dive that culminated in a hard landing on one shoulder and an unplanned somersault into some brambles, and then she was rolling downhill. She came to a sliding, disheveled stop on her back seconds later, in a moonlit patch of grass. As Mandy and Kit giggled somewhere above, Willa silently performed a quick physical inventory, making sure she wasn't hurt. Other than a few bruises and a rip in her T-shirt, she was fine. She leaned up on one elbow and examined her surroundings.

A dark, eyeless face glared at her from just a few feet away.

Willa screamed and rolled over and scrambled away on her hands and knees, bumping into Kit's black Doc Marten's.

"Be quiet," Kit hissed. "You'll wake the dead."

Kit flashed Mandy a smile. Mandy squatted next to Willa and touched her shoulder. "It's just a stiff," she said. "No big deal."

Willa worked to catch her breath.

She eventually nodded and forced herself to stand. She didn't want to appear uncool or less cool, even if playing along would give her nightmares. This was the whole reason they had come. She couldn't chicken out.

Willa crept forward, joining Mandy and Kit. They were already hunkered down next to each other near the spot where Willa had landed. Willa peered over their shoulders.

On the ground, partially buried under a layer of fallen leaves and pine needles, was the shriveled corpse of a woman.

She lay spread-eagle, completely nude except for the tattered remains of what looked like a paper gown. Her skin was a dull white, waxy and almost fake somehow, stretched so tight over her frame that every bone in her slender torso was visible. Her breasts lay like deflated balloons and scraggles of copper-colored hair clung to her scalp in the wafting rays of moonlight. Her eye sockets were hollow and the skin of her face was discolored and peeling. A wooden stake with the number "23" printed on it in permanent marker had been planted in the ground beside her splayed right thigh.

The Body Farm.

That was what Kit had called this place when she first started talking about it last week. Willa realized she hadn't really believed it existed until this very moment.

"I d-don't understand," she whispered. The smell was in her stomach now, making her dinner roll. "Why do they do this?"

"They study how they rot." Kit said distractedly. Death was one of the few topics that got her to string together more than two words in a sentence these days. In fact, she'd been talking about this place all week, trying to coerce Willa and Mandy into coming out here. "How long it takes . . . which parts go first . . ."

"Yeah, but . . . why?"

"So forensics labs and the FBI can solve murders. Catch serial killers. Stuff like that."

"And they just leave them out in the woods like this?"

"They have to recreate the conditions that exist when someone dumps a dead body," Kit said. She snapped on her flashlight and pointed the beam at the woman's pale face. "That's why her eyes are gone. Probably got eaten by a bird."

A wave of nausea swept over Willa, but she couldn't look away. "How do they get the bodies? Who . . . who are these people?"

"Some of them were just homeless," Kit responded. "Some were people who died without any family or anyone to pay for their funeral. But mostly they're people who donated their bodies to science." Kit turned to face Willa. "They wanted to be here."

"Ugh." Mandy opened her mouth and stuck a finger dramatically down her gullet. "Talk about losers. I would never let my body be treated like that. I want a grave with a huge big tombstone so everyone can come and cry over me."

Kit stood up. "Let's go further. I wanna see more." She started off into the woods, carving through the dark with her flashlight. Willa stayed where she was until Mandy grabbed her hand and pulled her away.

Soon they were finding corpses all over the place, a ghastly array of all ages and races, arranged in rough groupings among the trees. Each body was laid out in its own unique position and allowed to undergo varying stages of decay. There was an old black man propped up against the base of a tree, fully dressed in a stained blue suit, eyes closed, so fresh he might only have been sleeping. Close by lay a young white boy lifelessly emerging from a shallow pit, his lower half buried in the ground and his bare torso visible, but dark with creeping rot. Further on was an Asian woman whose skull showed in flaky patches and then a body so skeletal they couldn't even determine its gender. Some of them had been shot or cut or burned before being set out to decompose, presumably to test the effects of such injuries on decayed flesh. They dangled from branches by nooses and lay in the trunks of old, rusted cars. They curled around one another in simulated mass graves, their ghoulish gestures reminiscent of scenes from a haunted house.

Whole rows of corpses lay side-by-side, wrapped in blankets and tarps and garbage bags. And still others couldn't be seen at all, their resting places marked only by freshly turned earth and a wooden stake with a number on it, to be dug back up at a later date.

The three girls wandered through these displays like visitors at a museum, so engrossed that they began to separate and drift apart. After the fifth or sixth grisly display, Willa found that she was no longer as scared or grossed out. She even stopped noticing the stench. When she came across bodies that had been medically mutilated—heads removed from necks, stomachs opened to the elements, torsos dismembered and the pieces set in piles to molder—she stopped to inspect each one and wondered at what they had been like before they died, who they were, what their existences had been like. It was also, then, less frightening, knowing that these deaths or stagings of death were created for scientific study.

Or maybe, she thought—as her mother often said—you can get used to anything if you try hard enough.

Willa lost track of Mandy, but, after fifteen or twenty minutes of roaming among the dead, she stepped over a girl her own age with her rotted brains exposed through a hole in her skull and found Kit just a few steps away, hunched over yet another body, shoulders shaking as she wept soundlessly.

Her flashlight sat on the ground. The beam spilled across the corpse's face, giving Willa enough light to see its features. It was an older white man with short brown hair and a bushy mustache, stretched serenely across a bed of moss and creeping ground vines. The few times she had been to Kit's house, Willa had seen pictures mounted on the wall of Kit's father, and the dead man in the flashlight beam bore a slight, passing resemblance.

It had been a heart attack that claimed the life of Kit's father. The rumor around school was that she found the body while her mother was out of town on business, and had been so traumatized she hadn't even called the police until the next day.

In the months that followed the funeral, Kit's presence in the elite circles at the school diminished rapidly. Gone were the pretty clothes and the perfect hair and the good grades and the adoration of teachers. Her friends relegated her to a Goth or burnout status and stopped being seen with her; except Mandy, who somehow maintained her status among the popular girls while regularly huddling in private conversation with Kit between classes. And then one day the two of them approached the corner table in the cafeteria where Willa ate lunch alone and asked if she wanted to come and hang out with them after school.

Now, watching the girl weep over the corpse of a man who vaguely resembled her father, Willa's heart filled with sympathy. She still didn't feel like she knew her two new friends very well, especially Kit, but she eased forward, knelt, and put a hand on the girl's quaking shoulder.

"Kit," she whispered. "I'm really sorry about your dad."

Without warning, Kit turned and threw her arms around Willa, pulling her so close their chins rested on each other's shoulders. After getting over her surprise, Willa returned the embrace, rubbing Kit's upper back with her palm.

"Oh Willa." Kit's whole body shook with the force of her sobs, voice broken with snorts and gasps. "You're such a good friend. I'm so happy I picked you."

"Me too," Willa told her, noting the odd way Kit phrased their budding relationship.

Kit trembled and shook, her jitters intermittent and her breath curious. The noises she made hardly sounded like crying. In fact, it almost seemed as if she was giggling. "That's why," Kit replied between exhalations, "I'll make this as painless as possible."

Willa felt Kit's hands move at her back and she instinctively pulled away. Out of the corner of Willa's eye, a glint of silver flashed and pain lanced up her left arm. Willa fell back across the leaves and kicked out, landing a blow on Kit's shoulder that sent her sprawling in the opposite direction, across the body that looked like her father.

She put a hand to her upper arm. Blood dribbled from a small slash across her bicep. "W-why did you do that?"

Kit sat up, still snickering in that breathless, almost hysterical way. In her hand was a long, thin blade that looked like a kitchen knife, stained with Willa's blood.

"It can be so easy," Kit said, running a tongue across her lips. In the glow of the flashlight, her eyes were dark and wild, reminiscent of a shark's. "Like going to sleep. Just close your eyes and when you wake up . . . you'll be in heaven."

She lunged forward, bringing the knife down in an overhead arc. Willa rolled away without thinking, dodging the blade as it sank to the hilt in the soft ground where her neck had been. She leapt to her feet.

"Stop!" she cried, backing away with her hands held out to ward Kit off. "What are you doing?"

Kit pulled the knife from the soil and climbed slowly to her feet. The grin on her face was obscene.

Willa continued to back away, but made it only a few steps before she realized someone was standing behind her. Mandy stepped around her, saw the knife in Kit's hand, then looked back and forth between it and Willa. Her mouth fell open in shock.

"What the eff are you doing?" She stamped one immaculate Chuck Taylor on the ground in anger. *"You were gonna kill her without me!"*

"I was just gonna make her bleed her a little," Kit explained sheepishly. "We can still take turns stabbing her."

"You're joking," Willa said numbly. "This is just a joke. I don't like it."

"Poor little Willa," Mandy crooned. *"Did you really think we wanted to be your friends? I mean, you're pathetic. I'm gonna have to get new carpet just because you slept on it."*

"But . . . b-but I don't understand . . ."

"It's simple." Kit held up the knife and ran a finger down the blade. "We decided we want to kill someone. And guess what? You're that someone."

They came at her. Willa tried to run, but Mandy got a grip on her arm. She swiveled and jabbed one hand out blindly. The heel of her palm smashed into the other girl's makeup-covered face. Mandy's grip on her arm released as she clutched her nose. A single scarlet thread seeped between her manicured fingers.

"You effing bee," she snarled.

Then Willa was sprinting through the woods, cutting between trees and leaping over underbrush with a spryness that surprised even her. She had no idea which way she was headed, and the darkness closed in around her almost immediately, but she didn't stop or slow down. She just kept running.

Decaying corpses jutted from every corner of the blackness, but they were disinterested, impassive and incapable of pity. It occurred to her then that death itself was much easier than dying; the bodies around her confirmed it.

Willa slowed and stopped near a staging away from the main path. It was a young man, missing his lower jaw, a cheekbone and one eyeball. She stared for a moment, realizing he was probably very handsome before, like many of the boys she passed in the hall at school. She wondered what made him volunteer for this. Or what unfortunate twist in his life had left him without parents or family who might have seen to it that he received a proper funeral and burial, rather than donating his body for a gory slasher-movie display here at the Body Farm.

Willa heard the other two crashing after her, and saw the beams of their flashlights bobbing and bouncing through the dark.

Not smart, she thought. You're giving yourselves away.

Willa turned away from the young man to keep going and saw a weak glow filtering through the trees ahead. She could make out the shape of a small building. She saw it clearly a moment later: a tiny log cabin with electric lights burning in the windows. Perhaps the other two had been wrong; maybe there was someone here after all.

Willa reached the door and pounded against the wood. "Help me, please help!" she said, as loudly as she thought she could without immediately giving her location away.

There was no response. She tried the handle. The door swung

open, and she bolted inside.

On either side of the door, dim lamps cast a ghostly pallor across the interior of the cabin. It was only one narrow room, with wide bunk beds lining both walls, and no other way in or out.

And bodies. Bodies everywhere, all of them hacked and chewed apart. Two corpses lay face down in the floor at her feet, their backs utterly shredded, in a pool of dried black blood. More corpses were packed in each level of the beds with stained sheets thrown over them, two and three together, their limbs sprawled over one another and dangling off the sides. Some of their faces and chests were obliterated, sliced to ribbons.

An axe jutted from the wall to her left, the blade sunk deep into the wood.

This was another display, she realized. An experiment made to look like the scene of a grisly axe murder. Clearly, the high watermark in terms of the methodical, blood-soaked carnage at the facility. She was beginning to suspect the body farmers had serious issues.

Although probably not as serious as her new friends.

"Hurry up!" Mandy's voice, from somewhere outside. "We can't let her get away!"

"See if she went in there!" Kit ordered.

Willa stumbled forward, stepping over the corpses on the floor, and searched for a place to hide. As footsteps approached the cabin, she dove into the lower bunk of the second bed, scrambling over a stiff body and into the shadows beyond. She squeezed between two corpses occupying the bunk and wiggled beneath the sheets, burying herself in a sprawl of wooden limbs. On her left, a middle-aged woman whose head was split nearly in two gaped at her for a moment before sliding forward to thump against Willa's neck, splattering bits of putrid-smelling flesh and writhing maggots across her chest. Choking back a gag, she settled down and held her breath just as the door flew open.

Through half-closed eyes and the filter of the sheet, Willa saw

Mandy come into the room and survey the macabre setup. *"Gah-ross,"* she declared, turning the word into two syllables. Mandy held a blade now also, though smaller than Kit's and probably a paring knife. Mandy held it in front of her as she walked slowly down the middle of the cabin, toward the bunk beds.

"Where are you, you slut?" Mandy murmured. Her voice sounded stuffy and thick, presumably due to Willa's blow to her nose. A bloodstain now marred the front of Mandy's expensive sweater.

Mandy reached the first set of bunks and jabbed her knife into the sheets. The blade sank into the tangle of bodies again and again, each blow hard enough to make the bed springs creak. She did the same thing to the upper bunk, then the one on the opposite side, then moved to the bed where Willa hid.

As Mandy leaned in with the blade clutched in one fist, Willa shoved the woman with the split-open head into her face.

Mandy screamed around a mouthful of rotten flesh and flailed backward, dropping the knife. The corpse slid from the bed and thumped into the floor at her feet. Willa followed, leaping out of the bunk in a low crouch and hitting Mandy's midsection with her shoulder. Willa surged with all her might, driving Mandy toward the bed on the other side of the cabin. The homecoming queen's head hit the frame with a dull thud, and she collapsed into a heap next to the other bodies.

Willa backed away from Mandy in mute horror and turned to run . . . and then came to a lurching halt.

Kit stood in the cabin's only doorway, watching her. She stepped slowly inside and pushed the door closed with the tip of her knife.

"She never got it," Kit said solemnly, gesturing at Mandy's unconscious form. The sadistic smile was gone. Now she looked cool, contemplative, and a little sad. "Not really. When I told her what I wanted—needed—to do, she just thought it sounded like fun. A new way to be mean to someone she thought was beneath her. I would probably have killed her eventually—will kill her . . . if she's not already dead. She just didn't understand."

"Understand w-what?" The words were no more than a squeak.

"That death is pretty," Kit said. She squatted between the hacked bodies in front of the door, turning her head back and forth to gaze at them lovingly. "I used to be like Mandy. I used to think nice clothes and a good body made you beautiful. But then my dad died, and I saw none of that mattered. We're all going to die and rot away to nothing." She sighed. "I sat there all night when I found him, just staring at his body. He wasn't in it anymore. It was empty. There was something so pure about that. Something clean and . . . and simple. I loved him more than ever."

Willa clasped her hands in front of her. "Kit . . . please, listen, I think you need help . . ."

"That's why I wanted to see this place," Kit continued, ignoring Willa's plea. She stood and continued down the aisle through the middle of the cabin. Willa backed away. "I wanted to see all this beauty. And to share it with you. Don't you see, Willa? I'm not like Mandy. I want to help you. I know you hung out with us because you wanted to be popular. So people would think you're pretty, like Mandy."

Willa froze in the act of taking another step backward. "That's not true," she said stonily.

"But you don't need to be like Mandy to be pretty. I can make you as beautiful as them." Kit reached out and stroked the ravaged face of one of the corpses in the first bunk.

"I don't want to be like them." Willa's voice was surprisingly strong and clear. "Or Mandy. I just want to go home."

"You can't go home," Kit told her, pointing over her shoulder, into the upper corner of the room. A tiny red camera light burned in the gloom. "None of us can ever go home again."

Kit raised the knife, pointed it at Willa, and, with a bloodcurdling, mad scream, charged forward.

Willa stepped aside in the narrow space and grabbed Kit's wrist, fighting to keep the blade pointed away. Kit grunted and strained as she tried to maneuver the knife back around.

The two of them stayed locked like that for what felt like an eternity, grappling in the surreal butchery of the dead cabin, a perverse parody of their embrace just minutes before.

In desperation, Willa abruptly stopped pushing the blade away and pulled it toward her, twisting clear as it stabbed past her shoulder. The movement threw Kit off-balance and Willa plucked the blade from her hand as easily as picking a flower.

"You want someone to die so bad?" Willa screamed, plunging the knife into Kit's side.

Willa felt the blade push through flesh and glance off bone, saw the splash of red that coated her hands. Kit crumpled to the wooden floor, landing beside Mandy. A dark river poured from her side.

Kit's eyes twitched and then calmed, landing on the head-split woman's mangled, maggot-sprinkled face. A vacant smile spread across her features as the rise and fall of her chest slowed and then stopped altogether.

The body farm had new additions to its ranks. Two pretty ones.

Willa left them there, trudging back out of the cabin and into the night. She was suddenly exhausted and spent. She just wanted to rest.

After a few delirious moments, she happened back across the boy with no jaw or cheekbone. A familiar face.

Willa sat down in the grass next to his body and then lay next to him. As she stared at his incomplete features, a tear ran down her cheek.

The Interrogation
of Horace Chatham, Esq.

By Michael H. Price

Somebody offered the miserable bastidge a cigarette, which seemed to loosen him up somewhat.

We have a strict No-Tobacco Policy—no chaw, even—what with the Mayor's campaign to "bring this department into the twentieth century." He's a tee-totaler in a top hat, but he makes the rules.

New century be damned, what we really need around the decrepit old Station House is some new linoleum, so you can put that in your Pope and smike it. Cops is cops, so the saying goes, and someone's always bound to have a pack on him, whether City Hall likes it or not. Comes in handy when some miserable bastidge needs loosening up. And beats the Third Degree, which is a decidedly nineteenth century tactic that many a flatfoot still employs when he can. Anyhow, we needed to get the boy talking while the experience was still fresh in his mind. Such as his mind was.

Chinless, wall–eyed and none too bright, Horace Chatham was a familiar face around the Cop Shop; and not for any good reasons other than keeping him off the streets and away from his wife whenever his mean-drunk nature used to take hold. Horace had kept his nose pretty clean during the last several years, especially since Rose–Marie had hauled off and hauled out on him. He'd landed himself a good job as a laboratory flunky and all-'round go–fer with A&M's School of Anthropology, which is a big deal hereabouts and also elsewhere on account of its dean, Dr. Forrester Bonham, and his expeditions. Bonham makes a whole lot of noise in the international press with his comings and goings, and he usually brings back discoveries that make for good exhibits at the museum and also keep the funds and the gravy-swimming set rolling in. And never mind whether these Scientific Revelations change anybody's mind around these parts about any truer Origins of the Human Species.

But Bonham had turned hostile, and worse, toward Horace since their return from an Arctic exploration that was rumored to have yielded some kind of a breakthrough. Bonham claimed the ol' boy had loused up a valuable shipment, judging from some very Horace-like scrawls on a waybill. The professor had finally canned Horace for dereliction, then started pestering me to send some officers prowling around Horace's house on suspicion of outright theft. Bonham wouldn't go into detail—wanting no publicity that he hadn't engineered for his own important self—and we dismissed the idea, figuring the freight company was probably at fault, in any event. It just goes to show you; I should have listened to the stuffy old egghead.

Well, now, so then things kind of escalated to where nobody could ignore them, and next thing you know Horace Chatham was back as a guest among our good company. And this was more than a matter of his just sleeping off a bender in the Drunk Tank, the way he used to do. Stone-cold sober, he was, but frenzied and haggard—running his mouth like ninety per, once he'd got all loosened up, and gesturing as emphatically as a feller could when cuffed and leg–ironed. The District Court had fixed him up with a lawyer by now, but Horace had declared his intentions of making a statement to set the record straight. Which he did, in the presence of counsel, plus me and the arresting officers and a courthouse steno. And his account was something.

"Just like Sleepin' Beauty," he began. "Or is it Snow White? I always get them two gals mixed up with each another. Whichever, that's how she looked to me, when we finally got all dug down to the glacier. That's a big ol' block of ice, did y'know? I l'arnt that from Perfesser Bonham.

"See, Perfesser Bonham, he was right there on the spot when we found her. She was just as frozened–up as that ol' guy I seen in this movie 'bout a' ape–man, one time. 'Cept nowhere near as ugly. Perfesser Bonham, he made him a speech 'bout how 'portant it was, us findin' her like that, and then he called in the crew to cut out the block of ice that she was all frozened–up in.

"He said it was, like, if'n she'd been all iced over for as long as he reckoned, then we didn't want to thaw her out on the spot. Just under only the most controlled of lab'atory conditions,' like he said. So I ups an' says, like, well, now, sir, maybe all she needed was just a nice kiss to wake her up, and they all laughed like as if I'd said somethin' funny.

"Then, Perfesser Bonham, he told me, he says, 'Well, Horace! I'd never suspected such a romantic nature in you,' and then he says, 'Maybe if you'd shown such tender feelings all along, your wife wouldn't have walked out on you.' They all had 'em a' even bigger laugh over that. Not that I cared.

"On account of, I knowed somethin' that they didn't none of 'em have a clue about. See, they all thought she was frozened dead. Me, I knowed better.

"So then, Perfesser Bonham, he started talkin' about how he couldn't wait 'til he could go to cuttin' on her. *Die*–section, he says, and I've watched him do them die–sections. I knowed then and there, yes, I did, what I was gonna have to do.

"Y'all know how long I've been handlin' the lab shipments for the college. It was a piece o' cake, once we'd landed back home and they was all unloadin' their gear, for me to change up the freight records. Make it look like that big ol' ice–chest had got put off at the harbor in Houston. An' then, while the 'fesser sent the charter-flight people off to backtrack and find his mislaid cargo, it was just about as easy for me to dolly that shipment off behind the hangar and to my truck. They was all 'stracted, but I wasn't,

and just to make things look okay I went back and said I sure did
need to get on back home, now that we was back in town. Perfesser Bonham looked up long enough to say, like this: 'Homesick,
Horace? As though you had someone waiting for you!' And then
them college guys all had 'em another big laugh 'fore they went
back to cussin' out the flight-crew people.

"Better I should have had me a lab'atory, but lab or no lab, I
knowed I had to bring that ice–lady out of her glacier real gradual–like. So I used what I could 'member of my ol' Grammaw's
remedy for frostbite. Damp warsh–towels, li'l' handfuls of salt,
keep the room warm but not too warm. Like that. Worked, I guess,
but I still like to think it was the kiss that done the trick."

Horace's assigned lawyer—a greenhorn, new to the county
and by now no doubt wishing he had gone into some other line
of work—cringed at this disclosure and scrawled out a memo to
himself about an insanity defense. He might have been preparing
to rein in his motor-mouthed client, but Sergeant Grimes bellied
up and saved him the trouble: "Okay, Horace. This yarn of yours
is taking us nowhere, 'cept maybe off into Screwball City, so why
not just get to the point and 'fess up?"

"Well, now, sir," Horace answered, "I'm just tryin' to tell y'all
how it . . ."

The lawyer asserted himself: "He's as good as owned up to the
theft of the fossilized remains, Sergeant Grimes. I'd say this man is
rushing himself just fine, with no need of any coaching from you."

"Thank you, Mr.—uh, Lawyer," said Horace. "Anyways, I was
just gettin' to the part about how beautiful she looked, once she'd
thawed out and wokened up."

"'Beautiful,' huh? And it 'wokened up,' too?" interrupted
Grimes, turning to the rest of us. "Say, Chief, you and the boys
saw that putrefied thing when we arrived at the . . ."

"That'll do, Sergeant," I said, then: "Okay, Horace. It's your
story, so you tell it."

"Well, sir," continued Horace, "she had her all this thick mane of hair, like my Rose–Marie used to call 'plat'num blonde' and envied any woomin that come by it natural. I reckon this ice–gal, she must of been a fightin' woomin back in the Olden Times, on account of she had this rock–hatchet kind of a tommyhawk thing that'd been froze along with her. I went to easin' that thing out of her hand, just in case she was to come to in a fightin' mood. Good thing I did, too, 'cause she surely did come to in a fightin' mood.

"So I s'pose you could say I had to slap her around a li'l' bit—just to show her who's the boss, y'know?"

At this, the lawyer showed enough initiative, at least, to rise and clear his throat, as if to silence his heedless client. Sergeant Grimes moved in quicker, though.

"Yeah, I know!" said Grimes. "And for an ol' boy whose lawyer seems to be plotting an insanity defense, you really oughtn't be reminding the law of your history of domestic violence—crackpot fantasy or not."

"Anyhow," said Horace, "and I ain't plottin' me no kind of defense, on account of I know what really happened, and how come. But she seemed to like it—gettin' roughed up, y'know? So I guess them old stories 'bout how them cavemen treated their cave–wimmen must be true. Y'think?" If he meant that as a leading question, no one took the cue.

A pause, as if waiting, then: "One thing led to another, and the nex' thing you know, she's a–puttin' some lovin' on me like I never . . ."

"What?!" interrupted Grimes. "Say, listen—Chief, you can indulge this sicko all you please, and I'll play along, for the sake of a confession . . ."

"A statement, you mean," I said. "We don't call it a confession any longer."

"Yeah, sure, whatever," Grimes grumbled. "But if he's gonna veer off into some prehistoric necro kick—yeesh! Man, I say we just cut the gibberish and whup the truth out of him before this thing gets any sicker!"

"None of your whuppin' on my watch, Sergeant," I said, pulling Grimes to one side and lowering my tone. "And especially not on a man who's been through so much madness and bereavement lately. Even if he did bring it all down upon himself." Horace overheard and raised his voice in reply.

"Well, now, if you mean by me rescuin' that gal away from the perfesser—yeah, I reckon I did bring it all down.

"But she was hell on roller–skates from th' git–goin'," he continued. "I was aimin' to call in sick the next day, just so's I could keep uh' eye on her. But when I did call in sick, it was 'count of she already had me wore out to a frazzle.

"And I never seen the likes of sitch a' appetite! Cleaned out my 'frigerator, yes, she did. Found her hatchet, too, though I'd hid it good, an' then barged out of doors an' eaten up a couple'r three dogs 'fore I could catch up with her."

"Oh, hell's bells!" Grimes bellowed. "You mean that rash of animal mutilations?"

Horace continued, unfazed: "Well, so I beat on her some more, 'til I had her l'arned to stay indoors."

"Mmm-hmm," I said. "And I'll bet you could tell us a thing or two about that break–in at the college cafeteria, eh, Horace?"

"Aw—well, sir," he said, "you know a man's got to pervide for his own. But anyhow, when I finally reported back for work, they told me I didn't work there no more, and also that I'd better leave before 'Fesser Bonham caught sight of me on account of he suspicioned me for that lost cargo. But then the telephone rang, and it was for me, and I said, well, now, if'n I don't work here no more, then how come somebody's callin' for me on the telephone? Turned out it was a call from Rose–Marie.

"I'd long gived up on ever hearin' from Rose–Marie, ever again. But now, here she was, back in town, and callin' 'round 'til she found out where it was I was at. She allowed as how she'd got to thinkin' 'bout patchin' things up 'tween us, and she'd be waitin' for me at the house.

"And here, I hadn't even thought to change out the door–locks in all that time since she'd moved out. So I thanked 'em kindly for the use of their telephone, even if I didn't work there no more, and lit a shuck out for home.

"I reached there in jig–time—but so had Rose–Marie. And y'all know 'bout all there was left to tell.

"Seems like my cave–lady, she couldn't abide no intrudin' woomin. There was no reasonin' with her. Nor with myself, neither. I just wrenched that weapon of hers out of her fist, and—uhm, so that's when I got on th' 'phone to you–all, an'—well . . ."

Horace trailed off with that, then came around to a more practical concern: "Reckon what's gonna 'come of me? I mean, for makin' off with the perfesser's discovery like that, an' . . ."

"Easy, Horace," I said. "I figure Dr. Bonham is the least of your problems, just now—and he seems downright relieved, just to have reclaimed his box of bones . . ."

"Yeah," Grimes cut in. "Even after you'd busted the thing's skull all to smithereens! 'Cept hammerin' on some zillion-year-old ape–woman carcass is one whole hell of a lot less of a deal than tearin' into your ex–wife with a chiseled-stone blade—and then tryin' to go blame her murder on a fossilized cadaver!"

"Aw," Horace muttered, "but I told y'all . . ."

"Yes," I said, "you told us, all right, Horace. And once is all I need to hear it. Now, you just sit tight. You can confer all you like with your lawyer, maybe even get to know the guy, and there'll be a couple of doctors coming in to talk with you—and we'll just see where things go from there. You gonna be okay with that?"

"Yessir," Horace said, then: "Dang it all! Y'know, it just occurred to me—I never even got to find out what that ol' cave–gal's name was."

"It was probably *Ooola*," I said. "Saw it in the funny papers."

"What?"

"Nevermind."

Poor bastidge.

Redstick, Texas

By Tom Bont

"Hollingsworth," Angela mumbled into the phone. Moonlight shimmered through her window, and a blurry 5:02 a.m. glowed on the digital clock face.

"Agent Hollingsworth," a frantic voice babbled, "I . . . I need yer help and raht now!"

She sat up in bed. The voice sounded like . . . "Ambrose?"

"Yeah! I—"

"How the hell did you get this number?" She jumped up from the bed, and the wisps of dreamland evaporated.

"Yer business card."

Trick! grumbled through her head as she asked, "What do you want?"

"To confess . . . to everything! But you hafta' get me outta here!"

Angela's blood pressure spiked. She brought up a recording app on her phone and pushed the record button. The conversation wouldn't hold up in court, but it would certainly go a long way toward helping her case. "Daryl, I'm recording this conversation. Is that okay?"

"Yes. Fuckin', yes! Just come 'n get me!"

"Okay, repeat what you just said."

She recognized the sounds of fear as they crowded her ear, heavy breathing, smacking lips. "I said I wanna confess to every-thing, but you gotta help me! They're comin' for me!"

"Settle down, Daryl. Who's coming for you?"

"Crazies, I think." His voice faded as if he turned to look over his shoulder, away from the handset. "Hell, I don't know! I just know they got really big-assed dogs."

A tractor-trailer roared through the call's background. "Where are you?" She tapped the speaker button on her phone and set it next to her laptop.

"Outside Redstick, Texas."

She typed that into the web's mapping site but kept talking. "Okay, Daryl . . . go to the local police station. If you can't find that, there's a diner on the main strip. Should be open this time of morning."

"Okay, but yer comin' to get me though, raht?"

"Yes." She looked at the caller ID. "This number good to call you back?"

"No, it's a pay phone."

"A pay phone?"

"Yeah. It's an old gas station. North of town, I think."

"Okay, Daryl. Repeat what I want you to do."

"Go to the police and if they're closed, go to the diner."

"Good, Daryl. Good. We're coming." She hung up and then called her boss.

"Angela?" He sounded like he'd just finished his second cup of coffee. She hated morning people.

"Evan, listen to this . . ." While the recording played back, she glanced at her sleep-mangled, black hair in the mirror and decided with a grimace she didn't have time for a shower. And her eyes were going to have to go without makeup. She kicked her night-gown to the corner, put her hair into a ponytail, and took a "Marine Shower" as her brother used to say . . . lots of deodorant.

When the recording finished, Evan whistled lowly. "Why would he do that?"

"Something spooked him," she mumbled around her tooth-brush. "Maybe his conscience woke up. Don't really care though." Spit. "We got the bastard!"

"Ang, don't go off half-cocked. The U.S. Attorney refused to try it last time because the evidence was weak. We need a good confession or good evidence this time, or we'll both be reading fertilizer invoices for the rest of our careers."

"Afraid of a little bad publicity?" she teased.

"Damn right, I am. My wife likes that supervisor paycheck I bring home. Says it makes up for me not being there all the time."

"Don't worry. I want this twisted fuck nailed to the wall this time. If all I wanted was to see him off the streets, I'd have shot him in front of the courthouse."

She remembered the laughing look in his eyes that day, the day she knew he'd gotten away with murder. Her own blue eyes stared back at her from the mirror. "Teenagers, Evan. Those three girls were teenagers, for Christ's sake." She trailed off as the bloody scenes flashed before her. "I can't believe we can't find one damn witness."

"I know. But if you look up 'Average American Male' in the dictionary, his picture is listed by the definition. On top of that, no credit, lives in his truck, collects a disability check once a month. He's well-nigh invisible in a crowd. Hell, the only reason I knew he was in the courtroom last week is because he smelled bad."

"Smelled bad? Damn, you've got a sensitive nose."

He chuckled. "You even know where Redstick is?"

"North of Caddo Lake. Texas side of the border across from Fouke, Arkansas."

"You want me to send someone from Shreveport? They're closer than Fort Worth."

"Hell, no! This is my case."

"Alright. Besides, if anyone knows their way around a small town, it's you."

"You trying to make me quit?"

"Sorry. I forgot how much you like to hide your roots." Then he took a long, deep breath. "Alright. I'll call local law enforcement and have them hold Ambrose on a vagrancy charge until the U.S. Attorney okays his arrest. In the meantime, you go get that confession."

The lanky, wizened police chief walked up the sidewalk and stuck his hand out. "You must be Agent Hollingsworth. I'm Chief Wilcox."

He had a friendly enough look on his face but considering she was there to take custody of a child killer, he seemed too friendly in her opinion. She figured Evan hadn't filled him in on the particulars of the case.

"Thanks for your help, Chief." They shook hands, and through unspoken agreement, strode into his office, her legs taking two strides to his one.

"Aw, think nothing of it! And call me Jim. How was your drive?" he asked.

"Long. But fine, thanks. And call me Angela. My apologies for sounding impatient, but I really need to see Ambrose. Where are you keeping him?"

Jim took his hat off and scratched a balding pate. "We don't have him. He didn't show up here. An officer has been sitting at the diner since, um—" He pulled out a small notebook and flipped through a couple of pages. "Since Agent Evan Welch called this morning at 5:30."

"He . . ." Angela started. She began to seethe and turned in a slow circle. When she saw the women's bathroom, she made a beeline for it. "I'll be back in a minute."

Five minutes away, and no one went to get him! Maybe they should change the town's name to Redneck.

The thought brought a sarcastic snicker and turned the heat down on her boiling temper. She crammed a piece of gum into her mouth and chewed at it as if she was trying to gnaw through saddle leather, a habit she learned at the academy; it was better than opening her mouth when she shouldn't have. She stopped flexing her hands long enough to relieve her bladder and went back out into the main office. "Can you take me to the diner?"

"Sure," Jim said, "Not sure what you're looking for. My officer would have called if your suspect had shown up."

"I just want to look around, ask a few questions."

Jim rubbed his clean-shaven chin. "Yes, ma'am." He turned to an older woman sitting by a bank of telephones and an antiquated dispatch radio. She had a thick book in her hands, Stephen King's *Silver Bullet*. "Helen, I'll be at the Lucky Star."

"Surprise. Surprise." She never looked up from her book.

Redstick obviously didn't know how to petition the federal government for law enforcement cash, because Jim led her out to an older model Ford Expedition. It had seen better days, but Angela had to admit it was still comfortable. There was a child seat, a plushy snake, and a primary reader in the backseat. "You do much cop-type work out of your personal vehicle?"

Jim glanced over his shoulder as he snapped on his seat belt. "All of it . . . when I don't have the grandkids with me." A crooked grin crossed his face. "Don't see much trouble around here." He twisted the key in the ignition. "Occasional out of town hunter with a little too much beer in his belly and not enough brains in his head. And any of the kids who get in trouble, we just call their parents at the scene. Folks around here respect each other. And the law."

Idyllic, 1950s Americana. That was Redstick.

Three old men sat in front of the barbershop. The man pumping gas at the service station wore an attendant's uniform. Main Street was spotless and the local postman walked down it with a spring in his step like he enjoyed every minute of his job. When Angela and Chief Wilcox pulled up in front of the diner, Angela swore she smelled homemade apple pie.

The diner was full of an early lunch crowd. When the little bell mounted over the wood frame and glass door announced their arrival with a ting-a-ling-a-ling, most everyone turned from their meals and either waved or shouted a friendly greeting. To the left ran a long counter fronting the steamy kitchen behind it.

An officer in a steam-pressed uniform with creases so sharp they seemed aerodynamic met them right inside the doorway. Jim said, "Special Agent Angela Hollingsworth, this is Officer Danny McIver."

The officer grabbed her hand and shook it. "A real life FBI agent, here in Redstick? Heck, I ain't never woulda' guessed it!"

"Settle down, Danny. Don't shake her shootin' hand off."

"Well, that ain't my shootin' hand, but let's leave it there anyway, okay?" she said as she tested all of her fingers. Then she chastised herself; *did I really just say "ain't?"*

"Oh, sorry, ma'am." Danny spun around and quick-stepped over to a table. "Here, I been holdin' these seats for y'all in case you showed up."

Angela smiled and then said, "Thanks, but I'd like to talk to everyone if I may."

Jim lifted his hands into the air and raised his voice, "Can I have everyone's attention, please? This is Special Agent Hollingsworth with the FBI. She'd like to ask y'all a few questions."

As soon as all eyes were on her, she pulled a picture of Daryl Ambrose out of her briefcase and held it up. "I am looking for this man. He called me this morning from a gas station north of town. I need to know if anyone knows where he is or if anyone's seen him." She handed the picture to a young woman sitting near her. "Please pass it around, ma'am."

A man from the back of the room spoke up. "What did he do?"

"I'm not at liberty to say. This is an ongoing investigation, but I can assure you it is imperative we get him off the streets. He's driving a '97 Chevy supercab pickup. Red, but one of the passenger-side doors is blue."

An old woman sitting in the back spoke up in a voice that sounded like rusty nails being pulled from an old windowsill. "Bad folk don't last long 'round here," she cackled, and returned back to her plate of food.

"Why's that, ma'am?"

Danny grimaced, and Jim stepped up. "Thanks, Mrs. Haster." He leaned in and whispered in Angela's ear. "That's Ma Haster. She lost her marbles well over twenty years ago."

Angela stepped back and waited while everyone passed the picture around. She watched for reactions, trying to glean if any-

one was hiding anything or not. Short, jerky movements. Lip bit-
ing. Itchy noses. Avoiding looking at the picture. Bouncing knees.
Popping knuckles. Nothing.

When the picture made its way back, Jim stood up next to
her. "Thanks, everyone. If you see him, please call the police." He
turned to Angela. "You might as well eat while you're here. We
can stop by the 47 afterwards."

"The 47?"

"The gas station north of town. That's when old man Henshaw
built it, 1947, after the war. Lived in the back until he died about
twenty years ago. His son owns it now."

"I don't suppose it's got a security camera, does it?"

Danny spouted, "Oh crap!" He snatched his cell phone off his
belt and pulled up some pictures before handing it across the table
to Angela. "I forgot with all the excitement of actually meeting
you. There's a cash machine there. I called the bank and they sent
the pictures to me. That there's his truck!" Jim looked at Danny
with surprise on his face.

As she was forwarding the pictures to her email account, Jim's
radio squawked to life. "Chief, I got a report of a 10-45 David out
on Hobart Road with that early model, red Chevy pickup."

Jim looked over at Angela and keyed his microphone. "Definitely 45 David?"

"Affirmative. That's what Hobe said."

"Thanks, Helen. We're Code 3, lights only."

Angela dug through her memories from the academy. Code
10-45 David meant a dead body. Code 3 meant they were using
lights and siren, but Jim modified it to lights only. If the body was
at the same scene as Ambrose's truck, it might be Ambrose. She
hoped not. She wanted him to answer for his crimes. Death was
too easy for him. "Any ID on the body?"

Jim radioed Helen. "Helen, any ID on the 45 David?"

"Negative, Sheriff."

They climbed into the Expedition, and Angela noticed everyone in the diner watching them through the windows. Exciting

day in Redstick.

Angela and Jim drove out to the south of town and into a large thicket. The road they used had changed from asphalt to gravel a couple of miles back. From what Angela could see, that road traveled deeper and deeper into forest. "How long before we get there, you think?" she asked.

"Pretty soon."

"How do you know that?"

"This is Hobart Road," he said, pointing ahead. "We've been on ol' Hobe's land for about 10 minutes now. Any farther, and we'll be off his land."

Sure enough, they rounded a bend, and up ahead two trucks were parked by the side of the road. One was a large, four-wheel drive, painted camouflage, with two men in hunter's orange standing near it. The other was a burned out husk, little wisps of smoke still curling around it. Angela sat as far forward as her seatbelt would allow and peered through the windshield. "What the hell happened?"

"I'm not sure . . ."

Angela made a phone call. "Evan, I might need an Evidence Response Team in Redstick."

"Why?" he asked.

"I think we've found Ambrose's truck, and we've got a body."

"I can't authorize an ERT, Angela. The U.S. Attorney is waiting on the results of your interview. If he's dead, it's a local matter. Case closed for us. Sorry."

"You serious?"

"I'm afraid so. I've been on the phone with them all morning."

There was no way she was going to let that stand. If Ambrose was dead, she wanted to know why. "I'll be in touch," she said, hanging up and turning her phone off before Evan had a chance to order her back.

Before the wheels stopped rolling, Angela hopped out and rushed up to the burned out vehicle. She took note the cab was empty and then pulled a napkin from her pocket to wipe the char from the license plate. She slowly stood up. "It's his truck." She turned to the hunters. "Where's the body?"

The older of the two—she guessed the father of the younger one—looked at Jim as if he needed permission to speak.

"She's with the FBI, Hobe."

"Oh," Hobe grunted, scratching his salt and pepper beard. "About a hundred yards in, ma'am. Just follow that small trail next to the fence."

"Can you show me?"

"Yes, ma'am."

She looked at the muddy trail and then at her feet. She had her street shoes on, black with thick, rubber soles. They felt like tennis shoes, but they also suited the FBI's dress code. Unfortunately, they weren't designed to slog through the woods.

Suddenly, Jim dropped a pair of big-man-sized, hunting boots at her feet. "These should do the trick."

"Thanks," she said. "My field kit includes a pair, but it's all in the trunk of my car." As she put them on, she glanced at Hobe and his son's feet. Their boots were mud-free.

They came upon the body right where Hobe said it was. What they hadn't mentioned was the condition of the corpse. Angela wasn't a forensic pathologist, but it was clear to her that large carnivores had chewed on Ambrose's body. She crouched down next to it for a closer look. "Chief," she continued, "y'all got critter problems around these parts?"

Critter problem? Ugh! Her country roots were sneaking back into her speech the longer she spent in Hicksville.

The chief looked up from writing in his notebook. "Not that I've heard," he replied.

"Looks like you got one now," she mumbled as she scanned the landscape of the surrounding woods.

"This Ambrose?" he asked as he took his hat off and wiped his brow with his shirtsleeve. "Face looks kinda tore up."

"It's him. I recognize the tattoos on his arms. Three little, pink hearts. One for each of his victims."

Angela leaned back against a rather old, but still usable autopsy table. At the request of the FBI—well, she's in the FBI, right?—and in the spirit of interagency cooperation—she really needed their cooperation—the local coroner, Dr. Albert Monroe, moved the Ambrose autopsy to the top of the stack—a stack of one. He'd called her and Chief Wilcox to his office to discuss his findings the next day.

When they'd first brought the body to the coroner's office, the chief had suggested she head back to Fort Worth. "I'll forward the results to you once we've got 'em," he said, flashing a wide, white smile at her.

"I appreciate that, Chief, but if it's all the same to you, I'd like to hang around and see it to its end."

He bristled slightly. "Suit yourself. Mary-Beth's there next to the diner usually has a room available."

The room was barely two-star, and she was glad she only had to spend one night there. The air conditioner rattled, and the shower mold looked like it needed a good wire brushing. She didn't consider herself Susie Homemaker, but she did like a clean bathroom.

"Without getting into the medical details," Dr. Monroe began, "he died from an acute myocardial infarction brought on by severe cardiorespiratory exertion." At hers and Jim's confused looks, he translated. "He died from a heart attack due to long term exertion."

"What about the mutilations?" she asked.

"Sharp tooth trauma. Ha! Get it? Sharp tooth trauma?" Neither she nor Jim laughed. "Ahem. Pack of dogs got him after he died. It's all in the file. Here's your copy. I've already forwarded one to your office."

She looked at Jim. "Dogs."

"I guess you were right," he said. "Sounds like we do have an animal problem. Al, any idea how many, breeds, anything?"

"At least three. Probably the size of German Shepherds."

Jim rubbed his chin. "So, Ambrose ditches his truck, runs into the woods, panics about something . . . either gets lost or is chased by dogs . . . and dies from a heart attack. Then some dogs, maybe the ones chasing him, chew on his body."

"That's the only explanation I can come up with," Albert said.

Angela tensed up. "I don't buy it. He was ready to turn himself in! And he was only thirty-five years old. A little young for a heart attack."

Jim shrugged. "Maybe he changed his mind."

"And his truck," she said. "Why burn his truck?"

"Setup?" he offered.

"Setup? How?"

"He calls you and says someone's after him. Then, lo and behold, his truck is found torched and he's gone. You stop looking because you think whoever was chasing him, got him. Only instead of being gone on his terms, he stumbles on a pack of wild dogs. I have an official category for those types of situations."

"Yeah? What's that?"

"A win!" He shined that wide smile again. "This is a win, Angela. Take it and run."

Angela shook her head. "Eaten by dogs." She thumbed the coroner's report. "Thanks, gentlemen. I guess I'm done here. Could you ship the body to Fort Worth for burial? C.O.D."

"We can cremate it here," the doctor offered. "It'd be easier."

"No, it's our responsibility," Angela replied. "Thanks anyway."

She called Evan as soon as she got on the road and filled him in. "It's all bullshit. I ran deerhounds with my older brothers. I've seen what meat looks like after large breed dogs have had their way with it. The teeth marks on Ambrose were twice that size. The hunters didn't have mud on their boots. What, did they change boots before I got to the scene? Something's not right here."

"Does it really matter?" he asked. "We've got a child killer off the streets. The sheriff's right. This is a win, case closed. That's a notch in your belt even if you didn't personally collar him."

"Maybe you're right," she conceded.

Angela pulled a stick of gum from her pocket and shoved it into her mouth. The Tarrant County Chief Medical Examiner, Dr. Fred Sherman, was laughing at the report from Dr. Monroe. "Oh, yeah, Ambrose was definitely chewed on by something, but he was alive when it happened. Dr. Monroe is either incompetent or he's blind. Every test shows Ambrose died from blood loss. And my professional opinion is it was not a dog. I don't even think it was a wolf."

Around a stream of nervous gum smacking, Angela asked, "What was it then?"

"I have absolutely no clue. DNA says Canidae though."

"Cana-what?"

"Canids . . . dog, wolf, fox. You know. Can't narrow it down further than that."

"Why not?"

"Either the DNA has degraded too much to get a decent reading, or we have a prehistoric proto-wolf roaming around East Texas."

Angela stopped smacking. "Proto-wolf? What kind of critt . . . animal is that?"

"Something that was around before modern wolves evolved." He threw the pictures on his desk next to comparisons from other wolf and large dog attacks. "You were right about one thing; the fangs and claws that cut up Ambrose were larger than those on a large breed dog. In fact, they're larger than those found on the wolf skeletons from the La Brea Tar Pits in Los Angeles. That's what I'm saying. I'm not sure what killed him, but it wasn't anything in my taxonomical textbooks, and it damned sure wasn't a heart attack."

"I can't believe you managed to get time off tonight," Angela said as she swirled a large mass of spaghetti noodles onto her fork. She put the noodle ball into her mouth and then sliced a large meatball in half. The meatballs at Don Genti's were works of art.

"Got a new resident," Heather said. "He's taking Thursdays."

"Cute?"

"Yeah, in a kid brother kinda way." Heather stabbed a chicken piece with her fork and swished it around in the tomato sauce. "The nurses are all fawning over him." She chewed on the chicken and looked at Angela's bowl of noodles. "It doesn't even look like you've taken a bite yet."

"I know, right?" Angela said. "I never seem to make a dent in it." She raised her fork to her mouth and then suddenly stopped. She tilted her head to the side, stared at her bowl, and whispered, "Noodles."

"Huh," Heather said, interrupting her.

Angela shook her head. "It's nothing."

"You sure?"

"Yeah." But she continued to gaze at the noodles. They reminded her of the old woman from the Lucky Star.

Bad folk don't last long 'round here.

That's what she had said before turning back to her lunch—a large plate of spaghetti and meat sauce. And the look on Danny's face when she'd spoken.

In Angela's mind's eye, she saw him . . . grimace? No, that wasn't the right word.

Wince? Yes. He winced. It was just a string of words, but they were not innocuous.

What am I missing?

Sticks and stones break bones, but words reveal secrets. *Interrogation 101.*

With an inward groan and an outward sigh, she sat back in her chair.

"What's up?" Heather said.

"Nothing. Really!"

"Angela, I've known you since college. You aren't going to be good company tonight until you solve that puzzle. I got the check, now get!"

Angela stood up and hugged her friend. "Thanks, Heather. I'll call you tomorrow."

It was past ten by the time Angela got to the federal building. She went straight downstairs to Archives. The hallways were empty that time of night. The only ones left were guards and workaholics like her. She sat down at one of the terminals and typed "Redstick, Texas."

The results appeared on her screen. There were three pages of events surrounding that half-horse town? It was going to be a long night.

Most of the references on the screen were for boxes of files not yet digitized. She sent it all to the printer and spent the next three hours roaming the Lumber Yard, the Bureau's slang for the non-digitized warehouse of paper files. By 4:00 a.m. and three large, unsweet teas later, she'd put together a brief history of the town based on newspaper articles, Texas Ranger archives, and FBI reports.

Jeremiah McIver, a preacher from New England and immigrant from Scotland, founded Redstick, Texas in 1843. *An ancestor of Officer Danny, I bet.*

The population doubled when the railroad put a train stop there about ten years later.

She could have put together a thorough history of the town, but she was more interested in the crime reports. For instance, back in the 1800s, a Texas Ranger chased a gang of train robbers into the area. No one heard from the gang again. The Rangers made a note that perhaps they had a run in with the Baker Gang and lost. It wasn't until after the turn of the century that the reports increased in frequency, and it wasn't until she looked at the reports as a whole that she suspected there were more in the 19th century. They just weren't reported.

The ones that caught her attention were the disappearances. In 1905, a snake oil salesman on the run from authorities in Shreveport was last seen headed into the woods to the east of town. No one heard from him again either. Part of the Bonnie and Clyde Gang hid out in the area. When Clyde Barrow went to join them, they were nowhere to be found. According to one James Carter, a pianist at a downtown Dallas speakeasy, Mr. Barrow said, "That town scared the willies out of me, and I ain't going back."

During World War II, the Korean War, and the Vietnam War, all draftees from the area skipped out. The government never found them. A couple of oil and gas companies tried to drill in the area, and most of their crews quit within days of arriving. They said the townsfolk scared the bejesus out of them. Those who didn't formally quit, skipped town, and never picked up their last pay-check. The companies finally gave up.

And the latest: Ambrose turns up chewed to death in the woods outside of town by a prehistoric proto-wolf, the only victim she can find in the area that didn't disappear outright.

She sat back in her chair and reviewed the different reports. Disappearances happen all the time, especially during the time frames these were reported. *I'm missing something.*

She decided to look through the reports not as individual events, but incidents in a larger pattern. She sat up in her chair as she read the name of the police chief during two of the incidents. The name pulled at her.

Conrad Welch. As in Evan Welch?

Her trance broke at the sound of a door closing and the lights going out.

"Hello? I'm still here," she yelled.

No one answered back.

She used her cell phone light to make her way through the aisles of shelved cardboard boxes to the door to turn the lights back on. When she got back to her terminal, she saw that someone had rifled through her notes and the neat pile of ancient records she'd collected. She twisted her head and looked around. "Hello? Who's here?"

Evan's voice echoed back at her from her left. "You should've taken my advice, Ang! Should've taken the win!"

"Evan?" She drew her Glock and gripped it in the two-handed style she'd been trained to use. "You're from Redstick?"

"Yes." This time his voice was from behind.

Keep him talking. "Why didn't you tell me?" No answer. She released her pistol with one hand and pulled her phone from her pocket. She set it on the table and pushed record. "Did you have anything to do with Ambrose's death, Evan?"

"Does it matter how he died?"

Angela spun around. His voice was close. To her right.

"Right to a trial, Evan. We arrest them. We don't try them." She crept down the aisles closest to her terminal. "We're not vigilantes."

"He was a child killer!" His voice sounded like he was back on her left again.

He's traveling in a circle around the room. He's stalking me!

"Why don't you come out? Let's talk." She peeked over her shoulder. "Maybe you have a point. You did save the courts a bunch of time." That last sentence sat on her tongue like sour milk.

He laughed with a low grumble. Then the laughter turned into a growl. "Don't patronize me!" he yelled. His voice had changed timbre. It now sounded like he was talking through an empty paper towel tube. But there was something else there . . . pain . . . he whimpered in pain. But it was deep, guttural. *Primal.*

The logical part of her mind told her she was in danger, and the other part confirmed it by telling her to hide. She turned to make a mad dash for the door, but her feet rooted to the floor in primitive fear as a howl pierced the air. It grabbed a hold of her soul and made her wish for daylight, warmth and peaceful ignorance.

She stood in a shooter's pose, afraid to move, and continued to stare down the aisle.

Be small. Be insignificant. Hide!

A shadow stretched around the corner and a monster from forgotten nightmares followed it.

The creature was crouched but rangy. No clothing, though coarse, short, brown fur covered it. Huge teeth protruded down the sides of its blunt snout. It rose to its full height when it finished rounding the corner and walked toward her in a casual manner, as if coming to ask for directions.

It dragged its paw along the boxes on the shelves. When the

claws scraped across the metal framings, they dug in, leaving furrows as if they'd ploughed through warm butter. She risked a look into its eyes.

They glared back, inhuman and pale blue. She didn't remember Evan having blue eyes. The word *werewolf* jumped into her mind.

This is what killed Daryl Ambrose. And it was coming for her.

She wanted to yell, "Freeze! FBI! You're under arrest." But her training and self-discipline failed her. She tilted the barrel of her Glock upwards a smidgen. Just enough. The monster's eyes caught the movement and then widened in surprise as she pulled the trigger.

Although she was going for a center mass shot, through luck, the grace of God, or errant FBI training, the bullet found its mark in the center of the creature's forehead. The werewolf fell to the floor and Angela took a deep breath. She kept her weapon trained on it as it transformed into the human known as Evan Welch.

Deputy Assistant Director Stan Stevenson read from a stack of papers. "The conclusions of the Department of Justice's Office of the Inspector General are as follows:

Article One: Special Agent Angela Hollingsworth, acting on instinct and in the best interest of the American people, took it upon herself to question the official findings of the cause of death of Daryl Ambrose.

Article Two: Special Agent Angela Hollingsworth discovered a link between Supervisory Special Agent Evan Welch and Daryl Ambrose in Redstick, Texas.

Article Three: When Supervisory Special Agent Evan Welch discovered Special Agent Angela Hollingsworth had discovered the link between the two men, he portrayed the link as if he was responsible for a vigilante-style murder.

Article Four: It is assumed that Supervisory Special Agent Evan Welch had unlawful and nefarious purposes planned for Special Agent Angela Hollingsworth. This is evident from the recordings made by Special Agent Hollingsworth, the condition of the surveillance cameras in Archives, and the condition of Supervisory Special Agent Evan Welch's body; to wit, he was naked. This attack was staged to cover up the fact of his involvement, and any other as yet unknown facts.

Article Five: Special Agent Hollingsworth acted properly in self-defense against Supervisory Special Agent Evan Welch.

Therefore, it is the decision of this board, Special Agent Hollingsworth, that you be returned to active status and promoted in grade to Senior Special Agent, effective retroactively six weeks back from today to the night of the incident in question.

"And may I say," Deputy Assistant Director Stevenson continued, "Senior Special Agent, the American people and the Federal Bureau of Investigation owe you a great debt of gratitude for weeding out this cancer in our midst."

Angela continued to stand before the three-member board while their decision sank in. Not only did she stay out of prison, she kept her job. She never mentioned the werewolf, of course, and with the video cameras disabled, there would have been no one to believe her. In the beginning, her shooting review psychologist insisted he wasn't getting the whole story; and over the weeks, even Angela began to forget what she saw.

Wait, Senior Special . . . did he say promotion?

It made no sense. Promotions were highly coveted and extremely competitive. *Hush money?*

She broke out of her reverie only when her lawyer leaned in close. "Angela, forget about the—"

"Sir, I have one question," she said.

Stevenson looked up from his papers. "Yes?"

"The research I was performing in Archives, the coroner reports . . . was any of it ever recovered?"

"No, I'm afraid not. The investigating agents have been reprimanded for failing to properly tag all evidence. Unfortunately, no one knows where it has been placed." His smile was as sweet as Sunday ice cream. "I'm sure it will turn up eventually. And, as you know, Ambrose's body was cremated by mistake, a bureaucratic oversight, I'm told."

Angela paused for a few moments while her lawyer shifted from one foot to the other. "Yes, sir," she said.

"Good!" Stevenson said. "Now, what are we to do with you? Although you have been cleared, we here on the board are not so naïve as to believe you'll be able to find a comfortable working environment. You did after all shoot a fellow agent. Based on your experiences in this matter, and the initiative you've shown, I've decided to assign you to Task Force W."

An administrative assistant appeared at her side with a fingerprint-secured thumb drive. If plugged into a computer by a finger not containing the keyed print, a memory chip holding the decryption key would be destroyed.

"Task Force W, sir? I've never heard of it."

"Everything you need to know is on that thumb drive."

She put the drive in her pocket. "Yes, sir."

"Excellent. This hearing is adjourned. Congratulations, Senior Special Agent Hollingsworth."

Angela stood on the sidewalk across the street from the Lucky Star Diner for close to fifteen minutes before she decided to go in. No one seemed to recognize her, so she chose a table near the front window and ordered a chicken Caesar salad. Chief Wilcox walked in and sat down at her table as she finished eating. The waitress met him there with a cup of coffee.

"Good afternoon, Senior Special Agent Hollingsworth. Is there anything I can help you with?"

"You know my new rank." She pushed her empty salad bowl to the side of the table and took a sip from her tea. "You're well-informed for someone so far from civilization."

He sat back in his chair, crossed his legs, and placed a tooth-pick in the side of his mouth. "We like to keep up with current events. We even have this new-fangled thing called an internet that helps us with that."

"Hmm. I didn't think vigilantes cared about what happened in real law enforcement circles."

Jim chuckled. "Vigilantes?"

"Don't insult me, Chief." She put her tea down on the table. "How many people know what Welch was?"

"What do you mean? He was an FBI agent."

"Yes. But he also grew fur and howled at the moon, right?"

Suddenly, all conversation in the diner ceased, and everyone looked over at her table. The chief's eyes had turned pale blue—exactly like Evan's on the night she'd shot him.

Chief Wilcox removed the toothpick. His voice dropped to a guttural slur and he bared his fangs. "We aren't actually slaves to the moon, Senior Special Agent. But, in that case, yes, we killed Ambrose. We don't consider ourselves vigilantes though. We just have a strong sense of the natural order of things. We . . ." He waved his hand around to indicate everyone in town. "We keep out territory clean. And I think deep down you know what we did was right."

"Maybe, but did you have to . . . to eat him?"

"We only chewed. We didn't swallow."

"Thin difference, Chief."

She took her time as she reached into her purse, well within his line of sight, and pulled out a twenty-dollar bill. He didn't make any threatening moves; indeed, he continued to sit with his legs crossed, never flinching, nor tensing.

"You aren't upset? About me killing Evan?"

"Of course we are! But he made the mistake. He could've turned you. Made you . . . an ally, so to speak."

She hung her purse on her shoulder. "Why didn't Ambrose disappear like everyone else?"

"Evan said you would've turned this town upside down looking for him. And we couldn't make you disappear—"

"—because the FBI would have scraped Redstick off the map looking for me," she said.

"Probably."

"You played me. And Officer McIver did his part. He had me convinced he was competent, getting those pictures like he did."

"He is competent. Don't let that Barney Fife exterior fool you." The chief's fangs had receded. He shook his head. "Senior Special Agent. *Angela.* Please don't fear us. We're on the same side. We have our own community and we would like to keep it that way."

Angela took another sip of her tea.

Chief Wilcox continued. "There's no place else for us. We owe you. You could have dragged us into the investigation, but you didn't. Thank you."

Angela placed the $20 bill on the table and walked out to her car. As she started it, everyone on Main Street stepped out of their doorways. As she drove out of town, every set of eyes she made contact with had turned pale blue.

Minor Details

By Ernie Lee

Charley finished off his ham and eggs and buttered a final slice of golden toast. He tried to keep up with the steady drone going on behind him.

". . . and don't forget the Housemans are coming over tonight."

"Who?"

"The Housemans. The Housemans. Tonight, Charley. It's Friday. They are coming for dinner and dominoes. Don't be late," she said as she added potatoes and carrots to the crockpot. "And don't forget to take out the trash!"

Charley sighed and rose from his chair, drained the last of his coffee and headed for the back door . . . like every morning—with one minor detail. On his way through the kitchen, he stabbed Daisy in the throat with a steak knife.

He left her, bleeding out on the floor, and grabbed the black plastic garbage bag and took it to the curb. Thin, little plastic kitchen garbage bags—the neighborhood dogs would probably string trash all over the yard again. He kept telling Daisy to buy the heavy-duty kind.

He slid in behind the wheel of his Buick Skylark. Last of the model years. They don't make them like this anymore. He slowly backed down the concrete, and came to the end of his driveway. The black garbage bag was sitting on the curb just where he left it. It was another typical Friday morning—with one minor detail.

What now? Go north on Willow to the interstate? East on I-10 would take him to Florida. He loved Key West. It would take two days to get there, because he'd have to stop in Biloxi. West on I-10 would take him to California. He could cut off on the way and go to Las Vegas. He could drive straight through. There was not much to see on the way anyway. Of course he'd have to stop for gas and to eat. But if he drove all night, he could be there by morning. Vegas never sleeps anyway.

He pondered what to do as he backed into the street. He'd decide when he got to the on-ramp. Ah, freedom! He could go where he pleased, no one to tell him where to turn, who he was having dinner with or that the trash needed to be taken out.

Halfway down the Allen Parkway, red flashing lights appeared in his rearview mirror. Unbelievable! That was fast. He hadn't even made it to the interstate yet. Well, freedom was good while it lasted.

He dreaded the part that would come next—*all the hoopla.*

The trial.

The publicity.

The booking, and newspaper reporters everywhere.

He looked forward to the peacefulness of his little cell, where he might sit and read and try to write the story of why he did it.

The scream of the siren broke into his thoughts, and Charley dutifully slowed, and moved over to the curb. The siren screamed louder and louder, and squawked as the police car flew past Charley and kept going down the street. Charley shrugged and nodded his head.

He pulled the car back into traffic and kept driving. He guessed they had not found out yet. At the rail crossing on Industrial, he was just in time for the safety bar to come down. A few seconds more and he would have made it through. He would have been free and clear and well on his way—except for one minor detail.

He watched the rail cars flash by. Charley loved to watch for the spray paintings on the sides of the cars. It was the only form of graffiti he appreciated. Some of those things were real works of art. Some were gang tags, or stupid names written in clown-like, bubble typeface.

He saw one car with its side door open. "That would work," he mused.

A smile crept across his face.

He could just jump on board. Ride wherever the train was going. No one would find him, or even think to look for him on a freight train. Charley Thompson—rail rider. Who would think? He could jump off wherever he wanted. He thought that train would probably be in California by tomorrow night. He wouldn't even have to drive—just sit back and enjoy the view.

Lost in his dreams of California and the life of riding the rails, Charley was almost surprised to find himself pulling into his office parking lot. He slipped into his regular slot, and turned off the engine. He sat behind the wheel for a while weighing his options. He didn't even remember the last few minutes of his commute.

Should he back out and go on his way to whatever destiny awaited him? What if someone saw him pull in, and then pull out again? Wouldn't that seem suspicious? He didn't want to attract attention by doing something out of the ordinary. Everyone who knew Charley, knew that he was as regular as clockwork.

He slipped from behind the wheel, locked his door and went into the office—just like always—except for one minor detail.

He flicked on his computer, poured a cup of coffee, and read the morning news feed. Not much going on out there. He went through his e-mails and sorted out the work for the day. Pretty typical. He started working and the morning went by very smoothly, just like always—except for one minor detail.

At ten o'clock his phone rang! Charley didn't get many calls, so the ring startled him a little. Ms. Stevens wanted to see him in her office right away.

Charley got up from his desk and walked down the hall toward his boss's office. In fifteen years, he could only remember a couple of times he had been called to mahogany row—both of them bad news. Once, when he was a new employee, he was joking with the guys from the warehouse. He liked those guys, and they seemed to like him. He was more like them than he was like the other cube dwellers. Charley was still smoking then, and had gone out on the dock to have a cigarette. Pete came out and bummed a light, and said something about Ms. Pederson. Charley said something he thought was very complimentary about certain parts of her anatomy. From the look on Pete's face, he could tell that Ms. Pederson was standing right behind him. When he slowly turned around, Ms. Pederson was walking back into the building. The guys really gave Charley the business on that one—laughing, slapping each other's backs and calling Charley a dog. When he got back to his cube his phone rang, and he got called to the office for that one. Charley felt bad about that, but didn't know how to make it right. He was afraid to approach Ms. Pederson. She never went on the dock to smoke again that he could remember. She left the company soon after. Charley regretted that too. He hoped he wasn't the reason she left. She was a nice lady.

The other time he was called to the office was even worse. He was in the company bathroom, in the first stall when someone came in and stood at the urinal. Charley looked under the edge of the stall and could see a pair of cowboy boots that he thought he recognized. He thought it was Sammy. The man broke wind in the middle of his business, so Charley joked, "Hey! Your voice has changed, but your breath still smells the same!" There was no laughter from the other side of the wall. He thought the guys would love that one. When Charley left the men's room his phone rang again with a request to report to the office. Mr. Kimbrough, the District Manager, had not been amused!

Approaching the glass-walled office, he could see a man standing inside talking to Ms. Stevens. Coat and tie, neatly trimmed hair, piercing eyes. "Well," thought Charley, "the police have arrived to take me away." He would read Charley his rights, cuff his hands behind his back, and lead him to the squad car parked near the front door. Everyone would see. He would surrender without a fight. He knew he would not get away with it anyway—no need to make a fuss. It was what it was.

Entering the office, Charley paused in the doorway. "Come in, Charley. Charley, this is Mr. Wallcutt. Mr. Wallcutt, this is Charley Thompson." Greetings were exchanged. Charley waited for the inevitable flashing of the badge. Then, Ms. Stevens explained that Mr. Wallcutt was a company executive who had come to reward good employees with an incentive bonus. Charley was being awarded $1,500. It was unexpected, and a huge relief.

This was a great day indeed—except for one minor detail.

On his way back to his cubicle, Charley thought of calling Daisy to share the good news. He didn't often call in the middle of the day. Then he remembered.

Charley slowly realized that he now had no one with whom to share his good news. There was no one left in his life who would care one way or the other, except a few coworkers who would whine that they didn't get a bonus. Best to keep it quiet for now.

The rest of the boring day passed without incident. No SWAT teams swarmed the building. No screaming police cars blocked the streets or barricaded the employee parking lot. No commandos crashed through the windows on ropes. No one rushed to his cubicle to place him in handcuffs. No one read him his rights. No mob of reporters flashed cameras in his face as he tried to hide under a sweater pulled over his head. There was not even a phone call telling him of his wife's tragic death.

There was absolutely nothing out of the ordinary. It was a normal, typical, everyday sort of day—except for one minor detail.

On the way home, Charley remembered, for a change, the note in his pocket. "Pick up oven rolls," it said. Obediently, out of habit mostly, he stopped at the store and picked up a package of dinner rolls. In a departure from his normal behavior, Charley added extra large, heavy duty garbage bags to his shopping cart. He picked the kind contractors use to clean up industrial work sites. He selected the largest size he could find on the shelf. He figured he would need them.

He pulled into his driveway, and parked the Skylark.

Just as he thought. Stray dogs had ripped open the garbage bag he had put out that morning. He looked at the kitchen door. Everything was quiet. He went up on the porch to the door, and pushed it open. Everything was just as he left it this morning—except for one minor detail.

Charley inhaled the delicious aroma of roast beef from the crockpot as he entered the kitchen. He tossed the package of dinner rolls onto the kitchen counter next to the steaming pot. He carefully opened the box of extra large, heavy duty, contractor garbage bags. These babies could sure hold a lot of stuff.

He shook one bag out by waving it around the room and filling it with air. Everything that needed to be done had been done.

Except for one minor detail.

Daisy was near the oven and Charley looked down at her. After all she had been through, after all that had happened to her that day, she still looked so lovely. She was all dressed up. Her makeup was just so. He never loved her so much as right now. He leaned down and kissed her cheek.

"I'm so glad I didn't cut your throat," he said tenderly.

Daisy looked deep into his eyes, took off her oven cleaning gloves, and laughed. "And, I'm so glad I didn't poison your coffee!"

Daisy gave Charley a hug and kissed him on the lips. "I might have," she added. "If you'd have forgotten those rolls. Now go pick up that garbage in the front yard—we've got company coming!"

Taquache Nights

By David Robledo

Taquaches don't hiss. They rattle. Like a death rattle. They sound like the crackling or popping of dry mesquite wood in a white hot fire.

Taquaches (tah-kwa-ches)—otherwise known as possums or opossums—have cartoonishly large teeth that take up most of their cavernous mouths. Their angry bite can easily slice through a person's finger, bone and all, but they are mostly benign with dove-like innocent eyes and a gentle, breeze-like gait.

Kiki, an old, San Benito local, was a little fuzzy on why taquaches had started following him. But they weren't.

Taquache's had a bad habit of climbing into neighborhood trash cans to forage for food. Getting in was easy; getting out was very difficult. Many taquaches met their deaths in this fashion. Residents who discovered them often dispatched them with hoes or pitchforks. In one case a cruel lout had squirted lighter fluid on a taquache trapped in his trash can and roasted it alive.

Kiki was a reasonable soul, amicable to all. Though he kept finding taquaches in his trash, he bore them no ill will. He simply tilted his trash can sideways and allowed them to run along. His good will was uncommon.

After a couple of years, several local taquaches had grown quite comfortable with Kiki. At one time or another, he had liberated them all at least once. After ten years he was an ally.

So when Kiki came storming out of the San Benito City Hall on a Tuesday night in late June, a small mob of taquaches was waiting in the nearby shadows. He was fuming when he walked out of the meeting that was being held, the angry click of his ostrich boot heels echoing along the hallway's European granite floor. The corridor was flanked by drab rooms where countless backdoor deals had contributed to the bloodletting of public funds for decades.

That night the city council had gone too far, voting to close the doors of the San Benito Conjunto Music Hall of Fame and to lease the space to a private interest. Kiki was stupefied. Under the guise of economic development, the council was shuttering the only universe that San Benito had ever been the center of. Conjunto had begun in the community almost a century ago and had spread roots in a 300-mile radius on either side of the border.

For members of the council, which was comprised mostly of hourly wage earners with eyes only to the immediate, bottom line, their seats were seen more as promotions than civic mandates. And they felt ascendance to these positions signified their arrival as powerful players in a longstanding game of entitlement. They eagerly accepted gifts and bribes worth thousands of dollars in exchange for handing out contracts worth millions.

Kiki didn't begrudge anyone trying to make a few extra dollars, but the community's cultural heritage was at stake. He threw open the front glass doors of the city hall and cursed the council members for greedy fools. Then, he spit and turned toward the downtown Conjunto joints to have a bitter beer and hopefully commiserate with a sage voice, like Eva Ybarra's.

Eva knew. Eva knew and knew.

A small group of taquaches followed, rattling and crackling, but keeping to the dark corners and passageways.

Their ally was distraught. They would stay close.

Most people assume that taquaches are vegetarians, and in their natural habitat they mostly are. They invaded the South Texas region when the area became a mecca for citrus in the 1950s. Hundreds of thousands of acres here had been cleared of the mesquite, huisache, cactus, sabal palm, and other native growth to make way for citrus orchards that would help the region become a significant driver of the nation's economy.

The taquaches nestled into the agricultural fields and orchards of the Rio Grande Valley and feasted on the citrus bounty, famous worldwide for its crisp, dew-like flavor. And then three decades later the orchards and fields were razed to make way for suburbs and strip malls, but the taquaches continued to thrive, discovering sanctuary in the attics and crawl spaces of the new structures, and finding food in residential and commercial trash cans. They became fond of Valley delicacies, especially barbacoa, the slow roasted brain, eyes, cheek and tongue of cows that South Texans gorged on during Saturday and Sunday morning break-fasts, accenting the succulent fare with blood-red salsa and diced cilantro and onion.

Kiki's opposition to the city council had begun as feisty letters to the editor in the town newspaper and graduated to open confrontations at the council meetings. For a time Kiki's public harangues were famous, and dozens of San Benito residents would attend the meetings for the sole purpose of hearing him speak. But then the crowd would leave as soon as he was finished, as if what the council had to say was unimportant.

To quell the crowds that appreciated Kiki, the council passed a city ordinance that required a valid picture ID in order to be admitted to the meetings. Most San Benito residents were a) undocumented immigrants who had nonetheless lived their entire lives in the town; b) citizens with outstanding arrest warrants for traffic violations, especially the very expensive charge of driving without insurance; or c) folks who were afraid that the council was keeping a list of spectators in order to wreak personal revenge against them and their associates, which was indeed the case.

For the last decade or so, Kiki's chief nemesis had been a gringo behind most if not all of the city council's opportunities for lucrative corruption—Thomas Gurvitz, a private developer and construction contractor who somehow sat on the finance committees of nearly a dozen political subdivisions in the county, including a water corporation, two school districts, a community college and two museums. In all, Gurvitz pulled the trigger on publicly-funded construction and service contracts worth nearly a half billion dollars a year. And though his own company was never hired directly by the finance committees that he steered, he always benefitted in one way or another from each and every significant contract that required his consent.

For Gurvitz, politics was simply a matter of securing public resources for personal benefit. Unfortunately, many South Texas cities stagnated where his way of doing things was prevalent. Some neighborhoods lost water service, became infested with wild pit bulls and grew weeds so thickly in alleys that trash trucks couldn't pass. The school systems similarly dilapidated, gutted by mass hirings and firings as political cliques took hold of school boards and packed them with agreeable cronies.

Kiki understood that it was this deeply entrenched corruption that was keeping the people of his community and the community itself from advancing. He knew that resignation to the widespread dysfunction and the growing notion that your neighbors were somehow expedient were what was crushing his people. But he eschewed hopelessness. His beloved Conjunto had originated from the town's downtrodden communities. Conjunto had sprung from second-hand, beat-up instruments, the sweaty energy of poor migrants and the indomitable twangs of the quasi-literate and consistently disenfranchised. And then it went on to birth Tejano.

Kiki believed his people would endure the grime and ignominy for only so long, and then there would be a change. It was simply a matter of time.

Taquaches are among the oldest, most primitive mammals of the New World. Many scientists refer to them as "living fossils" because they have survived relatively unchanged for at least 50 million years. Their body is covered with fur, but their tail has scales. They are the only mammal in North America with a marsupium or pouch; and they are also the only mammal in North America—besides a human being—that has opposable thumbs.

Early evenings when he roamed the downtown alleys of San Benito, stopping in at cantinas to hear Conjunto and enjoy moderately priced Bud Lights, the taquaches followed him. They'd cluster and wait for him behind waste disposal bins in the poorly lit alleys, senses heightened by the booming, smoky songs of incorruptible voices and hardscrabble musicians. Kiki was sure his marsupial peers did not wait for him alone, but that they lingered so they could hear the border music that wafted through the rickety screen doors and patched windows that tumbled down the city's alleyways. He loved it and why shouldn't they? What true son or daughter of San Benito wouldn't? It was the greatest celebration of the culture and the purest exposition of their identity. This was why Kiki stormed out of the city council meeting. The city council members selling their souls was one thing, but watching them sell the soul of the community itself was quite another.

Kiki never fed the taquaches himself, under any circumstances. He respected the creatures. He didn't want his relationship with them to be influenced by or dependent upon his ability to provide them with food. He felt that such relationships were never those of true friends. He believed they were examples of pet-keeping or species monitoring. In his mind, feeding a pet created a lesser of otherwise equals at best, but more typically led to a worse outcome: slave-master dynamic.

In Meso-American mythology, the opossum is a tlaquache, the bringer of fire to mankind, a Promethean and Christ-like hero who steals the substance with its deft tail. For his efforts, the demons that guarded the fire ripped the tlacuache to pieces, but the tlacuache magically reconstituted itself to bring the gift to humankind. South Texans lost the "l" in tlacuache, replaced the "c" with a "q," and more casually refer to North America's only free-roaming marsupial as a *taquache*.

On the morning before the evening that Kiki stormed out of the San Benito City Hall, Thomas Gurvitz yawned and stretched his arms as he awoke in his million-dollar ranch house that edged a lake on a different outskirt of town than Kiki. A posh area with panoramic views, crystal clear (bleached) water and well-to-do residents with no dirt under their fingernails. He was a keeper of plenty and enjoyed the spoils. Gringo bingo, sure—but he was the gringo who called all the numbers. And he was excited with the promise of his next economic coup.

The city council meeting that evening would be a formality. The vote was bought and paid for and no matter how cleverly or eloquently Kiki engaged the members, the San Benito Conjunto Music Hall of Fame was ceasing operations. As the afternoon frittered away in the sun and the night came on dank and humid, Gurvitz could hardly suppress a smile.

The plan was disguised deep in an agenda item titled "Concession Agreements," which included agreements for leasing space at the baseball park to a snow cone business, leasing city land to a carnival that came to town each year, and other leases of city property and facilities that earned San Benito a few thousand dollars a month.

The council's first vote, however, was on an item titled "Freeway Exit." The city manager used a Power Point presentation to illustrate exactly where the freeway exit would start and where it would end. Kiki was pleasantly surprised to learn that the exit would lead directly to the existing site of the San Benito Conjunto Music Hall of Fame, a humble structure owned by the city and staffed by volunteers, mostly old timers who still played in Conjuntos. Kiki had worked hard to secure the use of the building, one of the few wins that he could count in his many wrangles with the council.

Kiki thought that the freeway exit would be an excellent development for the community. Though he was sure that Gurvitz was somehow benefitting from the deal, Kiki believed that the end result would bring more attention to the Hall of Fame and highlight their singular heritage. He was already envisioning a billboard and some facility upgrades; the freeway exit could be exactly the catalyst that San Benito needed to start down the path of New Orleans, Nashville, Austin, Seattle and other cities where music is at the heart of a lucrative tourist draw.

The council voted on the item quickly, all yeas and no nays, and then methodically moved on to the next piece of business.

As Kiki was imagining the possibilities of an exit ramp leading to the Hall of Fame, he noticed Gurvitz approaching the podium. This was discomfiting and Kiki immediately sensed something was wrong.

The city secretary read the next agenda item. Kiki did not hear everything she said, but he clearly heard her say " . . . 9191 Mingo Saldivar Road as a concession to Thomas Gurvitz Construction concern for 100 years at a cost of one dollar per year for economic development and the express requirement to build a *Hombres Hermanos* restaurant at the existing site."

The council voted again and, again, the vote passed unanimously.

9191 Mingo Saldivar Road.

It slowly dawned on Kiki that was the address of the San Benito Conjunto Music Hall of Fame. He scanned the room. All of the council members were smiling, and Gurvitz left the podium to shake hands with them.

Kiki was furious. He trembled with impotent rage. He stood up and pointed at Gurvitz.

"Pinche," he said. *"Pinche!"* That's all he could manage. He was shocked.

Gurvitz and the council stared back at Kiki for an uncomfortable moment, and then returned their attentions to one another.

Then, they resumed their congratulations of Gurvitz.

Kiki lowered his arm in disbelief and stammered under his breath. Then, he walked out.

"Apparent death," colloquially known as "playing dead," or playing possum, is a behavior in which an animal takes on the appearance of being dead, usually to protect itself. This form of animal deception is an adaptive behavior also known as "tonic immobility." Apparent death can be used as a defense mechanism and it occurs in a variety of animals, including humans.

Gurvitz knew that he should leave well enough alone, but he couldn't help himself. It couldn't have come off better. He decided to follow Kiki out to take full advantage of the opportunity to gloat. But he reconsidered. Even better, he thought, he could feign magnanimity. It would play better, be twice as satisfying and add insult to the no doubt mortal injury to his old foe's longstanding activism.

As Kiki exited the building, Gurvitz sped up his stride to catch him. "The old fool," he said.

Kiki was already headed for the downtown Conjunto joints when Gurvitz came out. His appearance gave the taquaches pause, but they simply followed farther back.

As Gurvitz pursued Kiki into the alleyway, the taquaches were directly behind him, anxious and curious.

When the taquaches lost sight of Kiki, they became alarmed. In an attempt to catch up, one of the larger ones attempted to cut across the alley before an upcoming turn and accidentally tripped Gurvitz. His head fell through the air like a bowling ball in a slow arch and struck the corner of a large metal trash bin owned by one of his shell companies.

Kiki heard a dull thud and a grunt and doubled back. He discovered Gurvitz lying in the alley.

The button-up shirt that Gurvitz wore displayed a large blood stain across its multi-colored diagonal stripes, and it looked like a large glob of dark magenta paint in the dimly lit alley. He was bleeding profusely from his forehead.

Barely conscious, Gurvitz tried to speak, but simply gurgled blood.

The taquaches began to press in on Gurvitz, smelling blood and expensive cologne. Gurvitz sputtered in terror and Kiki leaned down and tried to shoo the taquaches back and away. But some stayed.

Kiki's instinct to render aid quickly fizzled.

He realized that he wanted revenge against Gurvitz—a deep and long awaited revenge. He did not like the feeling, but he could not deny it.

"Help," Gurvitz spurted, blood running down his chin.

Kiki looked into his eyes for a moment and stood up.

"Yes," Kiki said. "Yes, I think so."

Gurvitz's eyes rolled back and his lower jaw slowly dropped and closed twice. He looked like a fat catfish noodled from a mud wall of the Rio and tossed up and left on the bank.

Gurvitz gasped once more and was gone.

As the taquaches slithered and writhed across the dead man's body, Kiki stepped back and watched one gouge an eyeball from Gurvitz's head. It stretched the optical fiber to its limit to break it free, and Kiki turned away. He heard the fiber snap as he rounded a corner farther down the alley.

Kiki walked down to one of his favorite Conjunto bars and ordered a Bud Light. Three beers and the right song later—"Besos Callejeros," by San Benito native Valerio Longoria—he exited the cantina and walked home. For the first time since he could remember, there were no taquaches to follow him.

At dawn the next day, a cook from a nearby restaurant was shocked to discover a dead Gringo spread eagle in the alley. She immediately called the police.

The corpse resembled the prominent Gurvitz exactly, except some of his parts were conspicuously absent. The skin that had covered the paunch of his abdomen was now splayed across the alley floor. Gurvitz's eyes were gone, and his tongue was gone, too.

That afternoon, the Cameron County coroner was astounded to find that the inside of Gurvitz's skull was picked perfectly clean, as a scientific specimen's might be, or a skull left in a desert for years. But the skull's exterior held all of the man's hair and scalp perfectly in place. The smaller taquaches had burrowed their heads into his skull from the back of his throat to gorge on uncooked, human barbacoa.

Too, Gurvitz's heart had been taken from his chest with precision. And the taquaches had gnawed a hole through his large belly so that they could reach his offal.

They took his lungs, liver, kidneys, all of his intestines, plus his gonads.

From his knees down, though, there was not a drop of blood to be seen. And Gurvitz's fancy Italian leather shoes were as shiny as they had been the evening before when he walked into the city council assembly chambers to vanquish Kiki.

Local authorities initially assumed Gurvitz's death was a cartel hit, but investigators were doubtful that cartel assassins would go to the trouble of cleanly and surgically removing organs from the victim's body. It didn't fit their MO.

With Gurvitz dead, the *Hombres Hermanos* franchising fell through and the new Mingo Saldivar Road exit was put on hold.

Bamfires

By Alan Beauvais

r you ascared of bamfires

i am.

mama says they aint real but I think they r jus as real as sanna claws. daddy jus laffs at me an I dont no if hes laffin cuz im scared or cuz i cant say the word rite. i toled him i saw one outside my windo one nite an he said it wuz prolly jus a coon. i know what a coon looks like an it werent no coon.

he wuz yung like me an he wanted to come in but i wuz scared to let him in cuz his face wuz real white an his eyes were black. big peeple think im jus bein silly but its true. i membered the movie an i held a cross with that man jesus on it to the window an he made a mean face at me an he runned away.

i almost wanted to let him in.

i hate bein little cuz win your little big peeple wont beleev you.

i hate beein little.

daddy works doin differnt things, I know cuz sometimes peeple ast me what he duz for a livin an i said well i didnt know so i ast him once what he did for a livin an he said differnt things so i said ok. but i think he fixes peeples prollems, cuz they bring im cars that need fixin an guns an other stuff, sometimes he shooshes me away an tells me to go play somewhere else so i do cuz i dont like it wen he gets mad.

mama stays in fort werth with reltivs when daddys havin his bad days thats what she calls em she tries to take me with her but I hide in the woods til she leevs.

she nos if she cant cach me daddy cant neether so she figures me ok. thother nite some men on moterbikes came an made a big fire and stayed late at nite playin loud music an drinkin beers an beein stoopid. i stayed bak in the trees an wached em like i always do. then i saw the bamfire he wuz small an skinny an reely wite an fast reely, reely fast. i dint see im till he wuz runnin an he grabbed a lil ole skinny biker man an dragged him skreemin into tha woods he wuz so fast an strong that they were in the woods afore ennyone new it. time they found his body his throte wuz tore out. they wuz all ascared. they started yellin bout bamfires an wanted to put a steak thru his hart. others yelled we cant do that to ole charlie an they all yelled for a long time bout it. but thats not the baddest part of it. the baddest part happened jus afore don they wuz all sleepin an i saw ole charlie get up an walk into the woods.

wen i waked in the morn the bikers were fightin about not putting a steak in ole charlies hart an screemin bout bamfires again an daddy looked ascared for the first time I ever saw.

daddy aint the same now he has his bad days all the times an when i say bamfire he tries to hit me in the mouf but i m too fast.

ole charlie came to my windo las nite, the boy with the blak eyes wuz with im. i toled them to go away they jus hissed at me like an ole tom cat we had once, the one daddy kilt with his shotgun one day when it scrached im an he got mad. but they kept wantin to come in so i got that cross again an i taped it to the windo glass an they got even madder. i dont know why they dont jus bust the windo an come in but i m glad they dont.

mama beleeves in that man on the cross, daddy dont an i dont no if i do but i no one thing them bamfires do, an they dont like im.

mama comed home! i was so happy I runned and yelled loud as i could. an mama hugged me but rite away she lookd all round an said what happened here? so i toled her bout ole charlie an the bamfires an that daddy been having all bad days since that nite an she got madder an madder. then daddy come out an they started fiting an i tried to stop daddy from hittin momma but he thru me across the yard like i was a little chiken. i hate beein little.

wen mama couldnt get up no more daddy carried her to the bed room and i wached thru the window when he thru her on the bed. i wached him drinkin more beers an went round thru the windo an sat with momma while she sleeped.

wen it got dark out, mama wuz still asleepin an i sat awake with the cross man in my hands for a long time. i looked in the front room an daddy wuz asleeped on the couch with a lot of beer cans all round him. wen i went bak to the bed room they wuz tappin at the windo.

i toled them to come to the front door. i went back to the front room an opened the door and toled them they could come in but not in the bed room. they comed in hissin at me cuz i still had the cross man in my hand an i wuz holdin it in front of me as i walked bakwards to the bed room. they smelled ded. they jumped on daddy an he waked up fightin but he wuz too drunked up. i went into the bed room to keep momma safe.

wen the sun came up in the morn, daddy wuz gone. i waked momma an toled her daddy's gone forever an she jus smiled. i toled her I wanted to go to the city with her an wanted never to come bak here again. She said why baby boy, r you still afraid of bamfires? i said no mama, i aint ascared of no bamfires no more. the end

Winging It

By Michael Baldwin

It's always an exciting time when a new class of airliner is put into service. The new Boeing 797s have been flying passengers for only a few days. Jeremy Slater is certainly interested, if not exactly excited, to be assigned to one of the new planes.

Jeremy is a sky marshal working for Homeland Security out of DFW International Airport. His job is to protect passengers and to prevent sky-jacking or sabotage of the commercial airliners he is assigned to.

Tonight he has been directed, on short notice, to take his first ride on a 797.

Jeremy had been due for two days off, but, at the last minute, the regularly scheduled sky marshal was unavailable. Jeremy was chosen to fill in. He didn't really mind the change in plans, because he's a dedicated professional and here was an opportunity to become acquainted with latest craft.

The 797 can carry about four hundred passengers, and will probably have nearly a full load tonight, flying from DFW to New York. It should be just a routine flight.

Jeremy boards early and is seated on the mid-plane exit row, just above the wing. He likes this row because it gives him extra leg room, and he can assist passengers in case of an emergency. The row has only two seats on each side of the center aisle rather than the standard three. The other seat is unassigned, so he will have extra space to maneuver if necessary. Also, he won't have to worry so much about concealing his service weapon, a laser-sighted SIG Sauer P229, with a 12-round magazine of .357 parabellum cartridges. The bullets are specially designed for lower velocity so they can't easily penetrate the walls of the plane. Sky marshals are highly trained and have the best marksmanship record among all federal law enforcement services.

Only the crew is supposed to know Jeremy is a sky marshal. To the other passengers, he is just one of them, blending in with no conspicuous or memorable qualities. That's deliberate, of course, because if people know or can easily figure out who he is, he may be targeted by terrorists.

Jeremy discreetly observes the passengers as they board the plane, searching for any indication of suspicious activity or atypical behavior. He makes mental note of several foreign-looking men, even though they show no terrorist characteristics; profiling is just automatic. But nothing arouses his suspicion. It's the usual chaotic scramble of passengers to locate their seats and find a vacant overhead space to stow their carry-ons.

One elderly lady nearby can't get her roller case into the overhead and the flight attendant struggles with it as well. Jeremy assists, rotating the case into the appropriate position (out of the twenty-four configuration possibilities) to make it fit. The flight attendant turns away to help someone else, so the elderly lady asks Jeremy to adjust the overhead light for her.

That done, he resumes his seat.

Finally, everyone is aboard and settled in their seats. On the 797, flight attendants don't physically demonstrate how to buckle seatbelts or show what to do in case of an emergency. They leave that to the video that is now playing on the seatback screens in front of every passenger. Jeremy ignores the familiar video and uses a small hand mirror to check for anything unusual behind him.

Nothing so far.

The takeoff from DFW is smooth and normal. Jeremy leans back, continuing to check his mirror occasionally. He finds nothing amiss. It looks like this flight will be another milk run. Then the plane enters a rainstorm.

Nothing serious, just some moderate precipitation. Jeremy idly wonders why the pilot doesn't announce it, but this isn't one of his normal crews.

Jeremy looks out his window along the broad wing. He is instantly shocked back into an upright position. *Something is moving. Something is on the wing that shouldn't be there.*

It's difficult to see through the blowing rain, but whatever it is—however impossibly—is plainly still there. And it's moving.

A momentary lapse in the wind and rain reveal a figure. Jeremy sees a human shape . . . out there . . . on the wing.

This is crazy, thinks Jeremy. *Am I losing it?*

Am I somehow hallucinating that old Twilight Zone episode?

There must be a rational explanation. He's a trained observer. It's not an optical illusion.

Jeremy considers the implications if what he's seeing is real.

He looks again.

The figure has moved closer to the cabin now. It's not possible.

Jeremy wipes his eyes and looks at it again. Yes, it is indeed, the *Twilight Zone* gremlin, exactly as he remembers it from the TV program. It's not possible.

It's madness of some sort he decides, but he's not going to have a nervous breakdown like William Shatner's character did. And he's sure not going to open the exit door at thirty thousand feet!

The gremlin is now using its claws to pry at the cowling of the engine, a jet turbine this time instead of the propeller from the TV program. Should he call the stewardess to be a witness to this? In the TV story, each time Shatner tries to get someone else to see the gremlin, it moves out of sight before they can observe it. They think he's crazy.

He can't risk a panic if someone else sees it. He can't jeopardize his professional reputation if they don't see it. But he can't just ignore it, either.

Jeremy fingers the gun in his waistband, considering the possibility of shooting the gremlin. But he knows it would be disastrous.

He continues to stare at the creature, which is still moving methodically down the wing. It even gazes at the window, leering directly at Jeremy with unmistakable menace.

Jeremy must do something.

But what?

"Would you like a drink of some kind?" asks the flight attendant.

She has stopped right beside him with the drink cart. "We have soft drinks, juice, water and beer," she continues. "Are you okay? You seem a bit anxious. The rain isn't a problem or the captain would have flown above it. So, don't worry. How about some coffee?"

"No!" blurts Jeremy. "I mean no thanks. I'm fine." God, he could use a double bourbon. "I was just interested to see how this new 797 handles in a storm. Does it have running lights on the wings so the pilots can see the engines at night?"

"Oh, I wouldn't know about that," says the attendant. "I could ask the captain if you think it's important." Then she bends toward him and whispers "You are the sky marshal, right?"

"Yes," he replies, "but don't bother the captain. I was just curious."

She smiles a little enigmatically and pushes the cart on down the aisle.

Jeremy peers out the window again. Nothing.

He moves closer and looks as far to the side as he can through the small port. Suddenly the creature's face is right there, menacingly pressed against the window, distorted by the glass. Its blazing red eyes sear into his.

Jeremy lurches away with a startled gasp.

He looks around to see if anyone noticed, and sees the flight attendant looking back at him. He shakes his head at her and hopes he doesn't look like a maniac.

He looks back to the window. The gremlin is no longer in view.

Jeremy thinks furiously.

Is this a terrorist tactic? Is someone trying to frighten or distract him?

The terrorists are becoming more tech savvy all the time. Could they have actually put something on the wing? More likely it's a projection of some kind. Yes, that's got to be it. But how? And why hasn't anyone else seen the creature?

His isn't the only view of the wing. Maybe others have seen it and, like him, haven't said anything.

Jeremy checks his rear view mirror again. The flight crew are passing out drinks and snacks. A few passengers are up and about, but nothing suspicious. He gets up and tries to casually walk the aisle to the rear restroom. It's occupied. He doesn't really need to use it. He just wants to see if anyone else is looking at the wing or appears nervous. Everything seems normal.

He returns to his seat and looks out the window. The gremlin is still out there.

Jeremy's frustration is morphing into anger.

There's got to be an explanation and a solution for this crazy situation. He unconsciously pounds his armrest. Then, his eyes widen. The creature is shambling toward the window. It is carrying a large wrench that could crack the window or disable the jet engine if it were tossed into the turbine. Now the gremlin is close and slowly swings the wrench back as if to smash the glass. Jeremy automatically grabs for his gun. Then he has an idea. He aims the gun at the gremlin and activates the laser sight. The red laser dot jitters about on the creature's grimacing visage. The gremlin snarls at him maliciously, then leaps into the air and is gone.

Jeremy collapses with relief. But now he is angry for a different reason. He gets up from his seat and asks the flight attendant to inform the captain that the sky marshal wants a word. She nods and goes to the intercom.

A minute later she motions him to follow her forward. The cockpit door opens and the flight attendant introduces Captain

Morris. He faces Jeremy quizzically. "You're not Marshal Danby. Show me your badge, please."

Jeremy shows Morris his badge and says "Danby was indisposed just before the flight. I was assigned to you without any briefing. I think that may have created a problem. I believe this new plane has some sort of anti-terrorist technology you've been testing on me. Maybe Danby knew about it, but I wasn't informed that the test would take place. It took me by surprise."

"Good God, I forgot all about the test," says Morris. "It must have been programmed to run automatically this trip rather than manually. Danby was supposed to observe and report. I'll bet it gave you quite a scare to see someone out on the wing like that. How did you figure it out?"

"Yes, it scared the crap out of me," Jeremy replied. "I thought it must either be real or I was having a psychotic episode. Then I got the idea to try to scare it by flashing the laser sight of my gun at it. The laser seemed to frighten it, but I noticed that the beam reflected back onto me, too. The beam should have gone through the window without reflecting back. I realized that the window must have a video screen built into it and what I saw must have been a video program. I reasoned it was some sort of distraction technique to thwart terrorists and I figured you would know about it."

"Wow, I guess we were lucky you didn't try to shoot through the window," Morris says. "Although you would have to be really psychotic to do that. You handled yourself very professionally. But it was a real screw-up on the part of Homeland Security not to inform you about this new system. By the way, which program did you see? Was it the angel or the Arab girl?"

"What? No, it was the gremlin from the old *Twilight Zone* episode."

"Gremlin?" Captain Morris answers. "I don't understand. That's not one of the programs in the system as far as I know. And I've been thoroughly briefed on it."

The two men stare intensely at each other for several seconds.

"In that case," Jeremy says, "you might want to check the condition of your port engine. I'm going to take another look out that window."

The Burned Boys

By Glen Coburn

After school that day, the new kid in town lay on the soft, cool grass of the soccer field. He focused his attention on the clean blue sky above. He gazed deeper and deeper until he convinced himself that he saw eternity. A Red-tailed Hawk circled silent and effortlessly. Soaring in the vast, cloudless sky it appeared in miniature. The kid lost himself and disappeared into forever. He stayed that way for a few minutes. Maybe five. Then, his reverie was cut short by the jangling approach of a bicycle. A lanky boy rolled to a stop alongside, got off his bike and propped it on its kickstand. The kid sensed the presence of a kindred spirit. A sweet faced, goofy boy with an honest smile put him at ease.

"Takin' a nap?"

"Sort of," Kevin replied. A piece of construction paper on the ground beside him displayed a drawing from afternoon art class. His new friend, Freddie bent down to take a look.

"Blue sky. Puffy clouds. And look at that! Is it a flying saucer?"

"That's right."

"What's your name?"

"Kevin. What's yours?"

"Freddie. Do you think flying saucers are real?"

"I do."

"Have you ever seen one?"

"Not yet."

Kevin was delighted to have a friend. For the last couple of months he had been a loner, having just moved to Edgevale, Texas, from Kansas City, Missouri. He hated his new home and resisted warming up to his classmates. His mother gave him permission to go out to Freddie's house.

Freddie lived way out in the country or at least that's what Kevin thought. It was actually just a couple miles beyond the outskirts of Edgevale. As the boys ventured into the flat prairie down a two-lane asphalt road, the open terrain was marked by barbed wire fence that flanked their path on either side.

In the distance Kevin spotted a two-story wood frame farm house, painted dark green. It was charming and well-tended but that didn't stop him from imagining that it was haunted. Two fiendish dormer windows peered down inviting him to come inside and play. The front of the house was adorned with an elevated wood porch. A short distance from the far side of the house, there stood a big, solid oak tree. It was Freddie's house and thirteen acres stretched from the house, down a hill and into a wooded patch with a creek running through it.

"Wow! This is the best place I've ever seen," Kevin shouted through panting breath. "You're a lucky dog to live out here."

"Speaking of dogs," Freddie said, as his good-natured white German Shepherd named Storm greeted them at the gate. Storm was so named because he was dumped outside Freddie's house during a thunder storm.

Freddie was excited to show his friend around. He felt like a guide in a foreign country. He got to re-explore his home through fresh eyes. Storm followed along.

Over by the oak tree, there was a garden twice as big as Kevin's front and back yards put together. The ground was meticulously cleared and tilled. There were rows of beets, cabbage, squash, green beans, peas, onions, peppers, bright red tomatoes, and even a few rows of corn. Kevin imagined there were also a few unmarked graves of unfortunate trespassers among the rows of vegetables. His dad had told him that country folks shoot first and ask questions later.

The property had been in Freddie's family for over a hundred years. The Lucas family was among the early settlers in the area. The farm house was built by Mr. Lucas' father in 1912 but the original barn burned to the ground ten years earlier in 1957. The new barn was made of corrugated metal with a gently sloping roof. It had a high ceiling and was divided in two. One space was full of farm implements. The other side was smaller and served as a shelter for the old horse named Red. Kevin had never seen a horse licking a hefty block of salt. He'd never even heard of a salt lick.

The section of the barn dedicated to utility was heavily-layered with tools and equipment. Like the fossil record, the tools that hadn't been used in a while were deeper in the collection. They were closest to the walls. Implements that had seen more recent use were up front and easily accessible. The mini-tractor and all its attachments were splayed out in a clearing. Kevin imagined the sharp, pointy, metal attachments as the stations of a torture chamber. A scythe that hung on a nearby bracket was suitable for the grim reaper. In the center of the space a tree stump provided a base for a heavy, rusted anvil. A horseshoe hammer was placed alongside the anvil. Like most boys his age, Kevin was drawn to instruments of noise and destruction. He wielded the hammer and slammed it upon the iron block. With clumsy precision he struck the anvil over and over even though Freddie pleaded with him to stop.

"What's the problem? It won't break."

"My dad hates it when I do that. He gets pretty mad. It's really hot in here anyway. Let's go down to the woods."

The boys ran down the hill, weaving and flailing like lunatics until they reached a brushy area on the edge of the tree line. Storm cantered along behind them. Freddie warned Kevin to keep an eye out for snakes.

"Be careful. You might step on a cottonmouth."

"A cottonmouth?" Kevin was stumped.

"A cottonmouth water-moccasin. It's a snake, a pit viper. They're poisonous," Freddie said. "In the grass, you won't see it until you're right up on it."

"You sure it's safe to be down here?" Kevin was terrified but careful not to show it.

"They mostly hang around the water. I've seen a few taking a snooze on the creek bed. They slither off pretty quick if you get close."

"That gives me the creeps." Kevin was not reassured.

Freddie led his friend to a fallen tree that made a bridge across a narrow, languid stream. The water was always shallow except after a heavy rain. During dry spells it was only ankle-deep. The natural bridge was a convenient way to cross but it was just precarious enough to offer a risk factor so the boys regarded it as a daring feat to make the crossing. Storm sat and watched but chose not to follow the boys.

Freddie was a cautious daredevil. His upraised arms were sturdy wings that imbued the boy with the keen balance of a tightrope walker. The rubber soles of his sneakers gripped the nubby bark. Nearing the far bank of the creek, Freddie entertained his friend with a playful wobble before leaping from the bridge to solid ground.

Kevin stepped onto the makeshift bridge. In a gesture of blind faith, he followed the lead of his mentor. Kevin's father was more comfortable indoors, so the boy had learned little of the possible adventures in the world of nature. Their trek through the leaves, branches and tangled vines was mystical. A spell was cast upon them by the breeze, the ripple of the creek and the deep, ancient earth beneath their feet.

The boys became the closest of friends. Weekends in the country alternated with weekends in town at Kevin's house. The cramped, noisy tract house was a rude contrast to the expansive serenity of the Lucas place. Kevin's family languished in a functional eleven-hundred square-foot home in a sea of sameness. Their subdivision was based on the A.B.C. plan. Every third house was identical.

The heart of Kevin's family home was the perpetual Motorola console color television. It was running during all waking hours unless there was nobody home. Kevin enjoyed playing in the street with the neighborhood wildlings, but he refused to introduce his best buddy to the unruly tribe.

In Kevin's cramped bedroom, the boys exercised their creative skills by staging violent and gruesome scenarios enacted by a legion of G.I. Joes. Kevin was the architect of these brutal dioramas. Freddie was a master of keeping the moving parts in sync. In the evenings, they played board games or Crazy Eights at the kitchen table. Kevin's younger sister was the third wheel. They let her win whenever she became suspicious that the game was rigged. The boys usually grew tired of being cooped up in the house, so they would spend many Saturday afternoons at the movies.

Sunday mornings were reserved for church. The Lucas family was a longtime fixture of the Redeemer's Bible Church. They never missed a Sunday. It inspired Kevin to become a regular churchgoer.

Years passed and Kevin and Freddie remained best friends into junior high school.

The Lucas' closest neighbors, the Dales, were about two miles down the road. The properties were adjacent, both on the north side of Bradfield Road. Freddie was enamored of Dr. Frank Dale because he had his own airplane hangar in the pasture next to his house. It was clearly visible from Freddie's back yard and he often admired it through the magnification of his binoculars. The structure, more of a shed than a hangar, housed Dr. Dale's Cessna 150. The top of the hangar was labeled "DALE" in thick capital letters that could be seen from high altitudes.

One sweltering Sunday afternoon, Mr. Lucas drove the boys down the road to conduct a close-up investigation of the plane. Dr. Dale opened the door of the single engine aircraft so the boys could get a full appreciation of the cockpit. Freddie already knew the details by heart but for Kevin it was like taking a peek inside a space capsule. He was fascinated by the instrument panel. His imagination ran wild as he studied the gauges, knobs, and switches. The tight quarters reminded Kevin of his dad's 1963 Falcon convertible, with its two bucket seats up front and confined rear bench seat. Dr. Dale informed the boys that he and his brother were taking their six-year-old sons up on the following Sunday. He said that from the Lucas' house they could watch the take-off and get a good view of the plane as it circled above the surrounding countryside.

The boys endured a week of utter boredom and, finally, Sunday arrived.

They practiced archery in Freddie's back yard. One bale of hay was stacked atop another. Kevin and Freddie took turns affixing paper targets to the bundled hay, which was placed about twenty yards away from the shooting station. Freddie held his beginner's longbow with confidence. With expert style and form, he drew the arrow into position and angled the bow upward to achieve the required arc. His arrows almost always struck somewhere on the target. Even his worst efforts at least met with the blocks of hay. In contrast, Kevin was horrible. He was lucky to maintain arrow placement on the string, and if he did draw the string and loose an arrow it was likely to land a glancing blow to the ground, far from the target.

Mr. Lucas received a phone call from Dr. Dale. He came out onto the back porch and gave the boys a shout. "Ten-minute warning." Then, he went back inside. Freddie grabbed his binoculars and the boys headed out to the pasture behind the house.

After a short wait, Dr. Dale and his brother and their boys climbed into the cabin. The engine started and the propeller kicked in, spinning so fast that the props disappeared. The plane slowly edged out as it lined up for takeoff. In position, it sped forward and began to lift off the ground hesitantly, like an ambitious flightless bird.

"I can't wait till I get my pilot's license," Freddie exclaimed. "We can fly anywhere you want."

"Forget it," Kevin said. "You'll never get me inside that tin can."

As the little plane pushed up higher, it let out a colossal backfire. The boys stood frozen as the soaring craft slowed, listed and then nosed downward. They watched in horror as the plane plummeted toward the ground in a full dive. And it was coming straight at them.

Kevin shoved Freddie and shouted "Run!"

Adrenaline pumping, they tore out like Olympic sprinters. They were still in a full stride when they heard the violent crash. The ground beneath them shook and they stumbled. Then, lungs heaving, the boys slowed their pace, turned and walked back.

"What should we do?" Freddie rattled. "Should we help?"

"Are you crazy? It's a plane crash!"

Dr. Dale and his brother managed to pull their broken bodies out of the wreckage. Then, they made a desperate attempt to free the boys from the back of the crumpled fuselage.

Freddie started to jog toward the crash site in an ill-considered effort to help, but Kevin chased him down and tackled him. It wasn't safe. Patches of smoke and fire spewed from the twisted metal and within seconds the plane was engulfed in flames. The initial burst of fire tossed the Dale fathers away from the flames and onto the ground. Their boys were beyond rescue.

Mr. Lucas called the fire department when he heard the initial impact. He hurried outside and spotted Freddie and Kevin in the pasture near the burning fuselage. He jogged toward them and shouted for them to get back to the house. Mr. Lucas put the boys on the front porch of the farm house and commanded them to stay put. The minutes that it took for the fire trucks and ambulances to arrive at the scene seemed like hours, and Kevin and Freddie were anxious and shaken by the horrifying event.

In the weeks that followed, the boys were celebrities at Cleaver Junior High. They shared their sensational tale with a constituency hungry for details of the most violent tragedy in the community's recent memory. There were fatal automobile accidents now and then but those were routine incidents compared to an aviation disaster. The grisly story of the young boys, crushed and burned to cinder was especially salacious because it was relatable. Although the victims went to a private school, they were close in age to the students at Cleaver. Kevin and Freddie used this grim tale to enhance their status and popularity. They even secured the attention of the eighth graders, who previously hounded and demeaned them almost daily. With each telling, the story was amplified and became bigger and more terrifying. The two pals were so enamored of their own popularity that they lost empathy for the dead boys.

The next time Kevin's dad drove him out to the Lucas homestead, the dads stood outside in quiet, solemn conversation. The boys watched from Freddie's window, which revealed a clear view of the driveway. They saw Mrs. Lucas come out and join the two dads in discussion.

"I bet they're talking about the plane crash," Freddie said.

"They're sure as heck not talking about the price of pork chops," Kevin replied. "Our parents hardly ever talk to each other. My dad barely stops the car when he lets me off out here."

"You think your dad's worried about you coming here so soon?"

"I'm pretty sure the only thing he's worried about is if he can get to Dallas before the beer store closes. So when can we go out to the crash site?"

"My dad says it's dangerous. He doesn't want us anywhere

near there."

"Then I guess we'll have to be sneaky."

Kevin was both creeped-out and thrilled when they visited the patch of scorched earth where the Cessna crashed. Tossed around in the rutted bed of dirt there were white, red, and gray shards of metal strewn about like sea shells on a beach.

"Is this it?" Kevin asked, his tone conveying his disappointment.

"This is what's left. They took most of the big pieces. My dad has a crate or two in the garage, and he's still gotta come out here with the tractor and scoop the rest of this stuff up."

"Those boys burned to a crisp right there. Imagine that." Kevin stepped closer.

"Don't. If you get hurt we'll be in big trouble.".

"What? I can't even take a souvenir?"

"A souvenir of death. Is that what you want? Are you a sicko?"

Kevin mulled over Freddie's reverent perspective and respected it. As they walked back to the house he was stricken with a touch of vertigo. Warm breath caressed the side of his neck, and a thin voice whispered his name. Kevin didn't see anything so he kept quiet.

That evening, Mrs. Lucas put the boys on the back porch to shell peas and shuck corn. Kevin enjoyed the work because it made him feel like a pioneer. And later, he experienced a sense of satisfaction when he saw the food on his plate and knew that he played a part in putting it there.

Storm lay beside the boys. His head rested on his outstretched paws but his ears were at attention. He perked up, turned his head and looked out toward the garden.

Storm growled and then whimpered. Kevin and Freddie set aside their shelling and shucking and crept slowly toward the far edge of the driveway. There was movement out past the squat, brick well house, between the oak tree and the garden.

"What was that?" Freddie asked.

"Where?"

"Look over by the tree."

The boys' jaws dropped. They saw what appeared to be a shadow weaving in and out alongside the thick tree trunk. Then, two dark figures bobbed up from behind the tree and moved toward the well house. The figures hesitated for an instant and appeared to look directly at Kevin and Freddie before disappearing behind the small brick structure.

"Holy shit," Kevin whispered. "Did you see that?"

"I sure did. And I think they saw us."

They kept their eyes fixed on the well house. Five minutes passed and nothing happened. There was no movement. Storm had gone silent but his gaze was still fixed on the structure.

"Maybe we should go inside," Freddie said. "They could be dangerous."

"Dangerous? What do you think, some armed robbers came out here to steal vegetables?"

Freddie laughed. The boys relaxed their stance.

Then, just as they let their guard down, the figures walked out, turning to look at the startled boys. Their nonchalant sideways glance was vaguely reminiscent of a picture of Bigfoot that Kevin had seen in a newspaper. The shadows moved through the garden and into the corn rows.

"Dad!" Freddie shouted. He turned and rushed toward the back door. Kevin followed. As they burst into the kitchen, Mr. Lucas came in from the den, open book in hand.

"Dad, we saw some guys out in the garden!"

Reading glasses still perched on the tip of his nose, Mr. Lucas closed his book and placed it on the kitchen table. "Are you two pullin' my leg?"

"No, Dad. They're out there. For real."

"So you both saw men in the garden?"

"They were boys," Kevin responded.

"Okay. Let's have a look. This better not be a trick." He smiled at Kevin. "I put down a good book for this."

"What if they come after us while he's way over there?" Freddie asked, as he watched his father go to his truck for a flashlight.

"They're gone," Kevin said.

"How do you know?"

"They already got our attention. That's all they really wanted."

"Look behind the well house, Dad," Freddie shouted. Mr. Lucas turned and aimed his flashlight so that it illuminated the back of the little brick building and the oak tree beyond.

The search turned up nothing. He returned to the house.

Freddie's dad was understanding and patient. He did not reprimand the boys. "Okay, you hooligans, go upstairs and settle down."

"Yes, sir" they responded in unison.

Mr. Lucas shot Kevin a glance. "No ghost stories tonight."

"Yes, sir," Kevin answered.

The boys sat cross-legged, facing each other on the floor, and played poker until after midnight. Freddie periodically went to the window, peering out toward the driveway and beyond. The house was old and prone to creaks and pops. Every hour the grandfather clock chimed in the den. It was dark and empty downstairs. Anyone or anything could slink and slither about quietly down there but the stair steps would betray even a soft footfall.

At 2:15 a.m., Kevin was awakened by a loud banging. It was a heavy sound like steel against steel, echoing from the barn. Freddie was already awake and seated on the edge of Kevin's bed.

"Do you hear that?" Freddie whispered as he grasped Kevin's arm.

"How could I not? What is it?"

"Sounds like the anvil?"

Kevin sat up next to Freddie. They leapt from the bed and ran to the window.

Clang. Clang. Clang. Three times. It stopped for a bit, then started again. Mr. Lucas came into the room wearing rumpled pajamas. He saw the boys at the window.

"What the heck is that? See anything out there?"

"Too dark," Kevin responded.

"Somebody sure is makin' a racket." Mr. Lucas was irritated but too good-natured to fly off the handle. "I better put some clothes on." He calmly turned and went back down the hallway.

The boys stumbled about as they picked up their discarded jeans and pulled them over their boxers. They hurried into the hallway and bounded down the stairs, snatching flashlights from the pantry. Mr. Lucas appeared carrying a shotgun. He went out to the back yard with the determined boys in tow. They watched as he pulled two 12-gauge shotgun shells from his pocket and steadily placed one in each barrel.

Mr. Lucas and the two boys headed over to the gate that opened to the pasture. Storm patrolled just in front of the search team. Kevin and Freddie revealed the path ahead with beams roaming like drunken klieg lights. Mr. Lucas held the stock of the gun snuggly against his right shoulder. His left hand gripped the barrels, which were angled toward the ground, but at the ready. As they trekked toward their destination, the clanging continued. When they drew close to the barn, the noise abated and countryside fell silent. Mr. Lucas tread softly to a halt. The boys fell in line. Storm stood at attention.

"They must know we're out here," Freddie remarked.

"If they decide to make a run for it, there's only one way outta' that barn," Kevin added.

"Hush," Mr. Lucas instructed.

In the still, quiet night, Kevin sensed the rapid thumping in his chest. Mr. Lucas cocked both barrels and lifted the gun into firing position. The boys held their flashlights steady, beams focused on the barn's entrance. The silence was broken as the clanging started up again. The boys went crazy.

"Shoot a monkey!" Mr. Lucas exclaimed. It was his harshest expletive.

"Holy moly!" shouted Freddie.

Shotgun trained, Mr. Lucas walked toward the barn door.

"You boys stay behind me and keep those flashlights aimed at that door."

The dog barked ferociously at the unseen intruder.

Freddie's dad came up to the opening. The banging ceased just as the boys illumined the interior darkness with slowly scanning beams of light. Storm calmed a bit and his bark shifted to a mild yawl as they went inside to survey the problem.

Mr. Lucas held his gun in place and took a careful look around. "Put your hands in the air and show yourself," he ordered. "You've had your fun. Now come on out. There's no damage done. You're not in any serious trouble . . . yet."

Behind Mr. Lucas, the boys made a thorough sweep of the room with the beams of their flashlights. The hammer lay there on the anvil where the unseen perpetrator had left it. Kevin panned his light down, onto the packed dirt floor below. Freddie followed suit.

Fanned out like carefully placed playing cards, strips and shards of metal from Dr. Dale's airplane wreckage circled the anvil forming a red and white mosaic. The pieces were not tossed about randomly. This project had been assembled with creative deliberation. And it had taken a while.

"You boys touch the crate this stuff was gathered up in?"

"No, sir."

"Don't lie to me."

"We aren't, Daddy," Freddie responded. "We have no idea what's going on."

Perplexed and somewhat disappointed, Mr. Lucas and the boys headed back to the house. Storm ran ahead of them and waited on the back porch.

"What do we do now?" Freddie asked his dad.

"You boys are gonna' get some sleep."

"What if the noise starts up again?" Kevin asked.

"That darn troublemaker sure got my goat," Mr. Lucas said. "If he tries it again I'll call the Sheriff's office and get somebody to come out here and pick him up. He can bang on the bars at the jail house with a tin cup."

Kevin and Freddie were pretty keyed up. They got into their beds and whispered excitedly about the noises in the barn and the creepy figures in the garden. When the adrenaline rush drained away, the boys settled in for a few hours of light sleep.

Foggy-headed, Kevin soon awakened. A faint, perpetual clang drifted in and out. He recognized it as a memory of a sound and not the sound itself. But he sensed that it was more significant than just a remembering. It was not a replay. It was part of the present moment. A harbinger. He felt a presence in the room. It wasn't his friend. It wasn't Freddie's mom or dad. It was like what he sometimes experienced in his Meemaw's house in Missouri. A couple of times, while watching television in a small bedroom in the back of the house he had seen a man looking out the window. The man looked real but Kevin knew he wasn't. He didn't have the physical presence of a real live man. There was vagueness about him. He wasn't fully saturated.

The first time Kevin saw the man it was the middle of a Wednesday afternoon. The second time was on a Sunday after church. Kevin was sitting in a beanbag chair on the opposite side of the room. That time the man turned and looked at Kevin. The man's face was like a faded photograph.

Now, he felt something similar in Freddie's room, except this time it was sickening. In the room at Kevin's grandmother's house there was a feeling of sadness and confusion. It wasn't scary. As he lay there, he glimpsed something eerie on the side of the bed. Next to his left leg, thin, smoky tendrils formed the fingers of two hands that gripped the edge of the bed. An ill-defined shadow the size and shape of a cantaloupe crowned the flat surface of the bed. As it rose it was clearly the head of a young boy. Dark and featureless it continued to rise revealing shoulders and upper torso. It was like the child had been kneeling and he moved his body upward but remained on his knees. Silent, the shadow child studied Kevin. Kevin faced him squarely. He hoped if he appeared fearless and unfazed, the child would lose interest and go away.

Out of the corner of his eye, Kevin saw the wispy gray fingers form on the right side of the bed. This time the shape was farther up the bed, next to Kevin's right shoulder. The specter slowly pushed itself up. This one rose up until it reached a standing position. The curious children examined him up and down. The standing boy cocked his head to one side. They watched intensely, waiting for Kevin to make a move, but he was stoic, motionless. A scream of terror welled up inside but he kept it to himself, pushing it down deep into a place where he could contain it. He let his eyelids slide shut. He made himself appear drowsy and pretended to fall asleep.

The next time he opened his eyes, the boys were gone. He didn't mention it to Freddie.

School was out.

Kevin and Freddie had just finished seventh grade, and summer was a welcome reward. Even better, the new school year would find the boys at the top of the junior high pecking order. It would be nine months of freedom from routine harassment. The unsettling events at the farm were a few months behind them and the boys had moved on.

Freddie's birthday was in June and Kevin rode his bike to his friend's house. When he pulled up, Storm ran out and greeted him with a couple of happy barks. Then, Storm ran alongside as he wheeled around to the back of the house.

"Get ready," Freddie said, appearing at the back door and leading Kevin to the garage. "You're about to be jealous."

"You got a new bike. I knew it. I'm gonna dump my piece of crap in a ditch and walk home."

Freddy opened the garage door slowly and Kevin glanced in.

"Holy shit!" Kevin exclaimed. Before him stood a red Sears mini-bike with a black seat. It was the most beautiful thing Kevin had ever laid eyes on. He moved in, circling it to admire every square inch. "Looks practically brand new."

"My dad bought it from a little old lady. She only rode it to church on Sundays."

Kevin laughed. "You had me there for a minute. I'd like to see my Meemaw kick up some dust on this baby."

Freddie stepped over and straddled the seat. He gave the starter cord an expert yank and the engine fired right up. With a subtle turn of his head, he invited Kevin to hop on back. The seat was long enough for two boys. Kevin climbed on behind his friend and they eased out of the garage into the driveway. Freddie fed the bike a healthy gulp of fuel and the boys ran circles around the house and then buzzed over to the gate that opened to the pasture. He pushed the bike to its limit. They picked up speed, leaving a dusty cloud in their wake. Freddie eased off the throttle and gingerly squeezed the brake lever as they reached the edge of the woods.

"Are we gonna park it here?"

"Park it? We just got to the fun part."

"Let's do it," Kevin responded, in a show of confidence.

Freddie surveyed the obstacle course ahead and boldly pulled the throttle, propelling the boys into the rugged patch of post oak and hackberry. Sparser at first, the improvised path was easy to maneuver. As they drew closer to the creek, Freddie slowed a bit to plot his course. Focusing on the fallen tree that connected the banks of the stream, the boy tightened his fist around the throttle grip. The bike lurched forward. Kevin suddenly realized that his friend was unhinged. He let go of the wild boy's shoulders and secured himself more firmly by throwing his arms around Freddie's waist.

The scooter hit the tree trunk at a rapid clip. The nubby tires bumped along the bark and the back of the bike slipped to the left. Kevin anticipated a plunge into the water below and prayed that the bike wouldn't land on top of him. In an instant, the front wheel leapt onto the packed dirt of the bank. The rear wheel held its precarious grip on the tree trunk and pushed the bike to safety.

Coming to a stop, the boys let out a raucous shout of victory. Freddie barely took time to catch his breath. He launched the little motor bike onward. As the boys ventured deeper, the space between the trees narrowed. Freddie was masterful in his approach, managing speed and balance. He cut the wheel left and right as he navigated the difficult terrain. Kevin wished he hadn't worn cut-offs as thin branches and sticky vines scratched his bare legs. Freddie brought the bike to a halt.

"I think we should turn back," Kevin said.

The engine began to sputter. It backfired issuing an acrid puff of gray smoke from the tailpipe. The motor shut down.

Feeling queasy, Kevin slid off the bike while Freddie gave an aggressive pull to the start cable. He tried a few more times without luck.

Kevin was dizzy and suddenly awash in a mild melancholy. He realized he'd known about this place from the beginning. The veil had been lifted here. The woods were full of mystery, but its secrets were unraveling. Freddie looked to Kevin for a reaction to their predicament and realized his friend was out of sorts. Kevin was pale and his manner distant, the flesh under each eye had darkened.

"Are you okay?"

Kevin bent down, heaved, and threw up.

"Oh man, you musta had some bad clams." Freddie said in jest. Kevin didn't laugh.

"Listen." Kevin wiped his mouth, looking around, appraising the situation.

"Listen to what? I don't hear anything."

"Exactly," Kevin said. "Shouldn't we be hearing birds and bugs? Leaves rustling in the wind?" A chill brushed across him and he looked sharply to the left. About thirty feet away in the deep woods, two boys stood amidst the heavy brush and tangled vines. It was nearly as dark as night in the space around them. From far away, the sound of a hammer on an anvil reached their ears. They stood side by side, focused on Kevin and Freddie. One boy was slightly taller than the other. Kevin recognized them immediately. Long ago, when he first saw them, they were wispy shadow figures; but now they were fully formed. Their skin was like a black charcoal shell, crackled and streaked with pink and red. In contrast, their eyes glowed light yellow.

"It's the burned boys," Kevin muttered.

"What?"

"It's the Dale boys."

"How do you . . ."

The darkness surrounding the sinister figures billowed outward, overtaking the woods around them. Freddie jumped on the bike and pulled the starter cable repeatedly. Kevin stood frozen, his eyes fixed on the dark figures.

The ink-like fog grew closer. Freddie jerked hard on the pull start and pumped the throttle grip. The engine started, rough at first, but it steadied quickly. He turned the bike around. Kevin got on, securing his arms around Freddie's waist.

Heart racing, Freddie got the bike moving through the thicket. As they raced along, Kevin resisted the temptation to look back. He hoped they had receded back into the woods. The scare was too intense. It didn't feel like the little boys from the plane crash were out for fun. Their intention seemed tangibly menacing.

Kevin trusted his friend's sense of direction and his skills as a scooter pilot. They would make it back across the creek, up the hill and to the safety of the Lucas house. He winced at the sting of the switch-like branches slapping at his bare legs.

Confident that the worst was behind them, Kevin turned to take one last look back.

The blood drained from his face.

The burned boys were running just behind them. They sped up until they were moving along a path parallel to the bike, but Kevin couldn't tell Freddie. He wanted his friend's attention focused solely on getting them to safety.

The pool of darkness surrounding the burned boys glided along with them. When the creepy entities veered closer to the mini-bike, the dark, flowing mass crept into Freddie's peripheral vision. He turned his head to the right and got his first look at the terrifying black cloud and its occupants.

Freddie swerved and the scooter hit a large exposed tree root. The jolt knocked Kevin onto the ground. The bike tipped to the right and slammed into a tree, pinning Freddie in between.

A cloud of shadow swept over the scene. Kevin was face down in a tousled pile. He was banged up but not badly injured. He spit out dirt and leaves and turned himself face up. Like hellish statues, the burned boys stood at his feet. Their heads moved slowly, as if underwater. They were utterly disgusting. Kevin saw crisp, twisted patches of bark-like charred black flesh, exposed bone, and seared red meat. They were hairless. Noses and ears burned away. They peered at him with dead, black pupils in a pool of putrid yellow gel. Kevin scooted backward. With effort, he righted his achy body and got on his feet. Freddie was moaning in pain a short distance away.

"Leave us alone," Kevin growled at the burned boys.

Kevin was relieved as he heard a familiar bark draw near. With a swift gallop, Storm landed in front of the burned boys. He hunkered down, snarling, baring his fearsome teeth. With Storm blocking the hideous creatures, Kevin hurried over to his downed friend.

Freddie was in bad shape. Kevin pulled the bike off him and Freddie fell away from the tree. He cried out in agony. The most obvious injury was an awful sight but Kevin maintained his composure. Freddie's right leg was a mess; a bone was protruding. The open wound was an oozing mix of blood and dirt. Kevin pulled his t-shirt over his head, wrapped it around the wound and tied it snug. Freddie began screaming.

Kevin was determined to carry his friend to safety but it was going to be difficult. He hadn't experienced his growth spurt yet and he was a little soft and pudgy. Freddie was half a head taller and his body shape had changed. He had an athletic frame with undeveloped but solid muscle tone. Kevin gathered his resolve and prepared for the challenge of his life. He would get his friend out of these woods and back to the house.

He noticed that they were no longer in shadow. The darkness had lifted. Crossing on the fallen tree seemed unlikely. Walking across required balance, coordination, and concentration. The boys were too wrung out. Kevin could possibly hug the tree and shimmy across but Freddie's right leg was useless. He couldn't bend or drag it and even touching it was excruciating.

Easing Freddie to the ground, Kevin set out to find the narrowest stretch of the creek with the lowest banks. If he could get Freddie down to the creek bed, he could carry him across. Upon reaching the other side, Kevin would get himself on the bank and pull Freddie up by the arms. Then he could carry his screaming friend up the hill. This would at least alert Freddie's mother to get help.

About fifty yards upstream, Kevin found a decent spot for crossing. Once again, he pulled his friend's left arm around his shoulder and hoisted him upward. This time Freddie had trouble supporting his weight on his left leg. Curiously, he had stopped wailing. He must have gone into shock. Kevin kept Freddie upright, mostly. It was touch and go but they finally reached the prospective crossing.

Controlling Freddie's slide from the bank to the creek bed was tricky. Kevin had no choice but to ease him in legs first. If he put

Freddie in head first, the boy would probably drown. Leaning over the bank, Kevin placed his friend onto the edge of the creek just above the waterline. Kevin then positioned himself to get down from the bank and onto the creek bed. Before he could make his move, he heard a rustle in the woods behind him. Enraged, he shouted as he turned around.

"Why can't you leave us alone!"

The burned boys were nowhere in sight. Storm emerged from the woods and yapped anxiously.

Kevin lowered himself down into the water. It was no more than seven feet to the other side. He took a step to test the depth and then another. One of his feet immediately sunk into a mud hole. As Kevin tried to free his foot from the muck, he felt something in the water beside him. Nervously, he looked down into the murky pool. Just breaking the surface, the grinning face of a burned boy emerged. Kevin tried to pull away, but his foot was stuck. The burned boy re-submerged and Kevin felt a hand grasp his ankle. His foot was immediately freed, but he was so startled he swallowed creek water and began coughing. Flailing and splashing, he fought to right himself. The burned boy's face tipped up and rose out of the water, revealing shoulders and upper arms. It loosened its jaw and smiled at Kevin.

Kevin pulled Freddie into the water and gingerly drug him to the other side of the crossing. When he got him there, he shimmied up onto the muddy bank still holding on to Freddie. Then, as he turned to establish leverage and pull Freddie up, he felt a sharp pain in his side, and caught a glimpse of a black ribbon twisting away out of the corner of his eye.

Damn, he thought. You said they slither off pretty quick if you get close.

Kevin never let go of Freddy and began dragging him up onto the muddy bank. It was slow-going at first, but it got easier. Kevin looked down and saw the other, taller burned boy helping.

Kevin ignored the pain in his side and his fatigue. Freddie was now out cold and Kevin wrapped his arms around his neck and held them, and began dragging Freddy toward the house. Storm yammered and whined beside them. The burned boys followed for a moment, but stayed back in the woods.

Delirious and woozy, Kevin soldiered on through the forest, struggled up the hill and made it to the pasture fence. He was like a wounded, wheezing animal fleeing for his life, and for his friend's life too. But his muscles began to leaden. He felt himself seize up and he let Freddie slip to the ground.

He could hear Storm barking like crazy and Mrs. Lucas screaming, but they were suddenly far away.

Kevin lay on the soft, cool grass of the soccer field. On the ground beside him was a picture rendered in crayon. Had he drawn it? It featured two black silhouettes among trees. He focused his attention on the clean blue sky above. He gazed deeper and deeper until he convinced himself that he saw eternity. A Red-tailed Hawk circled silently and effortlessly. Soaring in the vast, cloudless sky, it appeared in miniature. The mighty bird lost its detail and its path became a crayon line. Heavy down the middle, feathered on its edges. The traveling mark grew smudgy until it shattered into tiny shards, flying off in every direction. Then the sky was empty. Kevin lost himself and disappeared into forever. And everything was white.

Sky of Brass, Land of Iron

By Joe McKinney

For Robert Garza, it started on a cool, breezy night in early May. He was driving home on Texas Farm Route 181 when he saw the first one moving across the road from left to right with a slow, loping gait.

At first he didn't recognize it as a coyote. It didn't look right. It didn't move right. Coyotes were supposed to move like dogs. But there was something different about this one. It almost seemed to hop. More like a rat than a dog. Garza watched it move across the road and thought it was odd, but not particularly alarming.

Two more went by, disappearing into the cedar thicket off to his right.

A fourth went by a moment later.

He waited to see if there were any more, but none came. The night was perfectly still and quiet, save for the burbling exhaust of his idling truck. He could smell the faint tinge of wood smoke on the night breeze.

He shook his head and chuckled, dismissing the encounter as just another strange thing you sometimes see on empty country roads in the middle of the night.

He drove on.

At the time, it didn't occur to him to worry.

Garza's best friend was a man named Frank Resendez. They'd known each other for almost ten years, going back to when Garza was a rookie detective assigned to the San Antonio Police Department's Homicide Unit and Resendez was his sergeant. It was Resendez, in fact, who'd talked Garza into moving his family out to Espada Ridge.

Garza would be the first to admit that Resendez was a genius. And he wasn't alone in that belief, either. He'd watched, like the kid brother of somebody famous, as Resendez's skill as an investigator and police administrator made him a law enforcement legend all across South Texas. Those same skills also earned Resendez the coveted lieutenant's position overseeing San Antonio's Homicide Unit, a job he still held, and did exceedingly well, despite everything else he had on his plate. For as successful as he was in police circles, he was even more successful writing about it. His textbook, *Criminal Investigations for the Texas Peace Officer*, was now in its fourth edition, and the money he made from that allowed him to reinvent himself yet again—this time as a major player in South Texas real estate.

Now, looking out over the 3,400 acres that Resendez planned to turn into the Espada Ridge Estates, Garza felt a renewed awe for the scope of the man's vision. It was beautiful, but hard country. Espada Ridge formed a fat crescent around the north corner of Worther Lake. Its gently rolling hills were densely covered with cedar and hardy Spanish oaks, and close to the water. And there were occasional meadows that, in April, burst forth with wildflowers.

In a few places, Resendez had added old-fashioned split rail fences to demarcate available lots. And, of course, there was the lake itself. Right now, it was dappled with late afternoon sunshine, a rich tapestry of yellows and reds, a pool of molten bronze.

Resendez was showing him an old country church and the ruins of six small cottages he'd found while clearing the bottom ten acres of his land. "Impossible to say how old they are," Resendez said. "Too overgrown. I bet the place is probably crawling with rattlesnakes."

Garza nodded, suddenly mindful of where he stepped. The cottages themselves were nothing special, just small moldering derelicts waist deep in yellow alkali grass. None of them had roofs, and only one still had all four walls. The weather and the years had not been kind.

But the church was in better shape. It no longer had a front door, and few of the gravestones on its north lawn were still standing, but it retained enough of its former self that you could tell at a glance it was a church.

"This is what I wanted to show you," Resendez said, watching with pleasure at the fascination on Garza's face. "Go on, look inside."

Garza got as far as the front steps and stopped. "Oh Jesus," he said. He put a hand over his mouth and gagged. "Something's dead in there."

"It's a deer," Resendez said.

Garza glanced at Resendez, his face wrinkled in disgust. Even after twenty years of handling homicides, the smell of rotting flesh still rattled him.

"Go on, you big baby," Resendez said. "Go inside."

Gagging, Garza went. It took a moment for his eyes to adjust to the sudden darkness, but once they did, he saw that the church was as simple inside as out, no frills, no ornamentation. It was just a large, high-ceilinged, rectangular room with a couple pews. The dead deer lay across what had once been the altar, and swarming around its carcass was a vast gathering of flies. Clumps of them filled the shadows.

Resendez led him around the carcass to a small wooden box tucked back into a corner. The ancient black iron lock had been forced open. "One of my workers found this yesterday while he was clearing brush for me," Resendez said. "Go ahead. Open it."

Inside lay a small brown leather book. The back flap was water-damaged, but the spine was still somewhat supple, and the pages felt stiff as he thumbed through them. The handwriting was a thin, scrunched-together scrawl that didn't yield to easy translation. It looked like a series of journal entries, with an occasional list of names and dates. Some of the earliest were from the 1720s.

"It's in German," Garza said.

"Yeah, I was hoping you could translate it. That's what you did in the Army, right?"

Flies buzzed around them. Garza waved a hand to shoo them away. "That was twenty-five years ago," he said. "Rusty" didn't even come close to describing his comfort level with the German language. "I can try, I guess."

Resendez nodded and together they walked outside. The dusty haze of late afternoon wrapped around the trees. Resendez said something about wanting to know the history of the place.

But Garza was only half listening. He was watching a coyote about forty yards off, and it was watching him. Garza opened his mouth to say something about it, but the animal melted back into the cedar before he could get the words out.

He turned to Resendez. "Did you see that?"

Garza and his wife, Linda, both lay awake in bed, their eyes open in the dark, as their dog howled in the kitchen downstairs.

"Will you please go check on him?" Linda asked.

Garza grumbled something about strangling the damn dog with his bare hands and got dressed. On his way downstairs, he passed his daughter Sam's room. A white glow bordered the door. She was awake, of course, probably on her cell phone, or listening to music. For a moment he thought of getting her to do it. Guthrie was her dog, after all, and she was probably in there doing nothing, as usual.

"Screw it," he grumbled, and went down to shut the dog up himself.

Guthrie, a full grown chocolate lab ordinarily gentle as a kitten, stood in the kitchen by the back door, barking himself hoarse. His coat bristled down his spine and his lips pulled back over his teeth in a fairly convincing imitation of a tough-as-nails junkyard dog.

"Guthrie, shut up!"

The dog looked at him, whined once, then started barking even louder at the door. Garza watched him for a second, morbidly fascinated. He'd never acted like this. Not when they lived in the city.

Of course there Guthrie hadn't had ten acres of land to lord over.

A part of Garza wanted to slap the dog and be done with it. But another part of him recognized something hideous in his bark. At times it became a keening wail, almost feral, wolf-like. City dogs didn't make noises like that. And Guthrie, despite his new home, was decidedly a city dog.

Garza flipped on the kitchen light and Guthrie backed away from the door, his barks trailing off to a low, stuttering growl.

He turned on the floodlights for the backyard and looked through the window.

There was nothing there.

"Stupid dog," Garza said, and patted him on the head.

He looked outside again, his hand poised over the switch to turn out the lights, when he heard a low murmuring hum. He glanced at Guthrie, who was still growling, and then back at the yard.

There was nothing but grass and darkness beyond the trees. He hesitated for a moment, then opened the door and stepped outside—only to jump right back in and slam the door behind him.

A huge swarm of flies covered the outside of the door. He put his knuckles in his mouth to stifle the nausea threatening to overtake him.

"Jesus," he said. "Oh Jesus."

Though he was unbelievably tired, Garza stayed awake most of that night thinking about the church on Resendez's land, and the book he'd been given to translate.

It was curious that a building like was still standing. According to the book, the church had been there since at least 1728, for there had been a baptism in March of that year. Later entries showed the church was in constant use until 1848, when the last entry was made.

But the most curious thing about the book was that it only mentioned one surname: Kretschmer. Garza guessed that it was a family prayer book, which might explain why only that name was written there. The other alternative, that the little community had been so isolated that they only married each other, was too repugnant for him to dwell on.

He assumed it was a prayer book because the authors whose varied handwriting he could decipher all made mention of religious rites and ceremonies. He'd skimmed over them at first, only because he figured they described conventional ceremonies, like baptism and marriage. But when he began to read them in more detail, he realized they described activities so strange that they could only be Satanic in design. There were so many references to demons that Garza wondered if the community's isolation was voluntary, or perhaps forced on them by horrified neighbors.

He was enough of a modern man to dismiss most of what he read in the prayer book as hogwash. But there were constant references to flies that stirred something inside him. He was almost surprised to discover a superstitious side to his personality, but there it was. He read the numerous entries about the flies, and how the book said they were the eyes and ears of a demon called *"De Vermis,"* which Garza guessed meant "the worm," and he found himself thoroughly creeped out. It wasn't a feeling he enjoyed.

But he hadn't known any of that when he went to Resendez's house earlier that evening. At that time, shortly after touring the church and cottages on Resendez's land and before making it back to his place for dinner, he hadn't even opened the book yet. It wouldn't be until he was alone in his own study, while Sam was upstairs doing her homework and Linda was in the kitchen doing the dishes, that he learned about the demon the Kretschmers called *De Vermis.*

"I suppose the first thing we ought to do is figure out how old those structures are," Resendez had said. "Once we know that, we can make more informed decisions."

They were sitting in Resendez's study, looking over some maps of the land around the lake.

"Decisions about what, exactly?"

"Well, think about it, Robert. If it's just some cowboy church, we might as well bulldoze it and move on. But if it's something else, something older—maybe Spanish—we could use that."

"Why would it be Spanish? That book was in German."

"You know what I mean. I just want to know if we can use it somehow."

"Use how?"

Resendez smiled at him patiently. "We could market it. Maybe change the name of the development from Espada Ridge to something having to do with the church."

Garza started to speak, but suddenly stopped himself. It dawned on him that he and Resendez had very different ideas about their obligations.

"Do you think we have the right to do that?" Garza asked.

"What do you mean? Why wouldn't we?"

"Well, if it is a church, Spanish or otherwise, wouldn't it fall under some kind of historical preservation statute? The federal government's got laws that protect archeological artifacts."

Resendez waved the idea away with a dismissive flick of his hand. "This isn't like finding the Dead Sea Scrolls, Robert. It's just a little out of the way church the world forgot about. My point is we could use it to really give the development an identity. Make it something unique, you know?"

"Frank, I really think—"

"I'm not going to turn this thing over to a bunch of academics," Resendez interrupted, "and let them put the development on hold indefinitely. You know that's what they'd do. Remember when they were building the Walmart over off General Kirby

Parkway and they found that old Indian village? The academics got a court order to put a twenty-million-dollar building project on hold so they could dig around for a bunch of fucking arrowheads and cornhusk dolls. You think I want that?"

"No."

"Well, you're right. I don't. What I do want is for you to translate that book. Try to get me some answers."

And just like that, Garza realized he'd been given an order. There'd be no further discussion. The matter was closed.

"Hey, honey."

"Yes, dear?" Linda said. She was dropping spaghetti into a large pot of boiling water.

"We probably shouldn't put our garbage out on the back porch anymore. It attracts flies."

"Flies?"

"Yeah. Probably other things too. I think that's what Guthrie was barking at last night."

Linda looked puzzled. "I didn't put any garbage out back," she said. "We always put it out on the side, remember?"

Garza nodded. "Must have been Sam. I'll talk to her about it."

The little town of Bonheim stood about three miles South of Worther Lake. It was a quiet crossroads for the surrounding ranches, with a little eight-man police department under the command of Chief Pablo Delgado.

Delgado was a heavyset man in his early sixties with a sunburnt face and bald head. He'd been an assistant chief in Horizon City, and the chief's job at Bonheim was his retirement gig. Bonheim was a peaceful little town that didn't demand a lot from its police force, and that suited Delgado just fine. He preferred to be easygoing anyway, more like a benevolent grandpa than a serious lawman.

Garza knew that Delgado also happened to be the local expert on regional history, so he called Delgado, and the two agreed to meet in a little cafe in town.

"What kind of history do you want to know about?" Delgado asked as he managed to wrap his mouth around an enormous pulled pork sandwich that dripped red streams of barbecue sauce onto his plate.

That was a good question, Garza thought. He didn't really know. Or he did, he just didn't know how to bring it up. How does one break the ice when talking about demon worshipping in-breeders?

In the end he decided to come as close to the truth as he could.

"I've heard rumors about a family named Kretschmer that was supposed to live around these parts," he said. "Folks I've talked to said they lived up by the lake. Near my house."

The smile on Delgado's face slipped away like a greasy egg yolk running off a piece of toast, and Garza guessed he'd hit a nerve. The man put his sandwich down and wiped the barbecue sauce from the corner of his mouth. "How'd you find out about the Kretschmer family?"

"Just people talking," Garza said. "You know the way people talk. I figured if they used to live on my land, I wanted to know about it."

Delgado looked annoyed, or maybe skeptical. He said, "Well, that's the kind of thing I wish people wouldn't talk about. This area's got a lot of good, honest history. It doesn't need a scandal to make it interesting."

But Delgado seemed willing enough to talk about the scandal. After all the horrible things he'd read in that book, and the flies at his door and the coyotes that seemed to leer out of every dark pocket of cedar, Garza was keenly interested in the tale.

Most of it revolved around a man named Oswald Kretschmer, who fled Germany in the 1680s with his family to avoid religious persecution and ended up in Mexico. He relocated his family again to the area around Worther Lake sometime in the 1690s or early 1700s.

"They pretty much kept to themselves out there," Delgado explained. "Of course, at the time there really wasn't anybody else around for them to associate with. Most of the area was a giant Spanish land grant to one of their local governors. Empty except for a few half-starved Indian tribes.

"After Texas got its independence from Mexico, settlers started moving into the area and founded this town. People avoided the Kretschmers, mostly. Though, I did read a diary once that mentioned them. It said you could always tell the Kretschmer family on account of their eyes."

"Their eyes?" Garza asked. He was leaning forward despite himself, like he was hearing dirty gossip about what the pretty secretary in the office looked like naked.

"Said to be the iciest blue you ever saw. Every single member of that family had those eyes, apparently."

"And so what happened to them?"

"Nobody knows," Delgado said. "The Texas government took a census of the area when they tried to enlist local boys into the Confederate militias, and there's no record of them in it. My guess is they packed up and went somewhere where they could still be by themselves."

Garza sat back and scratched his head. "I'm afraid I don't see the scandal in all that."

"Well," Delgado said, and he obviously found this detail distasteful, "there's the part about them all marrying each other. It was just the one family, you know. Over the space of a hundred years or so, you're bound to end up with what the law calls marriages of consanguinity."

"In-breeding," Garza said.

Delgado nodded. "You know how that kind of thing gets people talking. There's more than a few references to them doing devil worship—and witchcraft too—but I think that's just people embellishing an already sordid story. The records I've seen mention birth defects and deformities and all the other things you'd expect from generations of in-breeding. Given the nature of the time it's only natural stories of witchcraft and such would start up."

Garza said he agreed, but his mind kept turning back to that book.

And the flies.

"You did what?" Resendez said. "Robert, what in the hell's wrong with you? I told you I didn't want a bunch of historians crawling all over this place."

"He's not a real historian, Frank. He's just an amateur—"

"I know who he is, Robert. What I want to know is why you'd do something like that. Don't you realize how much is at stake here? We both stand to make a lot of money if we do this right."

"I was just trying to find out about the history of this place. Like you asked me to do. And I didn't say a word about the buildings you found. As far as he knows, I was just following up on idle gossip I'd heard around town."

"You mean about that devil worshipping crap you found in that book?"

Garza nodded.

"That's great," Resendez said, and then he turned and looked out the window of his study, his gaze wandering over the acres of cedar to the lake beyond. At last he said, "You know, this isn't what I wanted when I asked you to help me give this place an identity."

"You got the truth, Frank."

"Bullshit," Resendez said. "There's no truth in that book. And none in Delgado's amateur history either. The truth is what we make it."

Garza was appalled. In all the years he'd known Resendez, he'd never once heard the man say something to suggest slippery ethics. He felt like one of his boyhood heroes had let him down. But that wasn't all. For the first time, he realized that some small part of his orderly, rational mind actually believed the stories he'd read about devil worship. Maybe there was a kernel of truth in it, at least. People who isolated themselves for religious reasons usually did it because they had some off-the-wall beliefs, didn't they?

"So what are you going to do, Frank?" Garza's voice strained, his lips thin as razorblades.

"I don't know yet," Resendez said, and turned back to the window. "Go home, Robert. We'll talk later."

The next day was Monday, and work was uncomfortable. Resendez, never one to hold a grudge or let a problem bog him down, was unusually cold, and he and Garza went most of the day without speaking more than a few grunts to each other.

Garza left work about six and drove home, taking Farm Route 181 like always. As he passed the new Methodist Church just south of Bonheim, still a half mile or so from his usual turn off, he saw one of the coyotes with the rat-like gait go bounding across the road in front of him, then disappear into the cedar off to his left.

He put on the brakes. A feeling had festered in his mind ever since he saw that coyote watching him near Resendez's church. He felt the coyotes and the flies and the church were somehow connected. His police training had prepared him to look for links between seemingly unrelated people and events, but this felt like a different kind of problem, like it wouldn't yield to conventional logic. He wasn't sure what the connection was, only that he believed one existed.

It was a cool night, and he'd been driving with the windows down. But watching the coyote shook him in a way he couldn't quite define, and he moved to roll up the windows.

He got the driver's side window secured, but when he reached over to roll up the passenger side, he stopped and jerked his hand back in horror. A huge humming mass of black, angry flies covered the whole door frame.

He backed against the driver's side door, fumbled blindly for the handle, and spilled out into the street, where he stood gaping at a living black carpet beating against his vehicle. They were actually rocking the truck.

After the shock wore off, Garza pulled out his fire extinguisher and turned it on the flies.

The chalky spray coated the insects, and they dropped to the road in powdery, white chunks. Their swollen bodies and still twitching wings disgusted him, but he mastered his nausea long enough to sweep the remaining flies onto the road with an old, greasy towel.

Something moved in the grass behind him. He turned, his right hand poised over the thumb snap on his holster, and saw a single coyote running with that familiar rat-like hop across the church lawn. It stopped about fifty feet away and watched him. Off in the distance, he could hear howling, a disconcerting chorus of yaps and long, mournful bays.

More coyotes came around the side of the building, moving fast. There was no point in pulling his gun. At the speed they moved, he'd probably empty the whole magazine without landing a single shot.

Instead of firing, he got back in his truck, dropped it into gear, and peeled out down the road as fast as the old Chevy would go.

When he looked in the rearview mirror, there was nothing but dust behind him.

When he arrived home, Linda was standing in the driveway. The look on her face said something was wrong. "She hasn't come home yet," Linda said.

"Sam?"

Linda nodded, near tears. "She was supposed to be home at four."

"Where'd she go?" But he had a sinking feeling that he already knew.

"She's out with Jenny and Margaret. They went horseback riding down by the lake."

"How long ago?"

"They left after lunch. I don't know."

Garza jumped back in his truck.

"Where are you going?"

"Call Chief Delgado," he told her. "Have him bring shotguns and a couple of his men. Tell him to meet me on Resendez's property down by the lake."

"Robert—"

"Go!" he said. "Hurry."

He dropped the truck in gear and sped away.

Garza raced down to the lake on a narrow dirt road he and Resendez had cut with a tractor the summer before. He took it as far as he could, then cut through the brush toward the church, his truck ripping through overhanging cedar branches the whole way.

He reached a large limestone outcropping and had to slow down so he could work the truck around it. When he did he heard Sam and Resendez's daughters screaming for help.

Their voices came from the trails above the church, and it sounded like they were getting closer.

Not thinking about anything except his daughter, he punched the gas and took the truck straight through the cedar and down the slope of the limestone outcropping. The old Chevy yawed in midair, making him feel weightless for a prolonged moment, and then hit the ground with a tremendous impact.

The truck bottomed out and stalled. It wouldn't start again. He jumped out, gun in hand, and scanned the trails on the hillside above the church.

"Daddy, Daddy," Sam screamed at him. He saw his little girl holding on to the horse for dear life. Resendez's daughters came up behind her.

He ran a few steps that way and stopped. Coyotes bounded down the hill on either side of the girls, moving through the brush so easily they seemed more like shadows than animals. In the gaps between the cedar trees he could see them snapping at the bellies of the horses.

"Samantha," he yelled. "This way. Come on. This way!"

The poor girl was barely holding on. She wasn't half the rider Resendez's daughters were, and as the horses jumped from the slope to the grassy ledge of limestone on the far side of the church, she nearly popped out of the saddle.

The coyotes snapped at her feet and at the horse's belly, but Garza couldn't risk a shot. Hitting a running dog-sized target at sixty yards with a pistol would be next to impossible, and he stood a better chance of hitting one of the girls by mistake.

"Make for that cottage," he yelled at her, and ran that way himself. It only had three walls, but it would have to do. At least that way the coyotes could only come at them from one side.

The girls raced for him and they met at the busted cottage wall. Garza shot at the coyote snapping at the horse's hooves. He missed the first shot and fired three more times. The last two shots sent the animal tumbling backwards over itself.

More coyotes raced across the grass, coming for them. He yanked Sam down and folded her into his arms while the other two girls jumped off their horses.

"Inside here," he said, packing them into the cottage. "Hurry."

He glanced inside the cottage as he pushed them inside and did a double take. Most of the floor was grown over with meadow grasses and wildflowers, but toward the back wall, someone had dug up fresh earth. There was a large mound of gray dirt and rock there, and a sizeable hole in the ground beyond it.

"There," he said.

"Daddy—"

"Go," he told her, and turned back just in time to see at least thirty coyotes going after the horses. The horses neighed and kicked. They punched the air with their hooves, their eyes rolling wildly, their lips pulled back, slinging long ropes of spit.

The coyotes tore the belly out of one of the horses and Garza couldn't look anymore. Its dying screams were enough. He backed into the cottage, moving toward the girls, who were already getting into the hole.

"Mr. Garza," Jenny said, "there's a tunnel down here."

"Get in," he said. "All of you."

"Daddy—"

"Go, Sam. I'm right behind you, baby."

They got down on their bellies and crawled into the darkness. He went after them, backing himself in just as one of the coyotes appeared at the rim.

In the fading evening light, all he saw was the jagged rows of its fangs. He fired with one hand, killing it. He backed further into the hole. Behind him he could hear the girls whimpering, saying his name. Sam tried to hold on to him. A coyote silhouette appeared at the entrance to the tunnel and more gathered behind it. He fired, putting it down, the bark of the Glock sounding like a cannon inside the tunnel.

"Get out of here!" he screamed at the snarling animals. "Get the hell away!"

He fired two more times. The coyotes outside the hole snapped and grabbed at their dead brethren blocking the entrance, and rather than drag the carcasses out of the way, they seemed more intent on ripping their way through.

But suddenly the cannibalistic tearing of flesh and the snarling growls stopped, and everything was silent save for the panicked shallow breathing of the girls behind him.

"Daddy," Sam said.

"Shhh, baby. Keep quiet."

He listened. From somewhere above him he heard voices shouting and men running. Then, like thunder, shotgun blasts. Several of them. A battle raged above them. And then, after a long time, that noise too went silent.

They huddled together in the dark, the girls crowding as close as they could to him. The moment seemed to go on forever.

Then, from the entrance, a thick Texas drawl: "Sergeant Garza, it's Officer Boller with the Bonheim Police Department. Y'all all right down there, sir?"

It was getting dark when they came out of the tunnel. Resendez stood there, a smoking shotgun in his hands. Chief Delgado was there, too. He had three of his officers with him. Resendez threw the shotgun on the ground and hugged his daughters. He steered them away from what was left of their horses, and then made arrangements for one of Delgado' officers to take them home.

When they were gone, Garza retrieved a flashlight from one of the other officers and pointed it down the tunnel where he and the girls had taken refuge. The light didn't reach the end of the tunnel. When he'd fired his pistol down there, the sound had carried a long ways, and now he knew the actual distance was farther than he thought.

Probably much farther.

The hole was fresh, the ground just recently overturned, but the tunnel was obviously much older. The earth was packed tight and dry. He crumbled it in his fist. It occurred to him the tunnel was probably the same age as the cottages and church.

He went back to the clearing between the buildings. Resendez stood there with Delgado and the other two officers. Delgado clearly had no idea what the hell was going on, but Resendez's face was set and unreadable.

"This tunnel connects all these buildings, doesn't it?" Garza asked.

Resendez nodded.

"How long have you known about this?"

Resendez looked away for a second, then said, "Since yesterday afternoon."

"And you didn't say anything about it?"

Resendez looked away again.

Delgado said, "Them coyotes. I've never seen so many in one place before. They're not supposed to act that way. Matter of fact, I don't think I've ever heard of a coyote going after anything bigger than a rabbit."

Garza glanced at him, but didn't respond. To Resendez he said, "What did you do?"

Resendez was silent.

"Answer me," Garza hissed. "What did you do?"

Delgado cocked his head in surprise. He glanced back and forth between the two of them.

"Watch your tone of voice with me, Sergeant," Resendez said, his face a mystery in the settling dark.

"Bullshit!" Garza shot back. "Don't try to pull rank on me. Not after what I just went through. Now you tell me what you fucking did."

Resendez glanced around. He drew a heavy breath and seemed to weigh the cost of telling what he knew. "There's a network of tunnels underneath here," he finally said. "They connect under the church. That seems to be the hub."

"What are they for?" Garza asked. "Do they go anywhere?"

Resendez nodded. "There's an entrance beneath the church."

"An entrance to what?"

Resendez just shook his head.

"It's that book, isn't it? It's all true."

Resendez hung his head in resigned acquiescence. The genie was out of the bottle, and they both knew it.

"What are ya'll talkin' about?" Delgado said.

Garza turned to him. "Do your men have enough flashlights and shotguns for all of us?"

Delgado still seemed uncertain. He looked to Resendez for guidance, but Resendez wouldn't look back.

Finally, Delgado said, "Yes, sir . . . we got plenty of fire power." He turned to one of the officers and said, "Bert, go and get the shotguns. Plenty of shells, too."

"What are you going to do?" Resendez asked.

"We're going down there. All of us."

"What good will that do?"

"I don't know," Garza said. "I really don't. But I think the book and those coyotes and these buildings are all connected, and I think whatever it is we're dealing with here is waiting for us down there beneath that church."

Resendez had done a lot of work in a short time. He'd peeled away the plank boards that made the floor of the altar and exposed a gaping pit leading down into darkness. Delgado and a young redheaded officer named Sturgis tried to light it up with flashlights, but only succeeded in casting an eerie, buttery glow on the ancient limestone steps.

"What are you fellas hoping to find down there?" Delgado asked.

Garza racked the shotgun, chambering a shell. "Let's go," he said. "Everybody stay sharp."

He climbed down the steps and made his way into the darkness, not even bothering to see if the others followed. The steps went down maybe thirty feet before leveling off into a tunnel. The flashlight beam hinted at other tunnels a short distance off, opening off the main passageway. Dried timbers were embedded into the walls like ribs, and he traced them with the light. Supports, Garza guessed, like the box frames miners use to prevent cave-ins. There was a faint, foul odor, like something lingering in the still air.

"Where do these tunnels lead?" he asked over his shoulder.

"The side tunnels on the right have collapsed," Resendez said. "I don't know how far back the main tunnel leads."

They went on silently, Garza in the lead, the others following. The tunnel opened up to a large, rectangular chamber, and there they stopped. Wooden platforms, the supports black with mold, ran along both side walls. In the middle of the chamber was a round stone wall, about knee-high, and inside boiled a dark, oily liquid. Toward the back of the chamber stood an altar, and as Garza looked around, Resendez made his way to it.

Once Resendez mounted the altar he turned and looked out over the chamber. As he did, a shudder spread through the air. They all sensed it. Garza staggered to one side. Flies buzzed in his ears. He swatted at them, but nothing was there. He felt dizzy, suddenly nauseous, and he thought he could see the ghostlike shapes of men and women and even children standing on the platforms, their eyes pointed at Resendez. He shook his head and blinked, trying to clear his mind, but couldn't. What at first he had taken for flies buzzing in his ears now sounded like voices. Slowly, those voices became a chorus that filled the air, and when Garza strained to listen, he found their cadence familiar. He knew the words they were chanting from the book Resendez had found.

The shotgun fell from Resendez's fingertips and clattered to the ground. His hands spread wide, as though in benediction. The ghostlike visions around him became more solid. The room seemed to brighten. The voices grew louder. Resendez muttered along with them, and Garza too felt a familiar rush pounding in his veins. The words were ancient, powerful. Garza yelled at Resendez from across the chamber, his voice unable to punch through the hazy veil that had enveloped them.

Resendez went on chanting. The words moved through him, so powerful they shook the walls.

The oil in the pit began to boil, and flies crawled out of the muck, taking to the air and attacking Delgado and Sturgis. Garza felt himself lensing in and out between two worlds, the world of Delgado and Sturgis screaming in pain on the one side, and the ghost world of the voices and Resendez on the other. The part of him that watched from the ghost world filled with the awe and love of the zealot. Yet that other part, the part still attached to the corporeal world, sensed an overpowering stench rising from the depths of the pit, and was nearly overcome by it.

He could sense the ghost world gaining strength, and as he looked out over the strangely similar faces of the men, women, and children of the Kretschmer family, he could see their fiercely penetrating blue eyes staring back at him.

Their cadence grew stronger. The room shook, and clods of earth and stone crashed down around them. Something vast rose from the depths of the pit, something old and powerful. Garza could sense it pushing its way up through the earth.

On the altar, Resendez was shaking. The man he had been now gone, something different stared back from his mad eyes.

Garza grabbed the man's shoulders, but Resendez shook him off. Any moment now the thing rising up through the earth would be free. *De Vermis*, Garza thought. He had to break whatever had a hold on his friend, but there didn't seem to be any way to reach him. Flies yawned out of the pit by the thousands. Their buzzing made Garza's skin vibrate. He yelled at Resendez, and though their faces were almost touching, they were miles away.

Garza grabbed the shotgun his friend had dropped and punched Resendez with it. Resendez seemed to hardly feel the blow at first, but then, as he looked up at Garza, pain entered his expression.

Garza pulled him up to his feet and wrapped Resendez's arm around his shoulders.

"Come on, man, we have to get out of here!"

As Garza led him down from the altar, he saw blurry shapes he knew were Delgado and his men standing by the pit.

He yelled a warning they didn't hear.

The stone wall collapsed and the boiling, oily liquid in the pit spilled over the ground. Garza yelled again, but not in time. Sturgis was snatched off his feet and pulled into the pit by a huge, blackened tentacle.

Delgado fell backwards, a scream dying on his lips.

"Move!" Garza shouted, and ran down from the altar with Resendez on his arm. "Move man! Move!"

He stopped long enough to grab Delgado's shirt and pull him to his feet. Then he pushed him to the door.

The three men ran for the surface.

From behind them, like thunder under the earth, something ancient struggled to break free.

They worked most of the night, packing the entrance beneath the church's altar with dynamite that Delgado and one of his men got from a nearby quarry. By morning they were ready to light the fuse.

The blast shook the lake and sent birds sprinting to the air. When it was done, and the land where the church had stood was just a smoking, crumbling crater in the ground, Garza went walking through the tall grass near the rim.

He walked until he saw a dead coyote, its legs bent under its body, the head twisted against the ground. Its eyes were open, bulging, and though no life lit them, they were still powerfully blue.

He stared into those eyes and thought of the thing he'd just faced. A great power had lurked beneath that church, something dark and ancient and evil beyond the narrow limits through which most men understood those words. Maybe it was still down there, waiting for another man like Resendez to open its way through the depths of rock and earth.

One thing eluded him though. The eyes of the coyote seemed hauntingly familiar. Other eyes that same color blue had stared at him from the ghost world Resendez had opened up, but he wouldn't believe—indeed, couldn't believe, if he had any prayer of holding on to the tattered remnants of his sanity—that they were the eyes of the Kretschmer family.

Still, there was no way to be sure.

Substitute Player

By Tom Alexander

Christ! What the hell happened to me? I can't see a bloody thing. Neck feels like someone took an axe to it, head's throbbing like a sonovabitch.

When I wake up like this I know I've been a bad boy. A very bad boy. Clean and sober for damn near twenty-six days; Bill was going to give me a chip next week. Guess I blew that.

Shit, I don't even remember falling off the goddamn wagon.

It's dark in here. Nothing but a small window up high letting in a little light. Smells oily . . . musty, like . . . Hell, I'm in a basement.

What the crap am I doing in a basement? I don't even know anyone who has a basement. *WHERE THE HELL AM I?*

Dammit, my head hurts. Can't think straight. Like I been up on stage too long and my brain is heading south, leaving behind one dried up lump of shit. Whatever I did last night, I swear I'll never do it again.

"Hello!" What the hell's the matter with my voice. "Anybody out there?"

Raspy, like one of them tough guys on the Sopranos. Jesus, I can't move my arms or legs. I can feel them . . . I think. I just can't move them. Somebody tied me up? I'm either bound so tightly or . . . I'm paralyzed from the neck down.

Floorboards creaking. Someone's walking upstairs. *"HEY, UP THERE!* I'm down in the basement." I can barely speak.

My mouth forms the words, but no sounds come out; like

playing a saxophone without blowing into it. Mentally I hear the notes, but the only real sound is the valves clicking.

Sax man, that's me. I'm a musician. Billy Churl, sitting in for my main man, Stu Kenderman. Stuey. Yeah, Stuey got me into this mess. He must have—every time I get totally whacked, Stuey is somehow involved. I was at Dallas' only Jazz bar, Strictly Taboo . . . I think. They serve Eye-talian food in the back room, and have a nice size bar in front with a small stage set off in one of the corners. Thursday night is Experimental Jazz night—whatever that means. Stuey had a cold so I sat in for him. So it must be Thursday. I think it's Thursday. Hell, it could be Sunday if I ended up pulling a real bender.

It's getting lighter in here; that or my eyes are adjusting to the dark. I'm definitely in some sort of basement. Overhead pipes, vents and conduit network running through the wooden beams that hold up the first floor. There's something next to me, I can see it out of the corner of my eye. Right next to me; definitely within reach—a body. Someone is out cold lying flat on his back right next to me.

He's breathing . . . barely. Sounds kind of funny, like someone trying to deflate a beach ball by squeezing the air out of it. If I could just move my arm I might be able to shake his ass awake and get some answers.

Useless, I can't even wiggle a finger. Above me I see a stairwell leading up to a door. My guess is to the kitchen.

More creaking. Man, someone big is walking up there.

Big?

Ahhh, shit. It's coming back to me. I have a fondness for large women. Mind you, I'm no chubby chaser; those bastards just want their momma. No, I just like big chicks because . . . well, hell, they try harder and they really seem to appreciate you being there.

Now, let's see, we were just finishing up our last set at Strictly Taboo when in walks some big blondie. The bar was clearing out, accept for the regulars . . . and Dolores. Big blondie's name was

Dolores. I remember because I said it was the same name as the Kathy Bates character in Stephen King's *Misery*.

She corrected me. "Her name wasn't Dolores. It was Annie Wilkes. You're thinking of *Dolores Claiborne*."

"Oh, yeah? Who was in that?"

"Kathy Bates."

"Kathy Bates? Well, what was that about?"

"How should I know? I don't like that shit."

"Too scary for you?"

"Hah!" she rolled her eyes at me and excused herself for the ladies room.

Attitude. I liked that. I leaned against the bar, smirking. A hand closed on my shoulder and I turned to see the bartender.

"Bud, that's a whole lot of woman. You sure you're man enough to handle her?"

"Ain't no hill for a stepper," I said. And then blondie was back. "Jesus, you pee fast."

Okay, I'm not the classiest guy in the world. Actually, I'm just one of those naturally occurring idiots who says really stupid things to girls and wonders why he can't get laid. Stupid things like, "Jesus, you pee fast" or "Did you color your hair?" or "Are you about to start your period?"

Dolores ignored the remark, staring at me like I was a side of beef ready to be butchered and smoked.

"You filling in for Stu?" she asked.

"Yeah. You know Stuey?"

She didn't answer. Her big blonde hair shaded her face hiding her eyes in the shadows. She was wearing a lot of make-up. I started to wonder if she was wearing a wig when she looked at me.

"Smoke?"

I nodded and we stepped outside.

Okay, so at that point I hadn't had a drink, so how the hell did I end up in Dolores' basement? Assuming of course the lead-footed person roaming around upstairs is Dolores and this is her place. I look over at the guy next to me; his clothes look familiar, I think he might have played in the band with me. He's still not moving. Shit, he's not even breathing anymore.

Holy crap on a stick, I'm lying next to a goddamn stiff!

I can't even tell who it is; his face is hidden in the shadows. Is it the bartender? Was he trying to get in on some of my action? What action? What the hell is going on?

A doorbell rings. The rafters creak and strain as I follow the sound of footsteps over to what must be the front door. The porch light comes on outside the basement window and a shaft of amber light illuminates a select portion of the basement. To my horror, a portion of the body next to me is now visible and I can see blood everywhere. I try screaming my lungs out, but it's no use; I make only a wet sound. Panic floods over me. I'm paralyzed, lying in a strange basement next to a corpse and judging by the amount of blood covering this poor sucker's shirt, I'd say someone slit his throat from ear to ear.

Christ almighty, get me the hell out of here!

Voices from above. I recognize one of them. Dolores. I did end up coming home with that fat murdering bitch. Only she didn't quite finish me off. Of course if I don't get my ass in gear and get some feeling back into my arms and legs then I'm toast. Upstairs I hear her speak to her visitor.

"No, George, I'm fine."

"You sure now? It sounded like an awful ruckus goin' on over here."

"I'm sorry, George. I'm really okay. Thanks."

"Okay, Dylan, if you say so."

Dylan? Did he say, "Dylan?"

"Good night, George."

I hear the door close. The porch light goes out plunging the basement mausoleum back into darkness.

Dylan?

Dylan?

Dylan. Oh shit. I've really screwed the pooch on this one.

We took her car back to her place. Dolores drove really fast. I remember her arm really slamming through them gears, like Mario Andretti on steroids. We zipped by a row of townhouses on the outskirts of Oak Lawn. That should have sent up warning bells right there, but I had cock blinders on so I couldn't think straight anyway. She pushed an automatic garage door opener and I saw one of the townhouse unit's garage door begin to lift. We zipped in and skidded to a halt before the door even finished rising. She clicked the door opener again and the door reversed direction and started to seal us in.

I always think of Indiana Jones when a garage door closes automatically. I have a secret urge to bolt for the door and slide under just before it closes. I wished I had followed that urge tonight.

Wait a minute . . . this isn't a basement I'm in, it's one of those multilevel units with the garage on the first floor. Sure enough, there's Andretti's car just past the stiff on the other side of the garage. Why is it so hard for me to remember? What did I do to end up on the garage floor in a puddle of motor oil?

I barely made it to the staircase before big blondie spins me around and rips open my pants. I said fat chicks try harder. That was an understatement. They think about sex so much (almost as much as guys do) that when they get some they really know how to tear it up. I've got a hummer going that's about to turn me inside out. She's literally got me pinned to the stairs, it's not just her weight either; I can tell this gal is strong, probably works out. I massage her shoulders; muscular, almost too muscular. Shame too, a girl who works out that much and still can't take off the pounds. Dolores is still at it when I notice the ticking.

Tick . . . Tick . . . A big clock ticks loudly on the far wall. The time reads ten 'til midnight. The DFD emblem is splashed across the face of the clock. Dallas Fire Department. What the hell? Hanging next to it is a firefighting outfit, complete with helmet and mask, air tank, fire-proof coat, axe, hoses . . . Christ, it's like a firefighting shrine.

Oh boy, I think I'm screwing around with a fireman's wife. And just where is Fire Marshall Bill? Is the door at the top of the stairs going to spring open and put me face to face with one of Big D's bravest? Why the hell did I just think of that?

You know I do this shit to myself all the time. Here I am getting one of the best blowjobs I've ever had and crap like this pops into my head. It really screws up my concentration. I swear, when I get out of this mess I'm definitely going to start seeing a shrink again.

Wait a minute. Don't tell me the stiff next to me is Fire Marshall Bill. Oh shit, maybe the door did spring open and put me face to face with one really pissed off rescue worker. What the hell happened? He must have caught me and Dolores doing the deed. But how the hell?

An overhead light clicks on and I hear more movement from upstairs. Probably Dolores. Lots of banging around; low thuds, like cabinet doors opening and closing. She's looking for something. What?

With the lights on I realize I'm not lying in a puddle of motor oil. Motor oil isn't red. It's blood. Lots of it. All coming from my dead friend who is . . . oh my God!

Where the hell is his head?

Someone has cut his head off and I'm lying right next to him. *GET ME THE HELL OUT OF HERE NOW!*

The banging around noise has stopped and I can hear that fat murdering bitch approaching the door at the top of stairs. She's going to come down any minute and finish me off next.

Dolores you psycho bitch, stay the hell away from Billygoat Churl. I'll mess you up.

You killed Fire Marshall Bill and now you're going to get rid of the witnesses.

I'm not paralyzed, I'm bound. Wrapped tightly like a mummy. I have to be. I can feel my elbows pinned to the sides of my body. If I can just wiggle something free.

The door opens and I can hear her walking down the stairs. Each step strains with her massive weight.

Please God, let her fat ass fall through the stairs and break her bulldog neck.

The DFD clock starts to chime. It's like something out of an old Hammer Horror movie; every step she takes, that damn clock gongs.

Dolores stops at the bottom of the stairs. The clock has also stopped. It's midnight. Twelve steps, twelve gongs. Silence now, except for the ticking. She's holding something. A bag. A big green garbage bag.

She stares at me from the base of the stairs. Thinking. Maybe she doesn't know that I can't move. That's it. She may outweigh me by a hundred pounds but I'm still a guy. That's it blondie stay away. I'm the one with the balls and I can kick your ass any sweet day of the week.

She's just staring at me. Worried; probably trying to calculate her next move—which is what I should be doing before she decides to tie that bag over my head and suffocate my ass.

I remember looking at the ticking clock as she took me deeper and deeper down her throat. I fondle and caress her head. I pull her blonde hair . . . I was right, it was a wig. But I didn't care, this chick was giving me the ride of my life. The wig fell off but she didn't stop. Hell, if anything she sped up, like the piston to a steam engine going full throttle. I felt the stubble on her skull. So she's bald, who cares; I'm ten seconds away from lift off. My finger traces a scar on the top of her head, which leads to another scar, then another, then what felt like stitches; sutures. I think that's what broke the spell, my hangnail got caught in one of those stiff black threads that was holding closed some recent incision running along the back of her skull. Surgery? Brain surgery? Judg-

ing by the road map running across her scalp, I'd say she's had a
lot of brain surgery.

Please God, don't let me look down.

I'm about to climax so if I look down now . . . which of course
is what I do.

I don't know what made me go limp first, the fact that this is
one of the ugliest freaks I've ever seen or that "she" was a "he."
Either way, I'm outta here.

I'm outta here is right.

Then why am I still here?

And why is Dolores or Dylan or whatever the hell you call
Frankenstein's monster slowly, cautiously approaching me with a
large green garbage bag. What did that bitch do to me?

I remember she . . . he . . . it trying to revive my sagging boner
but it soon stopped when it saw the look of horror on my face
(remember, I'm the not-so-subtle guy). I pushed her away, and I
think I called her a freak or something and then made a beeline
for the garage door. She ran off to the far wall and grabbed something, I don't know what it was. When I turned around to demand
she open the garage door, she swung something at me, a bat or an
axe . . .

Dolores knelt in front of me. I guess she's figured out I can't
move. Grabbing the top of my head she pulls me up by my hair.
Damn, she is strong to be able to lift me up with one hand. She's
putting me in the garbage sack, but how? I'm a full grown man
and can't fit . . .

Oh, no.

Sweet Jesus, no!

I finally recognize the headless body lying next to me.

It's mine

Bios

Tom Alexander graduated from SMU with a degree in broadcast film and currently works in the film industry. He has written numerous short stories and scripts and directed and produced award-winning short films. He wrote the original story for the Syfy Channel movie *Alien Train* and wrote and directed *The Dark Dealer* with filmmaker Wynn Winberg. He lives in Burbank, California.

Michael Baldwin, MLS, MPA, is a novelist and poet that currently resides in Benbrook. A former public library administrator and professor of American Government, he is the author of *Passing Strange* and *Murder Music* and has published three books of poetry, *Lone Star Heart, Counting Backward From Infinity* and *Scapes*.

Alan Beauvais is a songwriter and the current Director of Community Outreach for the Fort Worth Songwriters Association. He is a member of a writers group in Azle and lives in Reno, Texas.

E. R. Bills is an author, screenwriter and free-lance journalist from Aledo. He received a degree in journalism from Texas State University and his work has appeared in *Fort Worth Weekly*, *Fort Worth Magazine*, the *Fort Worth Star-Telegram*, the *Austin American-Statesman*, etc. He is the author of *Black Holocaust: The Paris Horror and a Legacy of Texas Terror*, *The 1910 Slocum Massacre: An Act of Genocide in East Texas* and *Texas Obscurities: Stories of the Peculiar, Exceptional and Nefarious*.

Tom Bont is the author of dozens of essays and articles and two books, including *Howlers: Lupus Rex*, appearing under his pseudonym, Tom Sutherland. Bont is a United States Navy veteran, has a degree in computer science from Louisiana Tech University, and lives in North Texas with his family.

David Bowles is a Mexican-American writer from South Texas, where he teaches at the University of Texas-Rio Grande Valley. He is the author of the Pura Belpré Honor Book *The Smoking Mirror*, and his work has been published in numerous venues including *Rattle*, *Strange Horizons*, *Apex Magazine*, *Metamorphoses*, *Translation Review*, the *Langdon Review of the Arts in Texas*, *Huizache*, *Axolotl*, *Concho River Review*, *Eye to the Telescope*, *Asymptote* and *BorderSenses*.

Glen Coburn, writer and director of cult horror spoof classic, *Bloodsuckers from Outer Space*, has written on a variety of topics including cars, travel and real estate. For the last two decades, he has enjoyed success as a commercial photographer specializing in advertising and architecture. He has a degree in journalism from Texas A&M-Commerce and currently resides in Dallas.

Russell C. Connor is a Fort Worth horror writer who started at the age of five. He is the author of two short story collections, four e-Novellas and nine novels. His book *Good Neighbors* won an Independent Publisher Award and his short fiction has appeared in *Black Petals*, *Burial Day* and *Beware the Dark*. He has been a member of the DFW Writers' Workshop since 2006 and his next novel, *Through the Deep Forest* (Vol.

1 of his Dark Filament Ephemeris series) hit the shelves on October 1st.

Misty Contreras is an editor and proofreader based out of Austin. She also has fifteen years experience in the creative arts.

Anna L. Davis is an author and editor who lives in the Dallas area. She has a degree in biology from the University of Texas-Dallas and experience in medical editing. Her debut novel, *Open Source*, is a cyberpunk, sci-fi thriller that explores the implications of human micro-chipping, brain implants and neuro hackers.

Carmen Gray has taught writing for over twenty years. Watching her daughter fight and survive a rare form of cancer compelled her to start crafting short stories and create her own poetry blog. She lives in Austin and her Mexican-American heritage and work with English Language Learners influence the characters and situations in her writing.

Joe R. Lansdale is the author of more than three dozen novels, including the Spur Award-winning *Paradise Sky*, the Edgar Award-winning *The Bottoms*, *Sunset and Sawdust* and *Honky Tonk Samurai*. His *Cold in July* received acclaimed film treatment in 2014, his *Bubba Ho-Tep* remains a cinema cult classic and his "Hap and Leonard" novels are currently enjoying series runs on the Sundance Channel. His writing has garnered eleven Bram Stoker Awards, the American Mystery Award, the British

Fantasy Award and the Grinzane Cavour Prize for Literature. He lives with his family in Nacogdoches.

Ernie Lee is an award-winning poet from Canyon Lake. He is a songwriter (BMI), storyteller and columnist. He is the author of *Aquasaurus, Where the Wild Rice Grows,* Him and the upcoming *Search for Aquasaurus*. He has also published technical professional books and academic guides related to public procurement for the University of Texas at Austin, and University of Texas-San Antonio.

Bret McCormick is an artist, writer and independent filmmaker. His short stories have appeared in many publications, including *Weirdbook, Bards and Sages* and the *Saturday Evening Post*. He is the author of *Hellfire* and *Headhunters from Outer Space*, and a partial listing of his motion picture credits can be found on imdb.com. He currently resides in Bedford.

Joe McKinney is a member of the San Antonio Police Department. He has worked as a patrol officer, a DWI Enforcement officer, disaster mitigation specialist, homicide detective, patrol supervisor

and the director of the City of San Antonio's 911 Call Center. He has a degree in American History from Trinity University and a Master's degree in English Literature from the University of Texas at San Antonio. His first novel, *Dead City*, is recognized as a seminal work in the zombie genre and he has won two Bram Stoker Awards. He is the author of over twenty books and a frequent guest at horror and mystery conventions. He resides in a little town outside San Antonio with his wife and children.

Stephen Patrick is an award-winning storyteller living in the Dallas area. His writing ranges from historical to horror and he has published over two dozen stories in various venues, including *Aphelion, Bewildering Stories* and the *Night Terrors Anthology* by Kayelle Press. He is a frequent panel guest at FENCON and ConDFW.

Michael H. Price is the lead author of the *Forgotten Horrors* books—the longest-running film-history franchise in commercial publishing, with ten volumes and counting and a variety of spinoff titles dealing with comedies, westerns, film noir, motion-picture

soundtracks and movie-related comic-book stories. His other projects include the *Comics from the Gone World* titles; *Leo Kragg: Prowler* (with Timothy Truman and John K. Snyder, III); the graphic-novel adaptation of Herk Harvey's classic movie *Carnival of Souls* (with Todd Camp); the *Chilling Archives of Horror Comics* series (with Craig Yoe); and various titles in the Library of American Comics project including *Dick Tracy, Flash Gordon* and *Little Orphan Annie*. Price is the founding president of the original Fort Worth Film Festival and a board member of the Fort Worth Public Library Foundation.

David Robledo is a writer, researcher, and environmental marketing specialist in Brownsville, Texas. He is the founder of the Texas Food Revolution, a group of loosely affiliated chefs and home cooks who celebrate local food in the Rio Grande Valley. And he also established and managed several other Valley farmers' markets in the region. His writing spans fiction, journalism and

academic research in the field of archetypal psychology.